CRUCIBLE

BOOK ONE OF THE RISE OF DANIEL

GREG S. BAKER

Crucibles of God
A Rise of Daniel Novel
Book One

by

Greg S. Baker

Copyright © 2022

ISBN: 9798440595309
Independently Published

First Edition

All Scripture quotations are from the King James Bible.

All rights reserved. No part of this publication may be reproduced or transmitted in any form or by any means, electronic or mechanical, including photocopy, recording, or any information storage retrieval system, without permission in writing from the copyright owner.

This is a work of fiction based on the Holy Scriptures as presented in the King James Bible. All characters and events resembling real people and events outside the Scriptures are wholly coincidental.

Other Books by Greg S. Baker

Biblical Fiction Novels

The Davidic Chronicles
- *Anointed*
- *Valiant*
- *Fugitive*
- *Delivered*
- *King*

The Rise of Daniel
- *Crucibles of God*
- *Children of the Captivity*
- *Revealer of Secrets*
- *Arising Wrath*

Adventure/Fantasy Novels

Isle of the Phoenix Novels
- *The Phoenix Quest*
- *In the Dragon's Shadow*
- *Phoenix Flame*
- *Rise of the Dragon Spawn*
- More to come…

Christian and Christian Living

- *The Generational Warrior – The Battlefield Manual for First-Generation Christians*
- *Fitly Spoken – Developing Effective Communication and Social Skills*
- *Restoring a Fallen Christian – Rebuilding Lives for the Cause of Christ*
- *The Great Tribulation and the Day of the Lord: Reconciling the Premillennial Approach to Revelation*
- *The Gospel of Manhood According to Dad – A Young Man's Guide to Becoming a Man*
- *Rediscovering the Character of Manhood – A Young Man's Guide to Building Integrity*
- *Stressin' Over Stress – Six Ways to Handle Stress*

www.GregSBaker.com

To Kyle, my son, who reminds me most of Daniel.

ACKNOWLEDGMENTS

This journey into Daniel's world has been an eye-opening experience for me. I've learned so much and feel my relationship with God has grown stronger as a result. But this journey wasn't taken alone.

My dad, Keith Baker, walked nearly each step of the way with me. His talks, advice, and attention to detail were invaluable.

My beta-reading team added so much insight and value, and I truly appreciate each of them taking the time to invest in this work: Diane Fraizer, Elizabeth Speer, Rich Menninger, Nobel Macaden, Gayle Wilson, and of course, my mom, Debbie Baker.

My dear wife, Liberty, helped with the editing and providing most of the encouragement I needed along the way.

CHARACTERS

Because this work follows the Old Testament Scriptures, there are characters who share the same name. This list will hopefully be an aid to the reader. Only the characters in the main story are included here, not those mentioned in the prologue or epilogue.

HEBREWS (JEWS)

Ahikam – Chief temple scribe
Azariah (1) (Abednego) – Daniel's friend
Azariah (2) – High priest in Jerusalem
Baruch – Jeremiah's scribe
Buzi – Ezekiel's father
Daniel (Belteshazzar) – Main character
Delaiah – Prince of Judah
Ebedmelech – A eunuch in King Jehoiakim's palace
Elishama – Court scribe; Hananiah's (1) and Mishael's father
Elnathan – Daniel's father
Ezekiel – Priest of the LORD
Gedaliah – Ahikam's son
Gemariah – Prince of Judah
Hananiah (1) (Shadrach) – Daniel's friend and cousin
Hananiah (2) – Son of Azur; a prophet
Ishi – Hebrew captive
Jeconiah – Daniel's nephew; King Jehoiakim's son
Jehoiakim – King of Jerusalem
Jehudi – Prince of Judah
Jerahmeel – Prince of Judah
Jeremiah – Main character
Jokim – Hebrew captive
Maachah – Hananiah and Mishael's mother
Mattaniah (Zedekiah) – King Jehoiakim's brother
Michaiah – Azariah's (Abednego's) father.
Mishael (Meshach) – Daniel's friend and cousin
Naam – Hebrew captive
Nehushta – Daniel's sister; King Jehoiakim's wife
Pashur – Governor of the temple
Seraiah – Azariah's (2), the high priest's, son
Shelemiah – Prince of Judah
Urijah – Prophet of the LORD
Ziph – Hebrew captive

CHALDEANS

Ashpenaz – Prince of the eunuchs
Baltasar – Priest of Marduk
Berosus – High priest of Marduk
Melzar – Steward to Ashpenaz
Nabushumlishir – Prince of Babylon; Nebuchadnezzar's brother
Nebuchadnezzar – Main character
Nebuzaradan – Captain of Nebuchadnezzar's guard

OTHERS

Ashur-uballit – Last Assyrian king
Pharaoh Necho – King of Egypt

JERUSALEM
In the Time of Daniel

An Artist's Rendering

PROLOGUE

105 YEARS EARLIER

A weighty chill lay heavy upon Isaiah's heart as he made his way up the slope to the king's palace. He could not stop thinking about what he must do—what the LORD his God required of him. The future pain and suffering that would result from the words the LORD had bidden him to speak aged him beyond his many years. He didn't want to speak them. For the moment he uttered them aloud, there would be no stopping what must come. But if he did not speak, the LORD would but find another to do His will. Better him than another.

That he must do this at all caused a simmering anger to build in his heart alongside his sadness, one that threatened to blossom into fury. Fury at the king of Judah for his thoughtless act of profaning the name of the LORD with his prideful heart.[1] The king had crossed a line, and now there would be no second chance and no undoing of the coming judgement. Isaiah drew comfort in only one thing: he would not be alive to see it.

The steps leading up to the king's palace sent painful aches rippling up his aging knees, and he was forced to brace his staff of olive wood against the limestones to help leverage himself upward toward the King's Court. The sun hung low in the west, bathing Jerusalem in shades of yellow and orange. From here, the prophet could see the western wall of the temple mount shining like a

---

[1] 2 Chronicles 32:25.

polished bell and admire the rising structure of the temple standing as a sentinel in all its magnificent glory.

Isaiah paused to stare at the sight—as much to revel in its beauty as to rest from his trek up from the lower valley and the Pool of Siloam. Never, Isaiah was sure, had there ever been a grander structure or a greater monument to the one true God. King Solomon had surely outdone himself in the construction. And someday, someday after he had been gathered to his fathers, the temple would lie in ruins. The course was set. The end inevitable—all because of one man's pride.

Turning away, the old prophet worked his way up the remaining steps, bypassing the guards who kept the entrance to the central courtyard of the palace. They bowed low as he ambled past. They didn't challenge him or stop him. They knew better.

The gardens inside caused most first-time visitors to stop and stare in awe—though not as majestic or ornate as the King's Garden near the Pool of Siloam, the gardens here were nevertheless a marvel of greenery and fertility. Isaiah had to admit, the king had done wonders for Jerusalem during his reign. He'd expanded the city to encompass much of the western hill, dug a tunnel to reroute water from the Gihon Spring to the Pool of Siloam on the southwest side of the City of David,[2] and raised the ground near the temple mount so that more could gather before its gates at the highest point of Mount Moriah. And all this didn't include the wealth that he had brought to the city.[3]

"A waste," he muttered to himself, making his way right down the middle of the garden toward the King's Court. The LORD had set him a task, and he would not fail to do it—no matter how distasteful.

But a voice brought him up short, and he turned to find a young woman of magnificent beauty bowing to him. Even to Isaiah's aged eyes, he could appreciate the glow of charm and femininity that shone off her like the sun.

---

[2] 2 Chronicles 32:30.
[3] 2 Chronicles 32:27-29.

PROLOGUE

Isaiah returned the bow as much as his body would let him. "My lady, I am honored that you would notice this humble servant of Jehovah."

She laughed, her voice like tinkling cymbals, and she shooed away the three servant girls lingering nearby. "I would speak with the great prophet in privacy," she ordered them.

Once the servants had stepped back out of earshot, she bowed her head to Isaiah. "You do yourself an injustice, O man of God. Your word is mighty in this house, and you are always welcome. Do you seek my husband, the king?"

Isaiah nodded gravely to Hephzibah. "I do. I must speak the word of the LORD to him."

Hephzibah hesitated, probably sensing that he bore ill tidings. She cast a furtive glance toward the King's Court. "He entertains ambassadors from a distant land."

"This I know, my lady."

She struggled with herself, clearly missing the heaviness in his tone, and finally put a hand on her stomach. Isaiah knew instinctively what she was going to ask and braced himself for it. King Hezekiah had other wives and daughters but no sons, and since Hephzibah was his first and most favored wife, she felt keenly this perceived failure in her duty.

"Do you come to speak of the future of his lineage?" she asked. "That I have not given a son to my husband has been a great grief to him. Am I…will I bear him a son?"

Hephzibah's anxiety twisted her face, creasing it with lines of worry. But even that could not dispel her beauty. One day, when Zion was restored, Isaiah imagined it would be compared to her beauty.[4] He cleared his throat, pushing aside his anger at her husband long enough to address her concern. "You shall bear a son," he said slowly, "and your husband, the king, will see his face. The line of David will continue. I have heard this at the mouth of the LORD."[5]

---

[4] Isaiah 62:4.
[5] 2 Kings 21:1.

The smile that blossomed on her face could have lit up the entire city. "Then you bring glad tidings, my lord!"

No, he did not, but he saw no reason to contradict her. She would find out soon enough. "As you say, but let me go, I pray. I must speak to the king."

"Of course, my lord. You must make haste."

Isaiah turned and walked away after another aching bow. The LORD had revealed to him the fate of Hephzibah's yet unborn son, and it chilled him to the bones. Dark days were coming to Judah. Dark indeed.

His anger surging again, he practically stalked toward the King's Court, his wrath lending his old bones strength. The guards standing before the bronze covered doors took one look at his face and blanched. They fumbled with the doors and only just succeeded in shoving them open before the aged prophet walked into them. There were stories of angry prophets, after all, angry enough to call fire down from heaven and consume all who stood against them. These guards were no fools.

Inside, a riot of sound washed over Isaiah. In one corner, musicians played enthusiastically on their harps, sackbuts, and dulcimers. Princes of Judah stood before the throne arrayed in their finest tunics and robes. After the LORD had turned back the armies of King Sennacherib by slaying nearly two-hundred thousand men in a single night,[6] wealth had poured into the city, enriching the princes. And that event wasn't the only source of riches. Nations had heard of King Hezekiah's miraculous recovery from a disease that was almost universally fatal. Thus, Judah had become a land of wonders, and the whole world wanted to understand her secrets. Which brought Isaiah to the reason for his visit to the king.

Isaiah marched between ornate columns that towered overhead into arches that supported glazed bricks carved with palm trees and seraphim. Two huge firepits to either side of the throne provided light, heat in the winter, and something on which to cook during

---

[6] 2 Kings 19:33-36.

feasts. And a feast was indeed in full swing. Gold cups filled with the best wine sparkled in the light. Silver platters of meat, bread, and grapes filled the tables placed strategically in the court for all to partake. Fresh water fish, imported from the sea to the north, and saltwater fish from the Great Sea to the west had been delicately cooked and seasoned with spices from far off Egypt. Incense and precious ointment scented the air. It was an amazing display of wealth from a city that had successfully defied the greatest power on earth: the mighty Assyrians.

And the king's guests, ambassadors from a far land that too felt the weight and yoke of the Assyrians, were soaking it all in. It was one thing to know these men were here, had engaged with the king, and had exchanged gifts, but it was altogether a different thing to see it with his own eyes. Isaiah virtually trembled in rage.

"My lord!" Isaiah's voice snapped over the noise like a fired catapult, disrupting the musicians who, sensing tension like a lion smells a wounded animal, stopped playing instantly. Conversation died across the court, and the man on the throne turned away from his guests to look down upon the prophet.

Isaiah didn't let him speak. He flung a hand toward the ambassadors and demanded, "What said these men to you, O king?"[7]

King Hezekiah had clearly set out to impress the visiting dignitaries. Isaiah couldn't remember the last time he'd seen the king arrayed in such finery. Even his gold crown had been reworked, possibly even recast, and embedded with rubies. He cut a fine figure, sitting upon his gold-covered throne and wearing a solid blue robe that must've cost a fortune.[8]

The king, clearly disturbed by Isaiah's visit, cast a sideways glance at his visitors. An interpreter was whispering furiously to them. The king stood from his throne and stepped down to where

---

[7] 2 Kings 20:14; Isaiah 39:3.
[8] Blue dye was among the most expensive to make, coming as it did from the digestive gland of a particular marine snail.

Isaiah waited. "Be at peace, my friend," Hezekiah said with a lowered voice. "These come from afar having heard about the LORD's mercy upon me in the matter of my illness and have come to hear the tale."[9]

Isaiah smoothed his white beard, trying hard to keep his fury in check. "The tale? The tale is the LORD's, my king. From where have they come?"

"From a far country, one called Babylon. Their king, Merodachbaladan, sent greetings and presents. He too fights against the yoke of Assyria and knows that our God has delivered our nation out of that nation's wicked hands and has delivered me from the sickness."[10] Hezekiah gestured, and a servant darted forward, bowed, and handed a scroll to the king, who showed it to Isaiah. "Here is the letter from King Merodachbaladan of Babylon."

Isaiah ignored it, fixing his stern eyes on the king, letting the full weight of his displeasure fall upon the man. The king was trying too hard to pacify Isaiah. Hezekiah *knew*.

"You say they have come to hear the tale of your deliverance, my king, then why are they here in your house and not kneeling before the LORD of Glory in *His* house, from whose hands came your deliverance? Tell me truly, my king, what have they seen in your house?"[11]

Some dread finally registered upon Hezekiah. His face drained of color and sweat beads formed on his brow. "There is nothing they have not seen," he whispered. "I have shown them all my treasures."

Isaiah had known this to be true. The LORD had told him before being sent to confront the king of Judah. But hearing it from the man's own lips, knowing what he now must say, tore Isaiah's heart out. In the back of his mind, he had hoped…had prayed…that it would be otherwise. But it was not to be.

Raising his voice so that all in the King's Court could hear, he cried, "Then hear the word of the LORD of Hosts!"

---

[9] 2 Kings 20:12; Isaiah 39:1.
[10] 2 Kings 20:14; Isaiah 39:3.
[11] 2 Kings 20:15; Isaiah 39:4.

PROLOGUE

The frantic whisperings, the shifting of sandaled feet, the clank of iron armor, and even the crackling of the fires all fell silent in the wake of that announcement. King Hezekiah stepped back, his eyes filling with fear.

"Behold, the days come when all that is in your house and the treasures that your fathers have laid up will be carried into Babylon." Isaiah's eyes swept the crowd of princes. "*Nothing* will be left, says the LORD."[12]

"What is this that you speak?" Hezekiah whispered with trembling lips. "What mean these words?"

"You know why the LORD speaks against you, my king. You have profaned the name of the LORD by showing the Babylonians *your* treasures and *your* house. Is not our God treasure enough? Are not His mercies blessing enough to proclaim to the nations? Why then have you lifted up your heart above the LORD?" Isaiah steadied himself, knowing what else must be said. "Know, king of Judah, and harken, princes of Judah, to the word of the LORD. Of your sons who will issue from you—" Isaiah deliberately let that phrase sink into Hezekiah's mind, knowing how desperate he was for an heir "—and that you will beget, shall be taken away and become eunuchs in the palace of the king of Babylon."[13]

For the longest moment, the only sound was the frantic, whispered translation of Isaiah's words to the Babylonian ambassadors. Then Hezekiah stumbled back, his hand groping for his throne. He sat down heavily on the golden seat, gripping the armrests with trembling hands.

"This," the king said hoarsely, "is the word of the LORD?"

Isaiah placed both his hands upon his staff and tried to look regal. "It is."

"Then good is the word of the LORD," Hezekiah said, the words choked out of him. "I shall have a son then?"

Isaiah offered a curt nod.

---

[12] 2 Kings 20:17; Isaiah 39:6.
[13] 2 Kings 20:18; Isaiah 39:7.

Hezekiah sucked in a deep breath. "Is it not good then that there be peace and truth in my days?"[14]

And that, Isaiah mused sadly, was why the LORD had spoken against Hezekiah. "Aye, in your days, perhaps. Howbeit, in the days of your son, and his son, and his…" Isaiah trailed off unable to finish. Those days would be dark indeed.

---

[14] 2 Kings 20:19; Isaiah 39:8.

1

PRESENT DAY

"Daniel! Daniel! Your father has returned!" The lad shouting wildly slid to a stop in a small cloud of dust, breathing heavily from his run through the narrow streets of Jerusalem, but his dark eyes glittered with excitement, and his olive-brown skin glowed in the afternoon light.

Daniel instinctively looked over his younger cousin's shoulder for his father. No one. And then he wished that Hananiah, Mishael's older and more practical brother, had come to deliver such news. Trying to wring coherency out of Mishael was often an exercise in frustration. He snapped up a hand to stop Mishael the moment the other opened his mouth again. The boy would talk endlessly about the most absurd details if permitted. This was too important to let him prattle on.

Daniel asked, "When did he come?"

At thirteen, it didn't take Mishael long to catch his breath. He began hopping from foot to foot, energy building like a boiling pot. "At midday! Come, Daniel! We must not delay! Your father has gone to see the king!"

Relief settled over Daniel, washing away an anxiety he had held close for a long time. His father had been gone for months, sent to Egypt at the behest of King Jehoiakim to return a criminal to justice. His whole family had been worried, knowing how dangerous the journey would be and how his success largely depended upon the favor of Pharaoh Necho.

Daniel started moving, his errand to the Tower of Hananeel forgotten. At a year older than Mishael, he was as nimble and light-footed as his cousin, and neither had problems navigating the narrow streets as they dashed away. To get to the king's palace, they had to make their way out of the City of David through the Valley Gate, descend into the central valley, and then make their way up the western hill to the king's palace that rested against the northern wall of the city.[1]

Daniel guessed his father had entered the city through the Corner Gate in the northwestern part of the city to avoid attention, and then made his way directly to the king's palace. Mishael's family lived in that part of the city, so it made sense that he would've discovered Elnathan's arrival before Daniel.

Excitement bubbled up within Daniel like a newborn spring. He dodged women carrying large jars of water atop their heads or shoulders, merchants who had found a niche in the street to hawk their wares, and priests making their way to the king's palace from the temple mount. Daniel hardly saw them, except to scowl darkly when he passed a priest of Baal or Molech walking openly on the streets of Jerusalem.

---

[1] Remnants of this wall have been found and named the Broad Wall.

Like his father, Elnathan, Daniel was a firm worshiper of Jehovah,[2] and it grieved him that King Jehoiakim had revived the idolatrous worship of these false gods—even if the king truly thought he had reason. Daniel had only been ten when King Josiah had died, but he still vividly remembered a time when only Jehovah's priests and servants walked Jerusalem's streets.

Daniel and Mishael flew down the steps of the Valley Gate and began the trek up the slope of the western hill of the city toward the palace. They made it in record time. Bounding up the steps to the courtyard, they gave a wave to the guards stationed at the entrance who nodded them on with hardly a glance. As princes of the kingdom, Daniel and Mishael were common faces around the palace. As the king's brother-in-law, the guards wouldn't dare stop Daniel from entering the palace unless the king himself had given the order.[3]

The courtyard had once housed a beautiful garden in King Hezekiah's day, but the trees and shrubs had long since been allowed to die off. Now the courtyard was used as a marshaling field for the king's guard. Barracks had been built along either side to house the men hired to protect the king. Not all of them were Hebrews, and some were Egyptian officials—spies really—who ensured that the annual tribute to Pharaoh Necho was delivered in a timely manner.[4] Daniel despised them, but there was nothing he could do about it.

The lads slowed down as they approached the large, bronze doors to the King's Court. They took a moment to get their

---

[2] For this portion of the series, Jehovah will be used instead of Yahweh. Both are correct, though Yahweh comes from the transliteration of the Aramaic translation of the Hebrew יהוה. Since Aramaic was only generally learned by the Jews during the Babylonian Captivity (though some of the nobles understood it [2 Kings 18:26]), Jehovah will be used.

[3] We have no knowledge of Daniel's lineage or family. All we know is that he was a prince, very likely related to the king in some manner (Daniel 1:3-4). For the purpose of this story, he is the king's brother-in-law after his older sister married the king. These relationships are fictitious.

[4] 2 Kings 23:33-35; 2 Chronicles 36:3.

breathing under control and then saluted the guards standing before the doors.

"Be wary, lads," the grizzled veteran on the left said in a fond voice. "The king's wrath has been kindled. Walk lightly."

The boys exchanged a glance. Mishael's face grew apprehensive immediately, but Daniel had witnessed the king's ire often and knew how to keep from running afoul of it. King Jehoiakim was *not* a popular king. In fact, when his father, King Josiah, had died, the people had anointed Jehoiakim's younger brother Jehoahaz as king instead.[5] Jehoiakim only ruled now because Pharaoh Necho had taken Jehoahaz captive to Egypt and put Jehoiakim on the throne.[6] That had been four years ago, but Jehoiakim had never forgotten or forgiven this slight from the people. Daniel wondered if the reinstatement of the worship of false gods was appeasement or retribution. Certainly, enough children had been sacrificed to the false gods to punish an entire generation.

"I will dance upon eggs, captain," Daniel said blithely, keeping his face serious.

The guard grinned, shook his head, and pulled one side of the door partially opened. "Be gone, scoundrel. The LORD bless me if I ever be promoted to captain!"

Daniel and Mishael slipped in and paused to take stock of the situation. The King's Court was filled with men for the most part. The few women in attendance stood in a group off to one side, among them the queen, Daniel's older sister, Nehushta. Daniel's father stood with arms folded near the front of the many officials, administrators, and princes of Judah. His weathered face had fallen flat, a sign, Daniel knew, of his displeasure. His thin lips were pressed so tightly together that they nearly disappeared into his gray-streaked beard. His hair had grown since he'd departed, looking ragged and shaggy. He hadn't even taken time to change. His dusty tunic looked travel stained, the blue tassels hanging from the fringe appeared

---

[5] 2 Kings 23:30-31; 2 Chronicles 36:1.
[6] 2 Kings 23:31-34; 2 Chronicles 36:3-4.

coated in brown dust. His eyes, however, never wavered as he watched the king.

Daniel moved slowly toward his father so as not to catch the attention of the man leaning forward on the throne. Not that he could, short of drawing a weapon. King Jehoiakim's attention was riveted on the prisoner standing in chains before him.

"You are worthy of death, Urijah!" Jehoiakim shouted at the prisoner, spittle splattering his dark beard. The king's hands gripped his bronze throne—Daniel had heard that it had once been gold—his knuckles turning white. The man teetered precariously on his seat.

Daniel gave a small start. He had not realized that his father had been tasked with returning the prophet instead of a criminal as he had supposed. His father had never said a word as to who he was to find or why. A sinking feeling found its way into Daniel's heart.

The prisoner had a resigned look upon his face, one that had gone beyond fear and anger. His matted beard hung in clumps from his drawn, nearly emaciated face. His eyes glowed with a feverish light that Daniel had seen on others who knew death was imminent.

"My lord," Urijah said in a surprisingly soft voice, "of what am I accused?"

Jehoiakim half came out of his seat. "Of what? Of what? Of treason!" The king's eyes wobbled as they shifted about, brushing over two of his immediate family members, Mattaniah[7] and Jeconiah, his younger brother and oldest son respectively. Both stood beside the throne in their official capacity of advisers to the king. Finally, the king's eyes settled onto a thin man with a snow-white beard. "Elishama, what record have you of Urijah the son of Shemaiah's words?"

The chief court scribe, who also was Hananiah's and Mishael's father, straightened as if someone had rammed a rod down his back. "My lord?"

---

[7] His name was changed later to Zedekiah.

The king's face darkened. "What words were spoken against his king!"

Elishama bobbed a bow and cleared his throat. "Urijah has spoken against this city and against the land, saying that Jerusalem will be overthrown and the land made desolate because you, my lord the king, have turned your back on Jehovah and served other gods."[8]

"I have not failed to worship the God of our fathers!" Jehoiakim roared, falling back into the throne. "Is not the temple repaired and the priesthood performing their daily duties?"

Urijah smiled. "T'was your father, O king, who repaired the temple of the LORD.[9] And as I passed through the Valley of Hinnom I beheld there an altar to Molech and smelled the flesh of our sons and daughters sacrificed upon the idol's arms.[10] Is there not also an altar to Osiris, god of the Egyptians, in the gates of the city? O king, why have you turned your back on the one true God of Israel and profaned His name?"

"You know not of what you speak," Jehoiakim hissed. "Was it not the gods of Egypt who overthrew my father and slew him? What strength was there in Jehovah that day? Did not the Assyrian gods overthrow Israel in the days of my father Hezekiah? Samaria is no more. The people who remain there are dogs of mixed blood, who scrounge a living among the rocks! Would you have *that* fate for Judah?"

Urijah shook his bedraggled head, and only then did Daniel begin to realize the seriousness of the conversation. The king had sacrificed children to Molech as Manasseh, his great-grandfather, had done before him.[11]

The captive prophet lifted up his voice and spoke in a ringing tone that sent chills down Daniel's spine, "Pharaoh Necho came forth at the word of the LORD God of Israel. Did he not send word

---

[8] Jeremiah 26:20.
[9] 2 Kings 22:3-7; 2 Chronicles 34:8-13.
[10] Jeremiah 7:31.
[11] 2 Kings 21:1-9; 2 Chronicles 33:1-9.

to your father to abide in Jerusalem and come not out against him—at the word of the LORD?"[12] The prophet drew himself up, and to Daniel, it was as if the king was the one in chains, not Urijah. "Remember, O king, the word of the LORD that came to Huldah, the prophetess. Because your father humbled himself before the LORD God of Israel, the evil written in the book of the law would not befall him while he yet lived.[13] Yet now, King Josiah lives no longer! Now will the curses written therein fall upon his children, upon *you*, O king!"

Daniel's father leaned closer to Daniel and whispered, "Stand fast, my son. The prophet has doomed himself. Do nothing rash."

Daniel glanced in surprise at his father. He didn't really understand. Prophets had a place of honor in his father's house. They were venerated and uplifted, and the prophet's words had struck a chord in Daniel's soul. He knew them for the truth. But looking at King Jehoiakim's face, Daniel knew his father was right.

With an inarticulate roar of rage, Jehoiakim flung himself out of his throne and tore out a sword from one of the guard's scabbards standing nearby. Urijah didn't resist. He had clearly known this would be his fate. He had already tried to run, and it had been Daniel's own father who had brought him back.

The sword plunged into Urijah's chest and came out his back in a spray of blood. Daniel stiffened in shock, his muscles bunching as he prepared to run to the prophet's aid. His father's hand tightened on his shoulder, keeping him rooted to the spot.

The dying prophet managed a feeble smile, blood staining his lips, and then he collapsed to the stone floor much like a sack of sticks.

The king stumbled back, leaving the sword embedded in the prophet's body. The only sound was the quiet sobbing of some of the queen's maids in the corner. No one else dared say a word—or

---

[12] 2 Kings 23:29-30; 2 Chronicles 35:20-25.
[13] 2 Kings 22:14-22; 2 Chronicles 34:22-33.

even breathe for that matter. No one dared even look in the manic eyes of the king, lest they share the prophet's fate.

Except for Daniel. He could not look away and so saw the cloud come over the king, a darkness as of an evil spirit that settled over him. Daniel knew then that everything the prophet had spoken would come to pass. Daniel glanced over at the crown prince, Jeconiah. They were blood related through Daniel's sister, King Jehoiakim's wife. This made the prince Daniel's nephew, though the other was but three years younger than Daniel. Perhaps this closeness in age had contributed to the quiet hostility they shared, but in truth, the real reason was that Jeconiah shared his father's evil heart. The eleven-year-old prince stared at the body of the prophet in the same way as his father: with cold satisfaction.

It was Mattaniah, Jehoiakim's brother, who broke the silence. The same age as Daniel, the dark-skinned lad had a scheming nature that had always rubbed Daniel wrong anytime they were together. Ambition bled off Mattaniah's chubby face as he took several steps forward and gestured to the body. "Urijah the son of Shemaiah has spoken treason against the king. He has paid with his life. Let him not rest with his fathers but be cast into the graves of the common people."

Jehoiakim nodded, seeming to relax in stages. "That is well spoken, brother. Let it be so." He gestured sharply, and two guards pushed their way forward to drag Urijah's body away, leaving a red stain on the white stones and broken tiles.

Elnathan pulled Daniel back deeper into the crowd until any words they spoke could not be overheard. Daniel jerked away from his father's grip. "Knew you this would happen?" he demanded of his father.

Elnathan's face tightened. To speak so to one's father could have him turned over to the elders of the city for punishment.[14] Some parts of Moses' Law had not been forgotten. But his father's face softened abruptly. "Nay, my son, I did not. The king bade me

---

[14] Deuteronomy 21:18-21.

only return him to Jerusalem.[15] I supposed the prophet would be imprisoned, not slain." He reached out and took Daniel's shoulder again. "Harken, my son. Go, find Jeremiah the prophet and tell him what befell here. I fear the king's wrath will fall upon him if he does not hide himself. He is in much danger."

Daniel's eyes widened. "Truly, Father?"

Elnathan nodded, his troubled face looking back toward the throne. "This is an ill deed. Jeremiah must be warned. Make haste, son, but tread lightly. Do not let the king's attention fall upon you."

A spike of determination rose in Daniel's breast. He glanced back toward the king, but the king wasn't looking at them. He was looking off into the distance, waging an internal war that Daniel could not possibly understand. Strangely, it was Mattaniah who was staring at Daniel and his father. Hatred brought the young man's eyes so close together that his eyebrows merged into a single line.

Daniel gave the king's youngest brother a flippant half bow and deliberately turned his back on him. He knew Mattaniah would be furious, but as far as Daniel was concerned, the prince could eat raw rats to ease his wrath. He wasn't the king and likely would never be. Not even King Jehoiakim trusted his scheming brother totally.

"Where will the prophet be?" Daniel whispered to his father.

Elhanan's eyes slid to another man not far away, a quiet man who watched the proceedings without so much as revealing anything on his face. He was one of the nobles. His father nodded in the man's direction. "Know you that fellow's brother?"[16]

Daniel thought for a moment. "Baruch?"

"Aye. Seek the prophet within his house. Hurry."

Daniel nodded and then slipped through the throng, sneaking outside.

"Where are you going, Daniel?"

Daniel whirled about and found Mishael hard on his heels. The lad's eyes danced with curiosity. No way around it now. Mishael

---

[15] Jeremiah 26:20-23.
[16] Jeremiah 32:12; Jeremiah 51:59.

would insist on coming. "We must warn Jeremiah the prophet," Daniel explained quietly. Then louder, he said, "So come and keep up if you can!" Daniel shot off, Mishael bounding after like a frolicky ibex.

Daniel didn't know how much time he had, but if his father's suspicions held true, Jeremiah was in imminent danger.

2

Jerusalem, after having been expanded by King Hezekiah, now covered much of the western hill, but it was to the City of David that Daniel now raced. In King David's day, the whole of Jerusalem encompassed the narrow ridge of the eastern hill, Mount Zion, and was overlooked by the taller Mount of Olives further to the east. Despite the defensibility of the ridge, it was the Gihon Spring, the main source of water, that had determined Jerusalem's ultimate location.

King Solomon had expanded the city further north to include Mount Moriah and there built the temple that dominated the highest place in the city. No matter how a worshiper went about it, he had to always ascend to the temple.

The narrow ridge upon which the City of David had been built was highly defensible. On three sides, steep slopes rose to the flattened top, which was surrounded by a sturdy wall. History said that Joab, King David's nephew and battle commander, had taken the city,[1] but only through subterfuge. Daniel had heard that Joab had used the Gihon Spring to infiltrate the city and open the gates, climbing up through a channel cut in the wall to bring water into the city.[2] King Solomon, as part of his expansion, had extended the walls to cover the spring, thus ending that vulnerability.

But after the Assyrians had destroyed Israel in the north, refugees had flooded south to Judah in Hezekiah's day, too many to house in the City of David. A city emerged almost overnight on the western hill. To protect them, Hezekiah built a massive wall that effectively quadrupled the size of Jerusalem, though he had to destroy some of the homes to provide the needed stone for the wall.[3] The new city was not as easily defended, and the walls Hezekiah had built were thicker and higher than those surrounding the City of David.

The western hill descended gently into the central valley, but once there, Daniel had to race up the steps that had been carved into the ridge leading up to the City of David. He was nearly out of breath by the time he reached the top. Merchants looked at him quizzically as he and Mishael darted past.

Baruch's house had been built next to the wall of the temple mount in the part of the city that Solomon had expanded. Jeremiah was a prophet, but he was also a Levite and a priest,[4] and so it was natural that the prophet would want to be close to the temple. It was said that the word of the LORD had come to Jeremiah as a child.[5] If true, it was a marvel that one so young would be called into Jehovah's service. Daniel fervently wished for a similar calling.

"What's going on?" Mishael gasped out, running alongside Daniel as they dodged people, carts, and animals. "Why is the prophet in danger?"

---

[1] 1 Chronicles 11:4-6.
[2] 2 Samuel 5:8.
[3] Isaiah 22:10.
[4] Jeremiah 1:1.
[5] Jeremiah 1:5-6.

Daniel shot his cousin an incredulous look. He knew Mishael to be highly intelligent. His father was the chief scribe of the King's Court, and the lad could already read and write and was learning the Chaldean tongue. His older brother, Hananiah spoke the Egyptian and Assyrian tongues already.

"You saw what happened," Daniel retorted.

"But Jeremiah is a priest!" Mishael protested. "The king would harm him not!"

"The king is fearful," Daniel puffed out as he ran. His own insight surprised him.

"What mean you?"

"The Egyptian army marched through the Shephelah[6] and Megiddo only last month. Know you where they were going?"

"Carchemish," Mishael breathed out, keeping pace. "To battle the Chaldeans."

"Aye, and no matter who is victorious, the victors will come here."

"But we already pay tribute to the Egyptians![7] Why would they come here?"

Daniel gave his cousin a tight smile that betrayed his cynicism. "They will wish to recoup their expenses."

Mishael fell silent. He knew the truth of Daniel's words. Every army in history sought to balance the cost of their campaigns at the expense of the people of the land in which they fought. It would be no different this time, and the outcome for the Egyptians was in serious doubt. The Chaldeans had emerged from Babylon like an angry lion, young, hungry, and set on slaughter. King Nabopolassar had defeated the Assyrians by entering into a league with the Medes and then sacking Nineveh. The aged but vengeful king of Babylon was now flexing his strength by pushing his armies to the west along the mighty Euphrates River, and Pharaoh Necho was determined to stop him.

---

[6] The Philistine plains near the Mediterranean Sea.
[7] 2 Kings 23:33; 2 Chronicles 36:3.

It was the most talked about subject in court.

And then there was Jeremiah the prophet and his words that Jerusalem would fall to the Chaldeans. No one wanted that. The Egyptians, at least, were willing to let the Hebrews live in peace as long as they paid the yearly tribute. Who knew what the Chaldeans would do. Rumor painted the Babylonian general, Nebuchadnezzar, son of King Nabopolassar, as a butcher bent on razing the land and slaughtering the inhabitants. No one wanted Jeremiah to be right.

Daniel came to a stumbling stop before a wooden door set in a white rock wall. The houses in Jerusalem were tightly built together, each sharing at least two walls with their neighbors. Most were two-story affairs with a flat roof accessed by a wooden ladder from within.

Daniel hailed the house. "Ho, Baruch! It is Daniel, son of Elnathan. I bring word from the King's Court."

The door opened to reveal a young man in his mid-twenties, wearing a dark and well-trimmed beard. He had dark eyes, brown skin, and a face only a mother could love. It looked like a blacksmith had taken a hammer and tried to flatten his face—mostly successfully with the exception of protruding, bony brows. The young man blinked owlishly in the afternoon light. Here was a man more accustomed to candlelight than sunlight. "Daniel?" His voice carried a gravelly quality as if he didn't use it all that often.

"It is I," Daniel replied impatiently. "I bring word to Jeremiah the prophet from my father, a warning."

Baruch glanced up and down the street. His eyes fell upon Mishael, who shrugged and offered a polite, but unabashed bow. "What word?" he finally asked Daniel.

Daniel had no intention of bandying words with Baruch. The urgency his father had pressed upon him overrode his normal good manners. He shoved past the startled young man, slipping inside before the scribe could lay a hand on him.

Mishael followed, crowding into the living space of the home, muttering apologetic words to the annoyed homeowner. "My lord,

Jeremiah," Daniel called, glancing all about, "I bring word from the King's Court. Urijah the prophet has been slain by the king's hand. My father fears for your safety and sent me to bring warning."

A man emerged from the shadows gathered behind a wooden ladder that ascended into the second story of the home. He wore a priestly robe and had a full beard. His eyes looked haunted, but his face bore the tightness of a man prepared to face his executioners. He looked older than his thirty-five years. In a voice heavy with emotion, Jeremiah asked, "Urijah has been slain?"

Daniel bowed deeply to the prophet. "Aye, my lord, by the king's own hand. My father fears for your life. He bids you to hide until the king's wrath is abated."

The prophet staggered to a low table and sat down heavily on a rug placed beneath it. "I knew this day would come," he breathed out. "It was not so in the days of King Josiah, but his son..." He trailed off, looking at the stone wall of the house. "I wished not to speak the words of the LORD. I wished not."[8]

Daniel and Mishael exchanged troubled looks. Neither thought to hear such words coming from a man of God. Daniel was wise enough, however, to realize that he had not yet walked in the prophet's steps, so he could not be a fair judge.

But then something changed behind Jeremiah's light-brown eyes, and he straightened abruptly. He looked at the three young men standing before him—two yet boys—and ran a hand over his eyes. "I would not speak these words, but I must. If the king and the princes of the land do not heed the words of the LORD, then all is lost. For the Chaldeans will prevail over the Egyptians, and the LORD will bring evil upon this city and upon its inhabitants. We must yield to the yoke of Babylon or be destroyed."

Daniel swallowed and shifted uncomfortably. The prophet spoke treason. No wonder King Jehoiakim wanted him dead. But it wasn't the first time Jeremiah had uttered such words. In fact, he'd been warning Judah of this since King Josiah died. Why would the

---

[8] Jeremiah 20:9.

king decide now to punish such words when he had not before? Something fundamental had changed in the king's mind, and Daniel wasn't sure what it was.

Mishael, ever quick to speak, burst out, "We are doomed then? Will the Chaldeans destroy all within the city? Should we flee, hide in the wilderness? I know of a place near Hebron, a place my father took my brother and me. Perhaps we could hide there. Or will the Chaldeans accept tribute as the Egyptians do? Should we—"

Daniel cleared his throat and gave his young cousin a hard look. The lad, fell silent, but he fairly squirmed with repressed words. Daniel turned back to the prophet, who was blinking at Mishael, likely trying to digest the barrage of words. Daniel asked, "Is there nothing that can be done to turn away the LORD's wrath?"

The prophet studied Daniel, seemingly surprised to find him still there. He stood back to his feet, coming several fingers below Daniel's own height. The prophet was not a man of great stature. "Nay, young one. The sins of King Manasseh cannot be lightly forgotten.[9] Nor will the LORD overlook the abominations of King Jehoiakim and the princes of Judah. Great evil comes." He started pacing, his hands clasped in front of him and his head bowed.

Baruch edged around the two lads and took a seat at the table, carefully rearranging a dozen candles to give him better light on what lay before him. A scroll of parchment lay open upon the tabletop next to a metal stylus and a clay bottle of ink. He picked up the pen and dipped the end in the ink and held it there, looking at the prophet in anticipation.

Daniel wasn't sure what was happening, but he fell silent and gave Mishael a commanding look lest his younger cousin begin talking again. If Mishael truly got started, it would take the combined forces of the Egyptian and Chaldean armies to stop him.

The prophet froze in mid stride abruptly and looked at the three of them. "We must save the ark of the LORD."

---

[9] 2 Kings 24:3.

Baruch began writing, but Jeremiah lurched forward and caught his hand.

"Nay, my friend, write this not. Leave no record of what we must do."

The scribe blinked. "What must we do, my lord?"

"My life is of no import. It is the ark that must be saved, for if not, the Chaldeans will surely destroy it or take it to Babylon, a trophy of their conquest. This must not come to pass."

All four turned to look at Baruch's northern wall. The slope of the house rose toward the north to meet a massive rock wall, the temple mount wall. Atop that massive platform built by King Hezekiah, stood Solomon's temple, and inside the Holy of Holies rested the ark of the LORD, the very seat of the presence of the LORD God of Israel.

Daniel had never seen it. The last time it had been removed from the most sacred place was when King Josiah had repaired the temple. It had been returned when the temple repairs had been completed,[10] and now, only the priests attended to it. A story of King David's day came to Daniel's mind. "Is this possible, my lord? Will not the LORD destroy any who come into His presence as He did Uzza, the son of Abinadab?"

Jeremiah shot Daniel a sharp look. "Uzza touched the ark in the pride of his heart, an act he would not have had to do if the ark had been carried with staves instead of driven in a cart. He forgot that the ark is holy." Jeremiah began pacing again. "I fear that the glory of the LORD has departed from the ark and Israel as it was in the days of Eli when his sons lost the ark to the Philistines."[11]

Daniel did not like hearing that. Was there truly no way to regain the LORD's favor? Was there no hope?

The prophet continued, "This must be done ere the Chaldeans come, for the LORD has spoken to me and has strengthened the might of the Chaldeans. Egypt and Assyria shall fall, for this is the

---

[10] 2 Chronicles 35:3.
[11] 1 Samuel 4:21.

day of the LORD God of hosts, a day of vengeance, that He may avenge Him of His adversaries. The sword shall devour, and it shall be satiated and made drunk with their blood, for the LORD God of hosts has a sacrifice in the north country by the river Euphrates."[12] The prophet seemed to shudder with those words, and even Daniel felt the weight of them. They carried the power of prophecy.

The prophet wiped sweat away from his brow and noted Baruch writing furiously. This time, Jeremiah didn't stop him. Only when he finished and set aside his pen did the prophet continue.

"What must be done to save the ark of the LORD must be done soon. The ark must be spirited away and hid until such a time as the LORD would reveal it."

Baruch pushed himself up from the table. "How may this be done? Of us here, only you are a priest of the LORD. Only you may enter into the presence of the LORD."

"Truly, I know not how this might be done or even if the LORD will permit it—nay, the LORD has put this in my heart. It will be permitted." He sucked in a deep breath. "There are others who will give us what aid they can." Jeremiah came to the table and leaned over it. "Seek out Ezekiel, the son of Buzi. He will lend us aid. As for me, I must seek an audience with Azariah, son of Hilkiah."

"The high priest?" Baruch looked stunned. "Will he harken unto you?"

"He must. Without his aid, we will not rescue the ark." The prophet's eyes flickered to the closed door. "And the king dare not come for me while I abide upon the temple mount. The LORD God of Israel still holds sway there."

"What words will you speak?"

Jeremiah stopped and faced Daniel and Mishael. He placed a hand on a shoulder of each boy, ignoring the scribe for the moment. "Fear not for me. Tell your father that I am safe for a time but repeat not what was said here of the ark. Do I have your pledge on this?"

---

[12] Jeremiah 46:1-10.

Daniel didn't hesitate. "I swear, my lord, not to say ought of the ark."

Mishael's mouth, however, hung open as he returned the prophet's look. The corner of Jeremiah's lips twitched beneath his dark beard. "I know you, Mishael, son of Elishama. All have heard of your true talent of *much* speech. Will you not pledge and tame your tongue this once?"

The lad nodded vigorously and then fell into a half bow. "I so pledge, my lord, upon my honor and the hope of Israel that I will not utter a word of what my ears have heard here! If I live a hundred years, yet will I not—"

"I thank you," Jeremiah interrupted, a smile finally blossomed on his face. It seemed to take years off his features. "It is a mighty vow indeed. See you to it then, Mishael, son of Elishama." He stepped back. "Now begone, the both of you. I thank you for your warning."

Daniel pulled his cousin out of the house and confronted him on the stone street. "Be mindful of your tongue, Mishael. You have given your pledge."

"I know it," the lad replied, a bit grumpily. "I know how to control my tongue despite what you and my brother may think. At the least, my mother believes I can hold my tongue when I must. Why then can you not? I tell you of a truth—"

"Then it is well," Daniel hastily interrupted, rubbing at his jaw line doubtfully and eyeing his cousin. Mishael looked to be fairly bursting with eagerness. Anyone who knew him would know with one glance that he had news he felt was important. Usually, it didn't take much to loosen his tongue. Daniel determined to keep an eye on his cousin, at least until the danger had passed along with whatever Jeremiah was going to do to save the ark. He felt a bit disappointed that he hadn't been asked to help. He'd have loved to lay eyes on the ark of the LORD and worship the LORD before it.

"Come," Daniel urged, "let us return."

They made their way south through the City of David and then west to the Valley Gate. They paused there to look over the expanded city of Jerusalem that covered the western hill, reflecting upon what the prophet had said about the coming evil. In his mind, Daniel couldn't conceive of such destruction, and he fervently prayed that the Lord would grant them mercy. For it wouldn't be only the city structures that would suffer, but the people too. He thought of his father, mother, and sister. Would they survive the coming horrors? Would he?

"Ho, Daniel! Ho, Mishael!"

Shaken out of his pensive reverie, Daniel looked down the steps leading into the central valley. A young man stood at the base of the stone steps waving up at them. This was Hananiah, Mishael's older brother.

"Ho, Hananiah," Daniel yelled back, starting down the steps.

Daniel and Mishael descended quickly. The three lads met upon a stone bridge underneath which a tiny trickle of water ran, the last remnant of a late spring rain. Hananiah, a quiet lad a year older than Daniel, kept looking over his shoulder. "Thank the Lord of Hosts that I found you," he said. "The king's brother seeks for you, Daniel."

"Mattaniah?" Daniel sighed. He had feared as much after giving the lad a mocking bow. He privately suspected that Mattaniah regularly ate rocks in order to perfect the stony grimace that he projected to the world. The fellow probably thought it made him kingly. It was an open secret to the sons of the princes of Judah that Mattaniah yearned to be king one day and resented the fact that his nephew, Jeconiah, was the crown prince. Not that King Jehoiakim would hear of such talk—not against his brother—and Mattaniah bore a well-oiled tongue that could speak out of both sides of his mouth at the same time.

Mattaniah was dangerous.

Daniel shifted from one foot to another, frowning. He didn't fear the king's brother, but he was intelligent enough to be wary. "Did he say why he seeks me?"

"Nay, only that you are commanded to present yourself to him immediately," Hananiah said, his face clouding over.

"I am summoned?" Daniel asked.

"Aye," Hananiah agreed.

Daniel squared his shoulders. He'd never backed down from confrontation before, and he didn't see a reason to begin now. "Then let us go see the king's brother." He marched off, sweeping the other two lads into his wake.

As brother-in-law to the king himself, Daniel enjoyed a bit of royal immunity from the conniving and backstabbing politics that had become the staple of Jehoiakim's court, but that didn't mean he was completely free of it. His father was one of the chief advisors to the throne, and as brother-in-law to the king, this meant Daniel was an obstacle to certain people.

Strangely, Hananiah and Mishael had decided to treat Daniel as the leader of a tiny faction among the sons of the princes who stood in opposition to the ambitions of the king's brother and even the king's eldest son. If it wasn't for the protection extended to Daniel by his father's position and his sister's love as the king's favorite wife, he might already be dead.

Well, so be it, then. It wouldn't be the first time Daniel had looked square into the fury of a storm and survived. He would trust in his God, so let the heathen rage!

3

With crossed arms and a cold smile, Nebuchadnezzar, crown prince of Babylon, commander of his father's armies, and most-favored of the god Marduk, watched the combined might of Assyrians and Egyptians marching directly toward him over the flat terrain with carnage in mind. He didn't mind. In fact, he relished the coming battle, knowing he would, at long last, finish what his father had started: utterly destroy the last remnant of the once mighty Assyrians. That the Egyptians had decided to join the Assyrians and march against him was their mistake. Pharaoh Necho should have known better. The Egyptian would pay the price for his presumption.

"Think you they know we are here?" Nebuzaradan asked.

Nebuchadnezzar gave the captain of his guard a wry look and turned back to study the approaching armies. He tugged thoughtfully on one of the braids woven into his beard. "Aye, Ashur-uballit doubtlessly informed Necho that we hold the city." The crown prince frowned. "Marduk grant us favor, but how I wish we could have put the edge of the sword to that snake's neck afore he slithered away."

Nebuzaradan shifted his sword and tightened straps on his scale armor. The approaching enemy would soon be in range. "I hear, my prince," he murmured, ever loyal, never contradicting. "But how could we know he would play the coward and abandon his wives and children to save his own skin?"

"It matters not," Nebuchadnezzar concluded, waving a hand. "He has emerged from his hole and will surely die this day. Harken, my servant. Do not be lulled into a trap or be dissuaded from our purpose. Necho is nothing. Defeat the Egyptian we will, but Ashur-uballit must die this day. The Assyrians must be no more. See you to it. Seek out the rogue wherever he hides and bring me to him. He will not escape as he did at Haran or when we first came against Carchemish."

Two days ago, Nebuchadnezzar had led a surprise attack against the fortified city of Carchemish. He had slipped his army across the Euphrates at night and then attacked the city before the Assyrians were fully prepared. The enemy had been routed and their surviving forces had fled south to meet up with Pharaoh Necho's approaching army. They had left behind their women and children.

And now, after having found allies, the cowardly Assyrians were finally returning, heading due north toward the captured city and using the Euphrates River to anchor their eastern flank.[1] The river would not protect the enemy. It would be their undoing. Nebuchadnezzar rolled his neck, loosening muscles. His smile, if he could have seen it, had a distinct reptilian cast.

From the broken city walls of Carchemish, Nebuchadnezzar watched the advancing enemy. The captured city rested atop a long, oblong hill that overlooked both the flat land to the west and south and the Euphrates River to the east. It had become the capital of the Assyrian remnant after Ashur-uballit had been defeated at Haran. The sly dog had fled here, to Carchemish, more than three years ago.

---

[1] Jeremiah 46:2.

It was only now that Nebuchadnezzar's father, King Nabopolassar, had pacified Urartu and established trade routes into the north that his attention had once again turned to the thorn known as Ashur-uballit. The king had sent his son, Nebuchadnezzar, to deal with him once and for all.

Which Nebuchadnezzar was suitably satisfied to do. And without the Medes this time. The Medes had been instrumental in the overthrow of Nineveh, the original Assyrian capital, but Nebuchadnezzar had never particularly liked them—despite having married the King of Media's daughter—and was happy to conduct this campaign without the Chaldean's uneasy ally.

"Prepare to sound, trumpeters," the prince commanded, holding up one hand.

To his left stood three men holding long ram's horns. Dressed in armor that followed the traditional Assyrian modes, they stood ready, watching their prince with steady eyes.

Nebuzaradan drew his sword and held it high. Midday sunlight glinted off the iron blade and off the sweat that coated his bronze-colored arm. Indeed, the sun beat down on everyone, the summer heat sweltering and casting shimmering waves of illusion that rolled over the plains and the approaching army.

"Steady!" Nebuchadnezzar said, his gray eyes narrowed to pierce the waves of heat that partially obscured the approaching army. "Steady…"

He waited another five minutes, allowing the enemy to march nearly to the base of the city. Chariots, horses, and rank after rank of foot soldiers marched right into the trap.

"Now!" Nebuchadnezzar clenched his raised fist tightly.

The trumpeters sounded, their horns blaring out a three-note signal while his captain of the guard waved his sword in the sunlight. From the west, dust rose into the clear sky: the upper jaw of Nebuchadnezzar's trap. Shouts went up from the enemy as they spotted the dust too. Time to spear the enemy upon the lower jaw and hold it there while the upper one snapped shut.

Whirling around, the prince leaped off the wall and ran to his battle horse. Mounting, he turned the trained animal toward one of the breaches in the wall. He strapped on his heavy shield, drew his sword, and slapped the horse's flanks with the flat of the blade. The horse snorted loudly, gathered itself, and then exploded over the rubble of the broken wall. The slope on the other side angled down steeply, but not so much that the horse couldn't navigate it, though it nearly slid down on its rump in a cloud of dust and dirt.

From other breaches, more horses appeared, and atop the remaining wall, a line of archers emerged, bows already drawn. A rain of death descended upon the enemy. Screams, curses, and prayers to their gods filled the air.

The Egyptian forces were already in disarray. Commanders were trying to adjust their defenses to counter the Chaldean chariot attack coming from the west, and they clearly had not expected a frontal attack from the city itself. The first signs of panic began to materialize in the enemy ranks.

Nebuchadnezzar and his calvary slammed into the front ranks of Egyptian foot soldiers while confusion abounded. His eyes glittering in battle lust, Nebuchadnezzar laid about him on either side, cutting flesh like a butcher carving up meat. Someone jabbed a spear at him, but he deflected it with his shield easily and spurred his horse forward. The heavy horse slammed into the foot solider, knocking him flat and then trampling the body into the blood-soaked dirt.

From the west, a massive body of chariots met the disorganized ranks of the Egyptians and mowed down entire ranks of the enemy. Meanwhile more arrows from the city walls rained down, and a flight of javelins flew over Nebuchadnezzar's head to kill the horses pulling the Egyptian chariots.

Nebuzaradan appeared at Nebuchadnezzar's side. Blood trickled from a scalp wound and the captain had lost his horse, but his expression remained unmoved. He could be strolling through a garden on a summer's eve for all the emotion he showed. "There, my lord!" the captain shouted, pointing with the tip of his sword.

Nebuchadnezzar looked. Milling chariots couldn't hide Necho's standard of Amun-ra, the Egyptian sun god. The standard depicted a flat disc of gold upon which was etched the head of a man wearing a hawk's headdress. And the Egyptian king himself stood high on his chariot holding aloft his royal scepter and shouting orders. He made quite the figure what with the sun gleaming off his bronze scale armor.

Next to the pharaoh, cowering as Nebuchadnezzar knew he would, was Ashur-uballit. The Assyrian king hunched low in the chariot next to the mighty pharaoh, eyes peering over the edge of the vehicle. Nebuchadnezzar muttered a prayer of vengeance to Marduk, and for good measure, another one to Nabu, Nebuchadnezzar's namesake, and urged his horse in that direction.

It didn't take long for Ashur-uballit to notice the approaching Chaldean prince. The man started gibbering inanely, motioning frantically at Nebuchadnezzar and tugging on Necho's arm. Necho yanked his arm free, a disgusted snarl clear upon his lips, but he did turn to look at where the man was pointing, and the two mighty leaders locked eyes.

Pharaoh Necho had dark brown skin, typical of northern Egyptians[2] and lacking the blacker skin of the Nubians who also fought among the Egyptian ranks. His face, lined already from his many battles, held no fear. His eyes never flinched or turned away from Nebuchadnezzar. The Chaldean prince's grin widened even more. Here was a true king, a worthy adversary—unlike the cockroach squatting at Necho's side.

Only one man stood between him and the enemy king. Nebuchadnezzar deflected a sword thrust with his shield and ran his own sword through his assailant's neck. He kicked the dead man aside without ever so much as blinking or his horse so much as breaking stride. Time to end this.

---

[2] Jeremiah 46:8-12.

But then warriors of pharaoh's bodyguard flowed together between the Chaldean prince and their master. These were elite fighters, likely descendants of the ancient Medjay.[3] Most had black skin that seemed almost dark blue in the bright sunlight. They possessed better armor and superior weapons than those Nebuchadnezzar had already faced among the Egyptians.

Nebuchadnezzar licked his lips as a thrill jolted his body. He'd always wanted to test himself against the Nubian weapons masters. Their fame had reached all the way to Babylon, and when Nebuchadnezzar had discovered that the Egyptians were marching against him, he had secretly hoped for this very outcome.

Still grinning, he slid off his horse and confronted the nearest Nubian warrior. The man's lips were pulled back into a snarl and his dark brown eyes held no fear. The warrior attacked immediately with a speed that defied description. Nebuchadnezzar barely deflected the attack with his shield, but the next one caught him and left a bloody cut down the length of his forearm. He grimaced as salty sweat burned in the cut.

The Nubian hadn't relaxed his snarl, except to lick his lips—in pleasure. Nebuchadnezzar knew right then that he was outmatched. This man had trained his entire life for this. He had done nothing else except fight, and to be appointed to the pharaoh's bodyguard meant no one was better, no one could compete—not one on one. For the first time, Nebuchadnezzar felt a measure of fear trickle into his brain. He could lose this fight. He could die.

Then the main force of Chaldeans caught up to him and a wall of spears, driven with the weight of a charging horse, cut the Nubians down. Sighing in relief, Nebuchadnezzar swore to offer a suitable sacrifice to Ishtar and Marduk when this was all over. He had been careless and nearly gotten himself killed. He berated himself for forgetting his own admonition not to get sidetracked.

---

[3] The Medjay were an ancient group of elite bodyguards to the pharaohs. They were last mentioned in Egyptian literature roughly 500 years before this story takes place.

With the collapse of the Nubians, the other Egyptian warriors panicked. They threw down their weapons and began fleeing southwest toward the Egyptian stronghold at Hamath. For a moment, Necho's chariot was vulnerable as his forces disintegrated around him. The Egyptian's eyes, though, had never left the Chaldean prince.

Necho's chariot driver whipped the horses into a frenzy, and the vehicle lurched away, but not before Necho gave Nebuchadnezzar a nod of respect and then shoved Ashur-uballit out the back. The Assyrian king screamed as he toppled out, his eyes bulging from his head. He hit the hard ground with enough force to lift a small cloud of dust. The abandoned king rolled over, hands raised in beseeching dismay. But Pharaoh Necho had turned his back and was carried rapidly away with the fleeing Egyptian army.[4]

It was a clever move by far. Necho knew that Nebuchadnezzar would pursue immediately if he took the embattled Assyrian king with him. By throwing him out of the chariot, he had created a temporary reprieve while the Chaldeans dealt with Ashur-uballit. Similar abandonments were happening all over the battlefield as the Egyptians betrayed the remaining Assyrians, using them as fodder to cover their retreat. It had the feel of a prearranged tactic for which the Chaldean prince gave silent tribute to Necho. The Egyptian was truly a wily adversary.

Slowly, the sounds of battle died off, leaving only the groans of the wounded and the feeble screams of the dying to lash at the ears. Nebuzaradan appeared next to Nebuchadnezzar once again. "I will call for the physician, my prince," he said, indicating the cut on Nebuchadnezzar's forearm.

"There is no need for haste," Nebuchadnezzar replied briskly, sheathing his sword. "The wound is but minor. Come." He pushed past his guard captain and strode over to where Ashur-uballit had risen shakily to his hands and knees and was trying to crawl away. He was surrounded by a dozen Chaldean soldiers who kept their

---

[4] Jeremiah 46:5-6.

distance. They knew better than to touch him. This man belonged to Nebuchadnezzar alone.

Nebuzaradan followed at the prince's shoulder as they came up to the Assyrian king—king no longer. The captain put a foot against the man's side and shoved, sending him sprawling onto the ground on his back. The defeated man stared stupidly up into the hot sky. "Mercy," he whispered in the Assyrian tongue. "Show mercy, son of Nabopolassar. Once your father offered me mercy as a king. I claim it in the name of your father."

Nebuchadnezzar regarded the fallen king without expression. The man had been an irritation, nothing more. But it was what he represented that mattered. Ashur-uballit was the last Assyrian king. With his death, the Assyrian power that had ruled the land for over three hundred years would be forever broken. The wrongs that Babylon had suffered under Assyrian rule would at last be avenged—and to think, it was the small Chaldean tribe that had emerged victorious over the once mighty Assyrians, conquered Nineveh, and brought their power to naught.

Nebuchadnezzar looked around at his men and gestured to the defeated man. "Flay him and stake his body wide to the ground beneath the sun. Nail his skin to the walls of Carchemish beside the skins of his wives and children." He paused, letting those words sink into the man's panicky and horror-filled mind. He then added, "Let Shamash, the sun god, pronounce judgment." He bent down to look Ashur-uballit in the eyes. The man's face had grown clammy with terror, his eyes rolling around senselessly. "Pray to Shamash for mercy, cowardly dog. If he grants you mercy, then who am I to say nay? But know, dog, he granted no mercy to your wives and children."

Ashur-uballit's mouth hung open, his tongue moving soundlessly while tears plowed muddy tracks down his dust-covered face. Disgusted, Nebuchadnezzar straightened and turned away, drawing Nebuzaradan to him as they walked back toward the city. Behind them, the first screams of the flaying reached his ears. It brought a satisfied smile to Nebuchadnezzar's lips. He'd waited a long time to hear that sound.

"What now, my prince?" Nebuzaradan asked, gathering up Nebuchadnezzar's horse and pulling it along behind the pair.

Nebuchadnezzar pulled off his helmet and wiped his brow free of sweat and handed his shield to one of the young warriors nearby. He yearned for the breeze found atop the king's palace in Babylon. Smoothing down his beard, he said, "Send word to Ashpenaz. Command him to ready my wives for I would be attended."

Nebuzaradan snapped an order and one of the commanders ran off toward the captured city. The master of Nebuchadnezzar's eunuchs was one of the most proficient and intelligent men he had ever met. The man would likely have things ready long before the messenger reached him. It had been a calculated risk bringing along some of his wives during the campaign against the Assyrian king. He'd only brought three, ones who had not yet given him either son or daughter. In truth, one of the reasons for bringing them was to have Ashpenaz's presence and advice. Nebuzaradan was a talented battle commander, but the master eunuch understood politics like no other. Nebuchadnezzar felt fortunate to have him, a gift from Nabu, the god of wisdom, no doubt.

"The Egyptians flee, my lord," Nebuzaradan said, bringing the conversation back around to what was important.

"We will pursue," Nebuchadnezzar replied. "Egypt has had its foot on the Levant[5] for long enough. I would deny them this road to Babylon."

"The Egyptian king surely flees to Hamath."[6]

"And we will pursue and destroy it." He stopped then and looked at the faithful captain of his guard who looked as calm as a cloudless day. "Fret not, Nebuzaradan, we will drive the Egyptians

---

[5] The Levant is the region along the eastern shore of the Mediterranean Sea. It includes Israel but also much more.

[6] An Egyptian stronghold. See 2 Kings 23:33.

back to their homeland, and if we must, we will burn it down around them and fill the Nile with their blood."

The captain's face cracked with a tight smile. "That is well, my prince. What of the vassal cities in the Levant?"

"They shall submit or be destroyed," Nebuchadnezzar said with hardly a thought. "But we must proceed with caution. It would not do to leave an enemy behind us as we pursue the Egyptians."

Nebuzaradan nodded. This was sound tactical judgement. "I hear tell of the Hebrews," he mentioned off hand. "There is a story of the land of Judah and their riches. Is this not written by Merodachbaladan?"

Nebuchadnezzar grunted. "Merodachbaladan was a fool."

The long dead king of Babylon had been solidly under the thumb of the Assyrians in those days. He had died under their thrall, a slave to their every whim.

"How so, my lord?"

"Merodachbaladan sought to throw off the yoke of the Assyrians, but in place of trusting Marduk and finding strength in his own people, he sought for deliverance in foreign lands and at the feet of other gods. There was indeed some business with the Hebrew God, but it came to naught."[7]

"Yet…I hear tell of their riches," Nebuzaradan hedged with a straight face.

Nebuchadnezzar glanced at him and couldn't suppress his own greedy smile. "Aye, you speak truly. Perchance it would behoove us to lay eyes on this city of the Hebrews."

Nebuzaradan's face finally showed a measure of emotion: avarice. "Jerusalem."

"Aye. Jerusalem."

---

[7] Isaiah 39:1-2.

4

Jeremiah couldn't stop pacing. The wait for Azariah had dragged on and on. The high priest knew the urgency of the matter, knew that Jeremiah brought word from the LORD God of Israel, so why was the man making him wait? It had been two days since Jeremiah had fled to the temple to avoid possible imprisonment. So far, King Jehoiakim had not made any overt moves to arrest Jeremiah, but that could change at any moment. He couldn't allow himself to be captured yet—not until his purpose had been accomplished and the ark of the LORD safe.

It had taken nearly two days to get a reply from Azariah that he was willing to meet. They'd agreed to meet in the entrance of the New Gate on the upper court of the temple mount. The high priest was late—by two hours.

"He will come, my lord," Baruch said from his stationary perch on the steps that led down to the lower court.

Jeremiah took that as a gentle admonition to have patience, but the matter was too urgent for any further delay. Already, word had come down from the far north of a battle brewing between the Egyptians and the Chaldeans. No one knew the outcome as of yet or even if the two had met on the field of battle—except for Jeremiah. The LORD had already spoken to him of the outcome.[1]

He stopped to stare at Baruch. "The Chaldeans come," he said softly. "They come."

Ezekiel, the son of Buzi,[2] in contrast to Jeremiah, stood as still as a statue while he waited with the two other men. Ezekiel was a stocky man, well groomed, with chiseled features framed by black hair and bright brown eyes. Where Jeremiah wore his emotions on his sleeve, Ezekiel let nothing of what he felt touch his face or his voice. He had to be the most enigmatic man Jeremiah had ever met. Only the man's devotion to the priesthood and to the God of Israel had convinced Jeremiah that he could be trusted.

That and the fact that the young priest truly believed the words Jeremiah had spoken.

"The high priest comes," Ezekiel said in a deep, resonating voice that sparked a bit of envy in Jeremiah. He wished for a voice like that.

Jeremiah turned to look. The high priest, trailed by three other priests, emerged onto the upper court from the southern stairs. One of the men was Pashur, head of the Levitical family of Immer and currently chief governor of the temple.[3] The one farthest to the left was the high priest's son, Seraiah,[4] who would one day follow his father in that office. Jeremiah didn't know the fourth man except in passing. All four paused for a moment to turn and face the temple. The bronze pillars to either side of the temple entrance shone like fire in the morning light. The three priests sang a psalm of praise to

---

[1] Jeremiah 46:1-12.
[2] Ezekiel 1:3.
[3] Jeremiah 20:1. There were 16 priestly orders set up by King David in 1 Chronicles 24. The Immer order was number 16 (24:14). The head of the order currently providing service to the temple was considered the chief governor (captain) of the temple.
[4] 1 Chronicles 6:13-14.

Jehovah, and only then did they move over to where Jeremiah waited impatiently.

"I beg your forgiveness," Azariah said as he came up before Jeremiah. His tone of voice indicated he was doing anything but begging. "The king required my presence to seek my counsel."

Jeremiah sighed within his spirit. If the king and high priest were colluding, his purpose would be in jeopardy. He had no idea how to rescue the ark without the high priest's aid.

Azariah adjusted his priestly robes, emphasizing the ephod and breastplate of his office.[5] Jeremiah wondered if the high priest had picked his position deliberately so that the sun would cause the precious gems in the breastplate to sparkle brilliantly.

"What word from the LORD?" Azariah said brusquely.

At this, other passing priests stopped what they were doing and began to gather around. A spike of fear shivered up Jeremiah's spine. The LORD had commanded him to speak these words in the court,[6] but he had hoped to do so only to the high priest—not to the entire priesthood!

He and the high priest, although not friends, had been at least friendly in times past. Surely, the high priest would heed his words. Surely! Swallowing his apprehension, Jeremiah straightened his shoulders and spoke, wishing silently that he had Ezekiel's voice, "Thus says the LORD: 'If you will not hearken to Me, to walk in My law, which I have set before you, to hearken to the words of My servants the prophets, whom I sent unto you, both rising up early, and sending them—but you have not hearkened—then will I make this house like Shiloh, and will make this city a curse to all the nations of the earth.'"[7]

There. He'd done it. Quick and easy. Still, he knew how it sounded, lifting up the prophets above that of the priests. No priest would take kindly to those words. And he was right.

---

[5] Exodus 28:2-43.
[6] Jeremiah 26:1-3.
[7] Jeremiah 26:4-6.

Azariah's face darkened like a thundercloud and the priests began angry murmuring among themselves.

"You lie!" shouted Pashur. "The prophets are not above the priests! You have not spoken in the name of the LORD! This is the LORD's city, His holy people! What you speak is blasphemy!"

A chorus of vengeful ayes erupted around Jeremiah who had taken several steps back. He looked around, but there was no escape; he was completely surrounded. Only Ezekiel stood like a bulwark against the growing fury.

This was not an unexpected result. Jeremiah had faced such doubters since he'd first heard the word of the LORD as a young lad. But this time, things were different. This time, the instruments of the LORD's wrath were coming…and his benefactor, King Josiah, was now dead.

Jeremiah flung out a hand, pointing to several men whispering together in the back of the crowd. They had their hair cut in a bowl-like style, shaved all the way around the sides to show the many tattoos that decorated their scalps. "Why then are the priests of Molech permitted to stand on holy ground?! Surely you can see that the glory of the LORD has departed this place. How can the land bear the abominations of our hands? The LORD will not abide such!"

Azariah threw a disgruntled look at the trio of Molech priests who did not appear bothered in the least by the prophet's words. And why should they? They had King Jehoiakim's favor while the high priest of the LORD was merely tolerated in court.

"They are nothing," Azariah spat out, turning back to Jeremiah. "The priests of the LORD remain true."

Jeremiah raised an eyebrow. His hand stabbed out again, this time toward the massive altar that rested atop a raised platform just to the north of the temple entrance. "Behold the evidence of your sin! Why does the altar grow cold? Did not the LORD our God command that the fire ever burn?"[8] He glared about him as best he could, but he secretly worried his face looked more petulant than

---

[8] Leviticus 6:13.

angry. "And why has meat sacrificed to idols been offered to the LORD and leavened bread eaten at this past Passover feast? What of the sabbaths? Have not the people labored on the most holy day, profaning the LORD's rest? What of the children offered to Molech? Innocent blood has been shed and the LORD will not hold us guiltless!"

Jeremiah tried his glare again, but he just didn't have the right face for it. Instead of cowering, the priests' necks stiffened. There was only one path to avoid the coming calamity, but even the notion of it left a bad taste in his mouth. How much more would these prideful priests resist?

"Even now," he said, "the Chaldeans come. They are the servants of the LORD, and we must yield to them or be destroyed!"

"The Chaldeans serve false gods!" Seraiah, son of the high priest, barked in clipped tones. "They be no servants of the LORD. Shall the true servants of the LORD serve the heathen? Nay, the LORD will defend His people! Your words are blasphemy! It is evil! Seek you to weaken our hearts? You betray your own people!"

Before Jeremiah could refute those words, Pashur pushed up before Jeremiah, his face contorted in rage. "You speak not for the LORD, Jeremiah son of Hilkiah. For these words, you deserve to die!"[9]

The prophet flinched in the face of this pronouncement. He'd been delivering the words of the LORD for many years, but this was the first time anyone had brought up killing him to his face. If the priests had the ammunition right then, they surely would have stoned Jeremiah to death.

"You have no cause!" Jeremiah shouted back, worried as the priests jostled closer to him. "I but speak the words of the LORD. I was forbidden from diminishing a single word!"[10]

Hands reached out and grabbed Jeremiah by the arms. He tried to yank himself free, but too many hands held him fast. Someone

---

[9] Jeremiah 26:8.
[10] Jeremiah 26:2.

slammed a fist into his side, causing the prophet to double over and nearly retch. Another fist struck him in the face. If it wasn't for the hands holding him up, he'd have collapsed entirely. His legs felt like willow branches, and bright spots appeared before his eyes.

Nothing else followed, thank Jehovah, but when he could see clearly, he found himself looking into the eyes of Azariah. The high priest had a hand up to stay his fellow priests from ripping Jeremiah apart, and Ezekiel was leaning in close and speaking softly into the high priest's ear. Azariah nodded. "Hold your wrath, Pashur." He set his eyes on his equally angry son. "Send word to the king and the princes of Judah of what was spoken here by…by this man. His fate belongs to all the people, not only us. They too must hear his words and judge for themselves if he is worthy of death."

A reprieve, even if a temporary one. Jeremiah breathed out a sigh, but he couldn't stop his legs from trembling, and the pain in his side made drawing breath a trial all its own. Ezekiel continued to stand beside him, though he stared off into the distance as if the events swirling around him were of little import.

Baruch, Jeremiah's *most* faithful servant, had disappeared. Well, he couldn't blame the scribe. The man too risked death by being so near the prophet. More people had gathered around, including priests of Ishtar and Baal. Their very presence on the temple mount sickened Jeremiah. And despite his personal danger, tears gathered in his eyes. He knew what was coming, and he knew the only way to avoid mass destruction was to serve the Chaldeans. But looking at the angry faces surrounding him, he knew they had hardened their hearts against this truth. They were blind to their own sins.

And Jeremiah wept for them.

An hour later, the princes of Judah had gathered, called by the high priest to bear witness to Jeremiah's words. The princes sat down in the new gate entrance, pulling Jeremiah down to the lower court so that they could look down upon him in judgement. His words were repeated—mostly accurately—to the princes who listened to them with stony, inscrutable faces.

Among the princes, Jeremiah spotted Daniel's father, Elnathan. With the prince was Elishama, the king's scribe, Ahikam, the temple scribe, Delaiah, and others. Of them all, he felt certain only Elnathan would look favorably upon him, but then again, it had been Elnathan that had fetched Urijah out of Egypt and delivered the prophet to his death.

Ahikam stood to his feet, all eyes turning to him. He was the chief scribe of the temple, tasked with recording all events and words spoken. A stone table had been set beneath a roof at which the scribe often sat to write down important events. Indeed, even now, an ink pot, pen, and scroll sat ready upon the stone top. The aging scribe gazed out over the crowd and let his eyes fall upon Jeremiah. He spoke in a raspy voice, "What say you, Jeremiah, the prophet of the LORD?"

Jeremiah shook off the hands that held him, his captors stepping back but also keeping him ringed inside the crowd to prevent him from running. He straightened his shoulders again, muttering a silent prayer to Jehovah for deliverance. Then looking around at the people, he said, "The LORD sent me to prophesy against this house and against this city all the words you have heard. I deny it not. But now, therefore, amend your ways and your doings, and obey the voice of the LORD your God. Mayhap the LORD will repent of the evil He has pronounced against you."[11]

Little chance of that last happening, Jeremiah knew. The sins of Manasseh and now King Jehoiakim had long stained the land. The people were blind to their own abominations, but he had to give them some measure of hope. Perhaps if they tried hard enough, the LORD would be merciful—in some capacity.

Taking a deep breath, he added, "As for me, I am in your hands. Do with me as seems good to you. But know for certain, that if you put me to death, you shall surely bring innocent blood upon yourselves, and upon this city, and upon the inhabitants thereof. For

---

[11] Jeremiah 26:12-13.

of a truth, the LORD has sent me to speak all these words in your ears."

That last bit had been a gamble. The mood in the temple court was toxic at best. Jeremiah had angered the priesthood, but he hoped his words would energize cooler heads. He certainly didn't want to end up like Urijah. In the days following Urijah's death at the hands of the king, Jeremiah had heard the details in full. There would be no reasoning with Jehoiakim if Jeremiah was turned over to the king.

Elnathan stood next. As father-in-law to the king, his words carried weight. He surveyed the crowd, the lines in his face deepening with some hidden emotion. "This man is not worthy to die. He has spoken to us in the name of the LORD our God.[12] Harken to his words, O Israel, and let us call upon the mercies of the LORD lest this evil befall us!"

The priests muttered darkly at this, especially Pashur, who looked ready to grab a sword and run Jeremiah through at that moment, but Elnathan held up both hands. When the murmurings died down, the prince looked over to his companion. "Ahikam, tell us of Micah, the Morasthite."

The temple scribe regained his feet, his graying hair and beard swaying with the motion. His son, Gedaliah, an enigmatic young man who always bore a serious expression but somehow always managed to be trustful of others, stood beside his father. Ahikam cleared his throat and answered Elnathan, "In the days of Hezekiah, king of Judah, Micah spoke to all the people of Judah, saying that Zion will be plowed like a field, Jerusalem will become a heap, and the mountain of the house of the LORD as the high places of a forest."[13]

Not a word was muttered. This was recorded history. Every priest had heard this story. Elnathan again addressed the assembly, "Did King Hezekiah and Judah put him at all to death? Nay! Did the king not fear the LORD and besought Him for mercy? And did not

---

[12] Jeremiah 26:16.
[13] Jeremiah 26:18.

the LORD repent of the evil which he had pronounced against them?" His eyes fell upon Azariah, the high priest. "By putting this man to death, might we not procure great evil against our souls?"[14] He sighed heavily. "I fear greatly that we have already set this doom upon ourselves, for it was I, along with certain others, who brought Urijah the prophet up from Egypt and stood in silence as his blood was shed for the words he spoke in the name of the LORD.[15] Elders and priests of Judah, I am silent no more. How can we turn away the coming wrath if we put this man to death?"

Many of the princes were nodding, looking troubled, and Jeremiah let out a breath he hadn't even known he'd been holding. Sentiment was turning. Urijah's recent death had shaken the princes. The priesthood might not like it, but they would not act against the princes openly. Some might appeal to the king, but the power of the unified might of the princes of Judah was not something to take lightly—even by a king.

Ahikam's raspy voice rose over the crowd. "This man is not worthy of death. The words he speaks might fall heavy upon our ears, but they are the words of the LORD. Let us seek to amend our ways and perhaps the LORD will show us mercy."

Deliberately, the aged scribe marched down the steps and took Jeremiah by the arm. With a slight tug, the pair began moving through the assembly. Ahikam had to stare down Pashur and Seraiah, who only parted reluctantly to let the pair through. Ezekiel followed, and after a muttered conversation with his son, so did Azariah, the high priest. The rest of the assembly began to disperse, some clearly irritated that they hadn't gotten a chance to shed Jeremiah's blood.

Somewhere along the way, Baruch reappeared, acting as if he'd never left to begin with. Indeed, a *most* faithful servant. Jeremiah thought about berating the cowardly scribe, but the young man had the most amazing memory, the perfect asset to help Jeremiah put

---

[14] Jeremiah 26:19.
[15] Jeremiah 26:20-23.

JEREMIAH

many of the words of the LORD into writing. Jeremiah dared not run him off, not now when the young scribe was most needed.

By the north wall of the temple mount near the tower of Hananeel, Azariah stepped in front of Jeremiah. The high priest's eyes, however, kept looking back at the dispersing crowd. "Do you truly think the LORD will show us mercy if we amend our ways?" he asked, again without looking at Jeremiah directly.

Jeremiah blinked in surprise and then winced, rubbing at the side of his face where someone had struck him. It would leave a bruise. "Mercy, aye, but not deliverance. The LORD means to give us into the hands of the Chaldeans. If we serve them, the LORD may yet be merciful and preserve this house and city."

Finally, the priest turned to look at Jeremiah squarely. The prophet saw pain and worry in the man's eyes. Surprised, the remaining words he wanted to say died on his lips. Here was a man in distress.

"The Egyptians may yet prevail over the Chaldeans," Azariah said softly. "There is yet hope."

"Pray for it then, but when word comes of the Chaldeans' approach, then you will know my words are true."

Azariah nodded. "So be it then."

The high priest took a deep breath and then turned to stare at the temple. Jeremiah joined him, feeling a strange camaraderie for the man who had nearly sentenced him to death. It was a strange world...a strange time. Solomon's temple, repaired and expanded by Hezekiah and Josiah, rose high into the sky. The gilded doors gleamed as did the two pillars that flanked the entrance. Inside rested the most holy object in Judah, the ark. Several priests were hard at work rekindling the fire beneath the altar. At least Jeremiah's words had had some effect.

"I fear for the house of the LORD," the high priest murmured. "I am growing old, and my son who will follow me one day secretly worships Ishtar, seeking to other gods for deliverance."

Jeremiah's knees wobbled at those words, and he had to catch himself. A worse scenario he could not imagine. But this was the chance Jeremiah had been waiting for. "I fear for the ark of the LORD. The Chaldeans will not relent when their eyes behold it. They will take it. I fear its destruction."

"Would the LORD permit this?" Ahikam asked, his raspy voiced raised in shock. "Surely not!"

Jeremiah and Ezekiel shared a knowing look. "What know you of the priest Eli and his days?" Jeremiah asked.

A profound silence fell upon the group. No one had to say anything. All knew the story of how the glory of the LORD had departed from Israel and the ark. The ark of the LORD had been captured and spent months in Philistia. And though the Philistines suffered greatly while the ark was in their charge, the LORD had allowed the ark to fall into their hands to begin with.[16]

"You think the LORD will turn His eyes away," Azariah finally said with a deep sigh.

"It is my fear," Jeremiah acknowledged. Already tears were gathering in his eyes.

The high priest turned back and noticed the tears. His face softened, and strangely, he reached out a comforting hand and placed it on Jeremiah's shoulder. "Then I share your fear. What must be done? Has the LORD spoken?"

"Nay, the LORD has not spoken, except to place this burden within my heart. He has not forbidden me this desire to rescue the ark afore the Chaldeans come."

"Mayhap we can hide it beneath the temple mount," Ahikam suggested, stepping up next to the pair and looking around. "Would that suffice?"

They thought about it. There were places that this could be done. And it didn't have to be the temple mount. It could be hidden anywhere in Jerusalem. It was Ezekiel who shook his head. "The ark cannot be hidden in the city without the priests or the king knowing.

---

[16] 1 Samuel 4-5.

JEREMIAH

Would the king stay silent, knowing that the ark might purchase his life and the lives of his sons when the Chaldeans come? And what of the priesthood? Already some secretly bow before Molech and Ishtar—as does your own son, my lord Azariah. You know this. How many might betray the ark for gain?"

Baruch spoke up for the first time. "Then let the ark be taken from here…far from here and hid until such a time as the LORD would restore it to Israel. Let only a few take it by night, secretly and with stealth. Let them go to a location only one knows." He looked steadily upon Jeremiah.

Azariah looked aghast. "You wish for the ark to be taken from the holy city?"

"Aye. If the glory of the LORD has truly departed, then what matter? I trust the prophet of the LORD in this. I advise he choose a place and tell no others, not even those who go with him. Let him take the ark and the altar of incense and hide them from the Chaldeans, lest they be lost."

Ahikam sucked in a deep breath, his aged face seeming to grow older as Jeremiah watched. "I too trust the prophet. I lend my support to this."

The high priest looked doubtful and scared. "I would not be known as the one who lost the ark of the LORD," he said at last. "If only one man knows where it is hidden, how shall it ever come to light again?"

"The LORD will see to it," Jeremiah said. "We must put our faith in the LORD."

Reluctantly, the high priest finally capitulated. "So be it." He said the words like a curse. "But I would not that the ark be without a house or a roof. Take, too, the tent of the LORD's presence, so that the ark may rest therein."

Some of the original tabernacle remained in the temple, the poles and cloth a reminder of a time of wandering for the people of Israel. The part that once was known as the Holy of Holies of the tabernacle had survived. It could be carried with little hassle, seeing as it was meant to be transported.

Jeremiah bowed. "That is well spoken, my lord. I will take Ezekiel here and Baruch. Detail servants to attend us. We will cover the ark so that they know not what we transport."

"Then we must secret the ark away," Azariah said softly. "This will not be an easy task."

Jeremiah took his turn placing a comforting hand upon the high priest's shoulder. "No one must know, especially the king and your son."

Heaving another sigh, Azariah dipped his head. "This I know. We must do this beyond the eyes of any who would betray the ark." He then stared steadily into Jeremiah's eyes. "If found out, you will be put to death."

Jeremiah flinched. He'd known that but had chosen to ignore the possibility until the high priest had decided to throw it in his face. He straightened. "It is but a small risk beside that of losing the ark. I will do this."

"Where will you go?"

Jeremiah turned to look due east. "To the mount of God."[17]

---

[17] See the Additional Explanations at the end of the book for a further discussion on the lost ark.

5

Trembling, Jeremiah placed a foot on the first golden step that led up to the inner sanctuary, the oracle,[1] and the Holy of Holies. Before him, at the top of the steps, a massive curtain hung. The two embroidered cherubs seemed to stare right at Jeremiah, a warning to proceed no farther, that he was unworthy and unholy to enter the presence of the LORD God of Israel. The blue, purple, and scarlet colors contrasted sharply with the golden steps, floor, and walls of the outer sanctuary.

Jeremiah could take it no more. He collapsed to his knees on the steps, his entire body trembling and tears staining his cheeks and beard. "I cannot," he whispered to his companions. "I am not worthy."

Azariah stopped as well, unwilling to rush the prophet, and nodded his understanding. Ezekiel and his father, Buzi, also paused, though they continued to bow and mutter prayers. At this time of

---

[1] 1 Kings 6:16-19.

night, no light streamed in from the windows high up to either side of the outer sanctuary, but the ten menorahs,[2] five on each side,[3] shed enough light on the reflective gold surfaces to clearly see.

Behind the four men sat the table of shewbread and the altar of incense—not the *real* altar of incense, but a replacement. Azariah had already removed the original altar of incense. It and the tent for the ark were waiting for Jeremiah north of the city, out of view of the watchmen atop the walls. Getting the ark there under the cover of night was now the priority. They didn't have much time, but all the time in the world would not erase the feeling that Jeremiah was, in some way, profaning the ark with his presence.

"The Lord will permit this," Azariah said in a tone that clearly indicated he wished otherwise. Jeremiah glanced up at him as the other continued, "I fear your prophesy has come to pass already. The glory of the Lord has departed this place. We may enter so that we may save the ark."

Jeremiah sighed. The priest was right. Not two weeks past, the celebration of Pentecost, the feast of first-fruits, had been a muted affair. The king had chosen to ignore his obligations and the people had shown only a token interest in one of the three main feasts of the year that honored the Lord God above everything. For the priesthood, it had been a disaster, and some had seen it as a sign that the God of Israel was in descendance. Rumors of open high places cropping up in the towns and villages had already made their way to Jerusalem, and as Jeremiah already knew, some of the priests were now serving other gods.

Climbing back to his feet, Jeremiah waited a moment until his legs felt strong enough to continue. "Then let us proceed," he whispered, fearful of speaking too loudly. "Time flees by the second."

---

[2] *Menorah* is Hebrew for lamp. They were candelabras with six branches to hold a candle each along with a seventh at the very center.
[3] 1 Kings 7:49.

JEREMIAH

They continued up to the curtain. Jeremiah didn't want to touch it, knowing that once he passed through, there would be no going back. But the high priest put a hand to one edge and drew it aside. Beyond were two folding doors overlayed in gold and elegantly engraved with cherubims, palm trees, and open flowers.[4] With solemn movements, Azariah pushed open each door, revealing the oracle within.

Typically, the high priest would pass the curtain first and then close it so that when he opened the doors, none might see within. Tonight was different. With the curtain withdrawn and the doors opened, all four men could see what lay beyond.

Jeremiah nearly squeezed his eyes shut, fearing to look upon a place that no man but the high priest had laid eyes upon since King Josiah's repairs.[5] But he did not. His eyes were drawn immediately to the covenant box, the mercy seat, that sat between two massive cherubs of gold. A wingtip each of the cherubs touched over the ark and the other wings stretched out to brush the wall to either side of the room. Jeremiah had never seen anything so incredible in all his life. The ark seemed to have a life of its own, a glow that overpowered all other light.

From floor to ceiling, each gold-covered wall had been engraved with more cherubims and palm trees. The whole oracle sparkled from the light that now filtered into the room from the menorahs. The cherubs had been carved with such intricacy and detail that their eyes appeared to follow Jeremiah as he moved reverently within the oracle.

"Come," Azariah beckoned, "we must hasten. The night will not protect us for long."

Knowing what must be done, Jeremiah moved with the priest and retrieved one of the poles used to transport the ark. Ezekiel and his father picked up the other one. Together, they slid the poles

---

[4] 1 Kings 6:31-35.
[5] 2 Chronicles 35:3, the last mention of the ark's physical location in Scripture.

through the eyelets on either side of the ark. Only then did Jeremiah look nervously back out into the outer sanctuary. He saw no one. The priests who normally tended to the menorahs had been sent home for the night.

His eyes slid back to the ark. His first thought was how *clean* the ark was. He expected to see dried blood, the result of the sprinkling of the blood on the mercy seat during the Day of Atonement. He'd never considered that someone might clean the ark between times. But it made the golden mercy seat where the glory of the LORD often resided feel…empty. That, more than anything, told Jeremiah that the word given to him by the LORD would truly come to pass. It made his lips quiver.

"We must cover the ark," Buzi said, speaking for the first time. Ezekiel's father matched his son when it came to expressionless faces. In fact, Buzi seemed an older version of his inscrutable son.

Idly, Jeremiah wondered if those stoic expressions would shatter if he jostled the ark. The prophet froze. How had such a thought found its way into his mind? He shuddered, glancing upward meekly and swallowing hard. Did God have a sense of humor? He sucked in his breath, fully expecting fire to fall from heaven and consume him. *What ails me?*

Tearing his mind away from this dangerous path of thought, he focused on the high priest who had retrieved a veil. He and Buzi carefully draped it over the ark. That done, Jeremiah and the high priest took up positions to the rear of the ark while Ezekiel and his father went to the front. Together, they lifted the ark, using the stout poles.

Jeremiah blinked in surprise. It was much lighter than he expected.[6] For some reason, he had believed something so holy to bear more weight. Together they left the oracle and set the ark down on the floor of the outer sanctuary while Azariah closed the doors

---

[6] Calculations vary and are in much dispute. One of the best I found determined that the ark weighed around 183 pounds. This comes out to roughly 46 pounds per man.

and drew the curtain across the opening. If they did this right, no one would even know the ark was gone.

Lifting the ark once again, they ventured out of the temple and into the upper court next to the altar. Jeremiah looked nervously around. Stars winked down at them from a clear sky. The altar glowed from the fire burning flames within, casting dim light across the courtyard. The vague shapes of the twin towers of Meah and Hananeel blotted out some of the stars to the north. No one was about. Ezekiel had been chosen as the altar attendant that night along with his father, so no one else had cause or reason to be around.

Except for the soldiers posted at the towers.

King Jehoiakim was rightly nervous about the outcome of the war between the Egyptians and the Chaldeans. Flaming torches and flickering shadows from the upper bulwarks of the towers told Jeremiah that men stood guard above.

Trying not to hurry, they turned and headed for the towers. There was a small exit beneath the Hananeel tower that allowed access to the land north of the wall. Another exit lay to the east, allowing one to enter the Kidron Valley, but it was to the north that Jeremiah must first go and then east toward Jericho. From there, he intended to cross the Jordan River and then travel on toward Mount Nebo where he would hide the ark.

The small postern gate located beneath the tower of Hananeel was used exclusively by the priesthood. It was a convenient way to bring in sacrifices and supplies without having to navigate through the main city. It also provided an easy way out while remaining unseen. Taking the ark through the city would surely be noticed.

As it was, they still had to contend with the guards on the tower. A voice floated down to them from above as they neared the tower entrance. "Who comes?"

Jeremiah heard the high priest mutter something unflattering under his breath. "It is I, Azariah son of Hilkiah, high priest of the

LORD!" he called up in a strained tone. It would not be well if they woke up the entire priesthood.

The ark bucked as someone shifted around on their pole.

It also would not be well if they dropped the ark, Jeremiah mused grimly.

Holding his breath, Jeremiah continued toward the tower entrance. The guards above would need to descend if they intended to bar the way.

"What business have you here at this time of night, priest?" The voice from above lacked the respect Jeremiah normally associated with the common people when addressing a priest—especially the *high* priest. When they didn't stop or respond, the voice barked, "Stand still! Go no farther!"

In the darkness, Jeremiah and Azariah exchanged worried looks. "Take the burden from me," the high priest whispered to Jeremiah. "I will arrest the guards' attention and give you opportunity to escape. The gate can be opened from within, but not from without. Once beyond the wall, you must make haste."

Jeremiah hesitated. He knew Azariah would not be going with him, but he had found comfort in the high priest's aid and presence. He shifted, lifting the pole up over his head so that it rested on his other shoulder. Now standing between the poles, he accepted the one from Azariah. The weight doubled, but not beyond what Jeremiah could bear for a time—as long as he didn't have to go too far. *This* was likely punishment for his rogue thoughts earlier.

"Where is the wagon hidden?" Jeremiah whispered as Azariah started away.

"Beyond the first rise. Seek the old road that once led to the hill cities of Gibeah." The high priest paused. "May the LORD God of our fathers bless your way and protect you."

Jeremiah bowed his head. "I thank you."

"Go then. Make haste." Azariah moved off, calling louder to the guards above, "Abide there! Must I chasten you then? Interfere with the duties of the LORD's priests at your own peril!" Azariah disappeared into the darkness and began climbing the stone stairs that wound toward the top of the tower.

"Let us go," Jeremiah hissed at his companions in front of him.

Ezekiel and his father moved quickly, causing Jeremiah to grunt as he was dragged forward. He carried double the weight, but with the threat of discovery looming near, he forced his weary legs to plow onward. They came to the gate beneath the tower, and there was a delay while Buzi relinquished his hold on the ark to leverage open the heavy door. It squealed alarmingly, and a query was shouted from above. The high priest's voice rose with it, anger lashing out at the guards.

Smiling wryly, Jeremiah felt a spike of satisfaction that he was not the target of those words this time.

Together, Jeremiah and Ezekiel carried the ark outside the temple mount for the first time since King Solomon had first brought the ark to his newly built temple. For a second time that night, Jeremiah expected fire to descend from heaven and consume him for his impudent act of stealing away the ark of the LORD. Nothing happened. He heard nothing except the voices raised in dispute high in the tower and crickets singing their lonely songs.

Buzi closed the gate and joined Jeremiah, taking one of the poles. "My son is young and strong," he explained. "He can carry his side without stumbling."

Jeremiah nodded, the gesture lost in the darkness. The path leading away from the postern gate, wound along the ridge and then cut over the top and down the northern side of the hill. In preparation for this night, Jeremiah and Ezekiel had walked it several times over the last few nights to familiarize themselves with the way. The only thing he didn't know was exactly where the wagon and the servants Azariah had hired waited.

They moved slowly, knowing that a misstep would spill all of them, including the ark, down the eastern slope toward the Kidron Valley. Not a pleasant prospect. After some time, Buzi gave the burden back to Jeremiah and went to the front of the ark to aid his son, who, though he had not uttered a word of complaint, was likely growing tired.

Jeremiah was in his mid-thirties, strong, and in the prime of his life, but carrying this much weight over rocky and rough ground made his shoulders scream in pain and his legs cry in protest with each step. The ark was meant to be carried by four men, not three.

The LORD was with them, however, and they found the wagon, Baruch, and six servants awaiting them on the old road out of sight of the walls of Jerusalem. The servants were a mixed group of men from other lands: Moabites, Philistines, and Ammonites. Jeremiah found it odd that none of them were Hebrews.

A cold thought penetrated Jeremiah's mind. Did the high priest expect him to kill these men after the ark was hidden? There had been more than a few unexplained deaths in the city since King Jehoiakim took power. The streets of Jerusalem were stained with blood. No. He would not be part of such atrocities even if it would preserve their secret.

The three priests set the ark down out of sight of the servants, and Jeremiah went alone to greet Baruch. The servants all started when he appeared as if emerging from the darkness like an avenging angel. They cringed away from him as if expecting to be beaten. The prophet frowned. They likely had been beaten. It was a wonder none of them had run off. But then again, where would they go? If caught, their lives would be forfeited.

Several oil lamps had been hung around the wagon and a small fire had been started on the far side of the road. They cast enough light to see by. "Ho, Baruch!"

After a violent start, the scribe heaved a sigh of relief. "Did all go well?"

"As well as it could," Jeremiah replied. He glanced at the crouched servants and pointed down the road. "Wait you there," he commanded. They flinched from his tone, so he felt compelled to add in a softer tone, "But fear not. We mean you no harm, and what you do this day will bring favor upon you, this I swear. Serve faithfully, and you will be rewarded."

The men looked at each other as if they could hardly believe their ears. In the dim light provided by the fire, Jeremiah could see their ribs standing starkly against their skin. When was the last time any of them had eaten? Strangers they might be, yet Jeremiah decided to feed them first chance he had.

"Go now," he said gently. "We will join you soon."

At the mention of "we," the men began to look around nervously, but they did move, walking slowly down the road toward the north. Jeremiah didn't want them to know what they would be transporting—not that they would recognize the ark anyway, being strangers in Israel. That, most likely, had been Azariah's true intent. But they could not fail to recognize something of immense value when they saw it. Best to keep the ark hidden, even from the servants.

He beckoned to Ezekiel and his father. They emerged from the darkness onto the road, illuminated like a faint sliver of land under the starlight. Baruch blanched when he laid eyes on the veiled ark, and he backed away, bowing several times and muttering prayers.

Jeremiah glanced into the wagon bed and spotted the dark shapes of the altar of incense and the tent already stowed within. All was in readiness.

Ezekiel regarded the wagon doubtfully. "Are we to put the ark therein?"

Jeremiah nodded. "It is the only way to keep eyes from knowing what we are about. You know what King Jehoiakim will do if he learns of this."

"But what of Uzza? The LORD made a breach upon him when he carried the ark of the LORD in a cart."

This was a sticky point, and Jeremiah knew it. He had, after all, been the first to bring up this point to the high priest. The ark was never meant to be transported in any manner other than by men bearing it on their shoulders. Of course, it was also always meant to be with the people of the LORD. Moving it under cover of darkness and stealing it away like this was…well, it was *wrong*. But Jeremiah didn't see what choice they had.

"There be too few of us to carry the ark for such a journey," he pointed out, and then cast a pointed look down the road. "The heathen servants must not know what we have, and neither must the inhabitants of the towns we pass through. This is not as David once did when he brought the ark to Jerusalem with music and dancing before all Israel. What we do here is in the dark of night. It is to save the ark that we do this." In his heart, he desperately wished it had never come to this point. Nay, it should have *never* come to this. Never. Sighing, he finished his argument, "And Uzza was smitten only when he touched the ark. It was for his profane touch that the LORD smote him. The ark rode in the cart for some time before Uzza touched it—as it did when the Philistines returned the ark to Israel. We will secure the ark in the wagon that none may know it is there and that none may touch it. All will be well."

The lie slid from his lips and rang harshly in his ears.

Ezekiel and his father regarded him with expressionless faces. Jeremiah didn't know if either believed him or not. But they were out of choices. The LORD had bidden him to do this. So do this he would.

Uneasily, Jeremiah felt compelled to add, "When we bring it yet again from its hidden place and return it to the house of our God, we will do so with music and dancing as David once did—carrying it upon our shoulders as commanded."

Still, neither father nor son changed expression, staring at him with emotionless eyes. *Curse those faces,* Jeremiah grumbled to himself. They were unnerving. Baruch wisely disappeared into the shadows beyond the fire. Finally, Buzi nodded to his son and the pair picked up the ark from either end and set it into the wagon. They pulled out the poles and stashed them beside the ark. Then they covered it all with enough camel hair blankets to obscure the ark's shape and tied everything down tight. Looking at it, Jeremiah knew it couldn't be hidden that they carried something large, but no one would know that the ark of the LORD rested therein without peering beneath the blankets.

Moving up to the pair of oxen tasked with pulling the wagon, Jeremiah took the lead halter and gently tugged. The docile beasts shambled forward, and they were off. Ezekiel smothered the fire while Jeremiah called for the servants to return. They would travel north for a bit and then head due east. Mount Nebo was a two-day journey, and Jeremiah vowed to be back in Jerusalem before a week was out.

He silently prayed for the city, hoping it would still be standing when he returned.

6

Daniel crept through the palace, keeping a watchful eye open for any sign of Mattaniah or Jeconiah. His run-in with Mattaniah several days back had not been pleasant. *Though it had been most enjoyable,* Daniel admitted to himself. He had liked frustrating the prince's ambitions. The king's younger brother had interrogated Daniel for thirty minutes regarding the prophet Jeremiah's location. Daniel had told him the truth.

As far as he knew, the prophet was on the temple mount. This had only enraged Mattaniah who had wanted to use the prophet to gain favor with his brother, the king. But there was a significant difference between Jeremiah and Urijah, the prophet the king had murdered. Jeremiah was also a priest. This gave him a degree of immunity, especially while he abided on the temple mount. The king wasn't yet powerful enough to go against the priesthood. But Daniel feared that fated day was coming soon.

But something about his conversation with the king's brother bothered Daniel. Mattaniah had seemed too eager, too determined to find the prophet. Something else was going on, and Daniel felt he needed to know about it since, whatever the young prince was concocting, Daniel's family would be directly involved.

He paused at the juncture of a long hallway that ran down the length of the far western wall of the palace. A maid or two scurried about, but he saw no signs of the two princes, Mattaniah or Jeconiah. This was the queen's wing of the palace, occupied by whichever wife was currently the favorite. Right now, that wife was Daniel's sister, the mother of Jeconiah. Since her marriage to the king, Daniel and his father had only rarely seen her or been able to talk to her. Jehoiakim guarded his wives jealously, and any man caught in the women's quarters who was not a eunuch could face summary execution.

Though Daniel was above twelve years of age when a boy was considered able to do a man's work, he was not near twenty where the law said he was a man.[1] He was counting on his blood relationship to the queen to allow him to talk his way out of any difficulty if it came to that. Keeping his head down, he slipped along the corridor of white stone. Windows let in light from outside and cedar planks, imported and installed by Jehoiakim,[2] lent a pleasant smell to the air.

Daniel hoped his sister would be able to give him some insight into what might be happening. Women were often overlooked and so they picked up things that no one else would hear. If his family was in danger, his sister would know.

At the end of the hall, he came to a cedar door. He glanced quickly about, and seeing no one, he knocked. And waited. And waited some more. No one answered. He knocked again, a little bit more forcibly. Still no one answered. Frowning now, he turned around and stared down the empty hallway. His sister might be attending the king. He should've checked on that first. *Fool!* But now

---

[1] Exodus 28:36; Numbers 1:3, 18, 32:11.
[2] Jeremiah 22:14-15.

without any reason to be in the women's quarters, he needed to leave quickly.

He started back down the hall but came to a sudden stop when angry voices carried to him from a crossing corridor. Voices coming his way. He darted to the side and opened the first door he came to. He peered inside. No one. Grinning in excitement, he slipped in and closed the door as gently as he could. Doors inside a building were still a luxury even for a prince of Judah. He always marveled at them, knowing he likely would never see such treasures anywhere else. But now he thanked Jehovah for Jehoiakim's vanity in putting cedar doors throughout the palace. It had provided him an easy place to hide. And listen.

He leaned against the door, trying to calm his racing heart. He'd recognized the voices. Pressing his ear to the wood, he held his breath. It took a bit, but the argument finally resolved into words he could understand. Then, against all odds, the arguers came to stop immediately beyond his door.

"You would do well to heed me," the first voice said in tones that reminded Daniel of an agitated snake. But then, Daniel had always seen Mattaniah that way.

"Father told me to beware of you," the second voice said doubtfully—Jeconiah's voice. Daniel didn't believe his younger nephew to be among the more mentally adept, and at times, the lad's foolishness was only matched by his cruelty. Unfortunately, his father, the king, doted on the little heathen.

Mattaniah laughed without any trace of humor, more like a hyena spotting its prey. "As well you should," the prince responded, exercising his well-oiled tongue. "My brother fears what the two of us could do together. He does know that in the day you become king, I will be your greatest ally—nay, nephew, look not so grim. I but speak the truth."

"It will be long before I am king. My father is in good health and not so aged. Speak not of the throne, *uncle!*" Daniel silently rejoiced in the vehemence he heard from his nephew. He wouldn't mind at all if a fight broke out between the two.

Mattaniah laughed again, this time darkly. "No one but the gods know what will be. But know this, there be ill tidings on the wind, my nephew. Word has come that the Egyptians have fallen before the might of the Chaldeans, and even now, the prince of Babylon comes this way with a mighty army. Your father will seek to defy them."

"As well he should," Jeconiah said stiffly. "Why should we bow before these Chaldean swine?"

"Aye, that is well spoken, but have you considered what opportunities may arise in such trying times? By Baal, nephew, what could you do if you were king?"

"My father is king!"

"Aye, but your father serves the Egyptians, and Pharaoh Necho has fled from before the face of this Nebuchadnezzar. Was it not Necho who put your father upon the throne?" Heat rose in Mattaniah's voice. "Did he not take your uncle, King Jehoahaz, down into Egypt and set your father in his stead? Think you that the Chaldean prince will look favorably upon your father for this? Tribute has been given to the Egyptians. Your father—my brother—is beholden to the pharaoh for his throne. The Chaldeans do know this." Mattaniah stopped, and there followed a heavy silence.

Daniel hardly breathed, straining to listen.

"Speak clearly," Jeconiah snapped suddenly. "Say it plain."

"I will then," Mattaniah said, his tone dropping low. Daniel tried to push his ear through the door. "The prince of Babylon may supplant your father so that he will no more be king. In that day, you must be ready to pledge yourself to Nebuchadnezzar so that he will give the throne of Judah to you. Then, with me at your side, we will strengthen Judah so that we may one day throw off the Chaldean yoke and be free from all tribute. Such power may fall to you, my nephew, but you must be ready to seize it when that day comes."

CRUCIBLES OF GOD

"Spoke you to my father of this?"

"Nay," Mattaniah scoffed. "We are but children in his eyes. He will not heed us. But you and I, we are brothers now. We must plan for the day when you ascend to the throne. Understand what this means? Those who oppose you will be at your mercy."

Daniel froze, hardly daring to breathe. This was what he had come to discover perhaps.

"Such as Daniel, the son of Elnathan," Jeconiah said softly, so softly that Daniel only heard it like the whisper on the wind.

"Such as Daniel and his ilk," Mattaniah agreed. "The brother of your mother has stayed true to the old God of Israel. But it is the new gods who will bring freedom and power to our hands."

"I would not see harm come to my mother," the younger prince hissed with sudden fire. "Mention her not."

"Had I? Your mother will become queen mother on the day you become king. Why would she oppose you, her son? Nay, she will say nothing if you slay Daniel and all those who oppose you."

Daniel swallowed. He'd been right. There was danger to him and to his family. He didn't believe for a moment that Mattaniah's ambitions stopped with Jeconiah's accession to the throne. No, Mattaniah wanted to be king himself, but Jeconiah was too foolish to realize this. For a moment, he thought of trying to warn his nephew, but dismissed it out of hand. Jeconiah hated Daniel. At Daniel's word in times past, the crown prince had been chastened publicly. No, Jeconiah would never let that pass.

But it was more than Daniel's family at risk. His friends, Hananiah and Mishael, would all be in danger on the day Jeconiah became king. He had to do something, but what? He chewed on a knuckle while the voices finally drifted away. He waited for a bit, and then opening the door, he poked his head slowly out. The two princes were gone, but he could still hear them talking in low tones in an adjoining hallway. Daniel guessed they'd come to the women's quarters because it would provide them more privacy for their conspiracy.

DANIEL

He tiptoed down the corridor and peeked around the corner at the first junction.

Jeconiah and Mattaniah had their heads close together as they walked back toward the main part of the palace. At fourteen, Mattaniah had hit one of his growth spurts and so towered over his eleven-year-old nephew. Jeconiah had better be careful. Mattaniah was a cunning dog, plotting and conniving to gain more power. In fact, Mattaniah was already married to one of the daughters of the princes, cementing his place among the royal elite.

Taking a breath, Daniel started across the corridor, intending to take a different route than the two princes. He was almost across when Mattaniah suddenly looked back. Daniel had a glimpse of narrowed eyes and a frown before he slipped out of sight. His heart thumping, he started to run, his sandals slapping on the stone much too loudly for his taste, but he made it to the outer courtyard without pursuit. Slowing down to a brisk walk, he left the palace.

He prayed he hadn't been recognized or things might get worse quickly. He needed to find his friends and make plans. His father would need to be told too, but what any of them could do was beyond Daniel. If he brought accusation against Mattaniah, the king's brother would simply deny it and somehow twist it around on Daniel. He needed witnesses, and even then, it would be doubtful that the king would move against his own brother and son. The two princes hadn't talked treason. They had only discussed what *might* happen.

And of putting me to death, Daniel thought wryly. Well, if he had to face down the crown prince's wrath, he'd do it. He began imagining various scenarios and how to defeat Jeconiah at his own game. A grin of exhilaration crept over his lips. He loved this sort of thing and believed God had placed him well to help fight idolatry and sin. He only wished this threat didn't extend to others as well.

He decided to talk to his friends first before his father. Maybe if all three of them put their heads together, they could come up with a plan. Elishama, Hananiah's and Mishael's father, lived nearby in the new city, just to the west of the palace. He would go there first.

But as he started, he caught a glimpse of a guard leaving the palace courtyard and falling in step some fifty paces behind. There was nothing overtly suspicious about the man. He was simply one of the palace guards, a mercenary hired by the king to help protect the palace. His conical helmet sported a dent, his spear looked dull, and his beard unkempt. An ugly red scar blemished his face above his left eye and his nose looked fat as if it had been oft broken. Daniel had seen him around before, but he had purposely avoided the mercenaries. Most of them were of other countries and made no secret that they followed false gods. This one was made memorable because he always portrayed a distasteful slovenliness that had set Daniel's teeth on edge. He supposed they'd exchanged no more than a dozen words in all the years the man had been around.

With a quirky grin, Daniel silently dubbed his pursuer Flat-nose.

Daniel kept walking, occasionally stopping to chat with a passerby. Flat-nose was still there, trailing at a discrete distance. He didn't appear threatening, but he was most certainly following. Daniel wondered what it meant. Had Mattaniah recognized him in the palace? Possibly. But Daniel doubted that the prince was certain of who he had seen. The glimpse had only been fleeting, and there was no way that Mattaniah could've known that Daniel had overheard his conspiracy. But then again, Mattaniah didn't need much of a reason.

Well, if you were going to step into a viper's pit, you might as well jump in and get it over with.

He whirled around to confront the guard, a social blunder under most circumstances. The man was Daniel's elder and so must be treated with the appropriate respect. Yet Flat-nose was clearly following him, so he felt justified in breaking social norms. But the moment he set himself to make the confrontation, his demand died on his lips.

DANIEL

The guard was gone.

Daniel stood in the middle of the street, rubbing his smooth chin in confusion. Where had the man gone? Flat-nose had been no more than half a street back. He peered into some of the shadows but saw no one hiding within. Strangely, the man's sudden disappearance bothered Daniel more than anything else. Where had he gone? More importantly, *why*?

He fingered one of the blue tassels hanging from his tunic[3] and began reciting under his breath, "Hear, O Israel, the LORD our God is one LORD, and you shall love the LORD your God with all your heart, and with all your soul, and with all your might."[4]

Turning slowly, he began walking again to find his friends, his mind troubled. He worried that the fellow was still back there, still watching. He'd find out soon enough, he vowed to himself. He took no more than a dozen steps or so when a whirling sound reached his ears. He glanced up and caught sight of Flat-nose standing upon the rooftops, a sling spinning rapidly in one hand. Daniel's eyes widened and he dove frantically forward.

He was almost quick enough. A stone missile coming with blinding speed grazed the back of his head and smashed into the wall of a house, sending chips of stone flying.

Daniel grunted as pain seared its way in a dozen directions from a spot at the back of his head. Through the agony, he screamed into the vaults of his mind, *Move!* While in the street, he was too easy of a target for the assassin. He had to move. But pain from the glancing shot had turned his muscles to liquid.

Faintly, the sound of a spinning sling reached his ears once more.

---

[3] Numbers 15:38-40.
[4] Deuteronomy 6:4-5.

7

D aniel did the only thing he could think of to do. He rolled. Another rock smashed into the rocky street where he'd just been, ricocheted into the wall above his head, and went bounding down the street in a clatter of noise. Someone nearby shouted a question, and Daniel heard an angry curse muttered from the rooftops.

Daniel scrambled to his feet and pressed himself against the wall closest to his assailant. He took deep breaths, trying to calm himself. The angle for another attack was all wrong. Flat-nose would need to reposition himself, but Daniel had no intention of waiting around to see what his attacker would do next.

He smiled wryly to himself. Despite the pain, he felt strangely more alive than ever. The danger thrilled him. He was no warrior, so he tossed aside his first thought of confronting the assassin. He studied his remaining options. He could flee straight up or down the street, but the moment he did, he would leave himself open for another attack. The street was narrow enough that he didn't have a lot of room to dodge. And he was hurt. Placing a hand to the back of his head, he felt wetness. Blood. Praise Jehovah it wasn't serious, but it hurt as if a chariot had run over him. Repeatedly.

He chuckled, his eyes brightening in anticipation. Hananiah would claim he was mad, but then Daniel's quiet friend sought out danger much like sheep sought out a hungry lion.

He listened and heard nothing. Which meant nothing. A sling could be brought up to speed within an incredibly short period of time, and a skilled slinger could thread a stone through a hole not much bigger than the stone itself. But if that were the case here, Daniel would already be dead. Which implied his assailant wasn't as proficient with the sling as he might be with other weapons.

Deciding on a course of action, Daniel leapt out into the open, eyes seeking the rooftops for any sign of Flat-nose. He balanced on the balls of his sandaled feet, preparing to jump out of the way, but the roofs were empty. Ah, just as he'd thought.

He spun, searching the shadows cast by the late afternoon sun and spotted a dark form moving stealthily toward him from up the street. Light glinted off bared metal. Very well, time to see if Flat-nose was as light of foot as a fourteen-year-old lad who had grown up running through the streets of the city. But Daniel couldn't resist a mocking salute first. "I commend your foolishness in attempting to slay a prince of the land, for I have seen your face, Flat-nose! Truly, I have seen its like only upon a diseased cur of unmentionable ancestry!"

With a laugh, Daniel spun and darted away, bounding down the slightly tiered street with the same grace as an ibex on a cliff trail. The solider spewed forth a dozen curses as he ran in pursuit, but he was laden down with his armor and Daniel had the dexterity and speed of youth. He soon left Flat-nose far in his wake.

To be sure, Daniel turned several corners and even doubled back to see if the assassin would show up, but the fellow didn't. For the moment, anyway, he was safe. Musing to himself, he began walking toward his original destination, seeking his friends. He wiped blood from the back of his head and winced. It hurt. Still, it had to be better than having half his head caved in by such a stone.

He found his two friends at the chief scribe's house. Elishama was gone, but his wife Maachah took one look at the blood running down the back of Daniel's neck and she immediately took charge while his friends stared at him in confused wonder.

"What happened?" Mishael demanded as his mother fetched water and bandages. "Did you fall? I wager you fell. Is that what happened? Or did you try to climb the wall? I wager you tried to climb the wall and slipped. Mayhap you—"

"Mishael," his mother snapped in a tolerant tone, "your tongue wags overmuch."

The lad snapped his mouth shut only with effort and managed to appear as if he had truly swallowed his own tongue. It failed to evoke any sympathy.

Hananiah folded his arms across his chest. "I sense a tale. What happened, Daniel?"

Maachah maneuvered Daniel onto a stool and she tsked irritably as she cleaned the wound. She muttered, "What will your mother think, young Daniel?" She stopped, her hand on his shoulder tightening. "This is a sling wound," she breathed out quietly.

"Tis?" Mishael couldn't help but speak up. "You were practicing with the sling?"

Daniel grinned, trying to put everyone at ease. "Nay. It is nothing. A mishap only."

"I know what I am about, young Daniel," Maachah reproved him. Daniel could hear her scowl with suspicion. "This was not done of your own hand."

Daniel thought fast. "Aye. The stone was slung from another hand, but it was nothing. A mishap, I say. Truly. The slinger does regret it." This last was true enough. Having failed in his mission, the assassin would not be pleased. Neither would the one who had hired him.

Maachah dabbed some wine on the wound to finish the cleaning. It stung and Daniel winced but bore under the administration with great dignity—or so he thought. But Mishael's barely suppressed laughter spoiled the effect somewhat.

"Hold this in place," the motherly woman ordered, pressing a bandage to his wound. He obeyed with his left hand. "You must hold it there until the bleeding abates."

Daniel stood and bowed in thanks. "As you command, good mother."

She sniffed and turned away, muttering something about foolish boys. Gratefully, Daniel allowed himself to be whisked outside by his friends before he could be lectured further. Hananiah's frown told Daniel that his friend, at least, hadn't believed his story. "Speak," the lad said stiffly. "I would know the truth."

Daniel glanced up and down the street. No one else was close enough to hear. "I was assailed in the streets," he said softly. "A hireling sent to slay me."

Hananiah glared at his younger brother who had opened his mouth again. The lad shut it with a click, cowed. Satisfied, the older lad looked at Daniel. "Know you the reason?"

"Aye. I overheard prince Jeconiah and prince Mattaniah speaking in conspiracy. They spoke of setting Jeconiah upon the throne of Judah."

"Treason?" Hananiah asked. "Wherefore? Jeconiah is crown prince already."

Daniel pulled his friends close together, still holding the bandage against his wounded head. "They spoke of turning to the Chaldeans." Quickly and in hushed tones, Daniel repeated what he had overheard in the palace.

"Think you that Mattaniah saw you then?" Hananiah asked after Daniel had finished. "It was he who sent the hireling?" The lad wasn't looking at Daniel anymore. He studied the street down toward the palace as if wondering if the assassin would make an appearance.

"Aye," Daniel agreed. "Chance cannot account for what happened. I had hoped not to be seen, but Mattaniah has quick eyes."

"He will try again," Mishael stated simply, sounding eager. "We must be watchful."

Daniel hoped there would be no further attempts on his life. While he didn't mind danger and often felt a thrill in those moments, he wasn't a fool.

"Nay," Hananiah said softly. Everyone looked at him, waiting for an explanation. The lad flushed under the attention. Finally, he shrugged and added reluctantly, "Mattaniah would dare not call attention to himself with a second attempt. You—we—are now on our guard. He would know this, and he would fear his brother, the king, learning of his ambitions through others."

"You speak of Mattaniah," Daniel said. "What of Jeconiah?"

"It is Mattaniah we must be wary of. It is he who has the mind for what he is about, not Jeconiah."

Daniel agreed. "And more, I think yet Mattaniah has plans beyond Jeconiah. He seeks the throne for himself—mark my words."

The other two nodded. They were all familiar with Mattaniah's ambitions. Mishael glanced from boy to boy. Apparently, he could stand it no longer and burst out, "Think you Mattaniah will seek to slay the king and mayhap Jeconiah?"

"I know not," Daniel admitted, "but I fear it is not without possibility. And I would not count against Mattaniah seeking to yet slay us. He holds bitterness and wrath as close companions."

The three exchanged somber looks.

"We must need seek allies," Hananiah added. "Among the sons of the princes, only we three stand against Mattaniah."

Strictly speaking, that wasn't true. Daniel knew that most of the other young princes disliked both Mattaniah and Jeconiah, but unlike Daniel and his friends, no one else dared stand up against them. Daniel's success had come only because of his relationship to the king through his sister. If not for that, King Jehoiakim would turn a blind eye to whatever his younger brother and favored son did to him.

But once either of the princes came to the throne…

Daniel stiffened his spine. He'd deal with that when and if the time came. In the meantime, there might yet be allies. "What of the prophet Jeremiah?" he asked. "Should we seek his aid?"

"Know you where the prophet is?" Mishael asked excitedly.

Daniel did not. There had been talk about hiding the ark at Baruch's house, but so far, he had heard nothing and so supposed the prophet's desire had come to nothing. If the ark was missing, surely, it would become known to all. The prophet was doubtlessly hiding. "I thought he resided upon the temple mount, but after the tumult of two days ago, no one can find the prophet or his scribe, Baruch. They have disappeared."

"Your father then," Hananiah said. "We must seek his aid."

True enough. Daniel's father must be warned. His sister, too. Then an idea struck him. "There yet may be a way," he said to the others. "Spread rumors that there are those among the princes who seek to fall away to the Chaldeans to supplant the king. When King Jehoiakim learns of it, he will seek out those responsible. Mattaniah and Jeconiah will be forced to lay aside their conspiracy lest it be discovered and made known to the king."

"Will not they know such rumors come from us?" Mishael asked. "I say we go before the king and say it plain. We will bear witness of the attack on your life"

"That will surely fail," Hananiah said. "Jeconiah is in favor with the king as is Mattaniah…for the most part. Any word spoken against them will be taken wrongly. I agree with Daniel. Spread the rumors. If the king learns of their misdeeds, let him do so on his own. In this way, we preserve our lives."

Daniel was glad for the endorsement of his plan, but he thought Hananiah's fear saw only the worst outcome. Daniel didn't think the king would slay them for speaking. Not yet anyway. And there might be a way to approach the king—through Daniel's sister, Nehushta. That path, he decided, would be one he walked alone. No sense in involving his friends.

"What of the hireling?" Mishael demanded. "Should we not know his whereabouts? He could lead us to his masters and then we would have evidence."

"That is well spoken," Daniel said, musing. "He was among the palace guards, one of the hired mercenaries. I have seen him about the palace grounds performing his duty."

"Describe him," Mishael said eagerly, ignoring his brother's frown. "We shall begin the hunt immediately."

Daniel held up a hand. "Care must be taken, Mishael. The man is most dangerous." He winced and checked his bandage. It looked like the blood was slowing down. "Most dangerous. He was slovenly, ill-kept. A flat nose. In truth, I noticed little to set him apart…wait…there was a scar above his left eye. Aye, I am sure of it. Look for the scar and the flat nose." He snagged Mishael's shoulder. "Heed me, Mishael. The man will shed blood without cause. Stay you well away from him if you discern his location."

"I will, Daniel. This I swear."

A vow that, Daniel felt sure, would be forgotten immediately. Mishael meant well, but much like his mouth, he tended to run amok much as a boulder crashing down a steep mountainside did.

"This," Hananiah said, "is our best recourse. Find the hireling and we can discover the evidence to take to the king."

The more Daniel thought about it, the more he liked it. "It is decided then," he said, clasping hands with Hananiah. Mishael joined in quickly. "Let us discover the hireling. The LORD bless our way and guide us to truth."

"Amen!" the two other lads shouted—well, Mishael shouted anyway.

But, as it happened, they never got the chance. The next day, Hananiah found Daniel at his house, practicing his writing with a piece of chalk and a heavy slate slab.

"Come. You must see," Hananiah said quietly from the doorway.

"What have you found?" Daniel replied, anxiously looking at his mother who worked near the cooking fire. If Hananiah had found the hireling already, then the LORD had surely blessed them.

"Come."

Something in his friend's voice convinced him all was not well. Daniel bade a hasty farewell to his mother and scurried after Hananiah who was already striding toward the palace like one set to disturb a beehive for the honey. Mixed feelings. Daniel caught up, but at a look at his friend's troubled face, he decided to wait to ask for more details.

They approached a market near the palace and a crowd of people had gathered about, looking at something upon the ground. Hananiah pushed his way apologetically to the forefront of the murmuring crowd, pulling Daniel along behind him. Once there, the lad pointed. "Is that your man?" he whispered.

Daniel's eyes went to the man lying on the ground. He easily recognized the scar and the broken nose. That was Flat-nose, the man who had tried to kill Daniel. But someone had found the guard first and added a new decoration to his disheveled features by slicing open his neck from ear to ear.

Which is what probably contributed to the large pool of blood beneath the dead man's head.

8

The city of Ashkelon burned. Nebuchadnezzar watched it from a hill just to the east of the city. Beyond the city, the waters of the Great Sea gleamed in the failing light of the sun. The red glow of the orb when mingled with the fires from the city seemed to set the horizon aflame. Nebuchadnezzar thought it a fitting sacrifice to Shamash, the sun god. The ancient city of the Philistines was no more. He had ordered it razed, the walls broken down, the fields sowed with salt, the inhabitants of the city slain, and everything else burned.

His soldiers had taken to the command with enthusiasm—exuberance might be a better word. The men had little enough plunder during this campaign thus far. Carchemish had been a poor city, the last refuge of the dying Assyrian dynasty. Hamish had been a true victory over the remaining Egyptian forces, but the city itself was more a military outpost and hardly worth the plunder gained there.

And Pharaoh Necho had escaped him.

NEBUCHADNEZZAR

Again!

The Egyptian king had abandoned his troops in the field at Hamish and fled south, using his vassal cities to aid him in quickly moving ever toward Egypt. Nebuchadnezzar had tracked him to Ashkelon where the wily Egyptian had sailed away across the Great Sea, escaping Nebuchadnezzar's grasp entirely. Nebuchadnezzar had let his fury get the better of him. To punish the king of Ashkelon and to allow his troops opportunity to shed some of their lust for wealth and women, he'd given the city into their hands entirely.

No one would escape.

"They bring the king of Ashkelon," Nebuzaradan said from beside him. His captain had overseen the destruction of the city's defenses and had accomplished the task with his usual brilliance, using a feint to draw defenders away from the main attack—which had also been a feint. In the end, as he knew it would be, Nebuzaradan had overwhelmed the confused enemy and easily breached the walls.

Nebuchadnezzar nodded in response, saying nothing until several of his other captains dragged a dark-skinned man of unusual height before him, tossing the battered man at his feet. If the man was upright, he would tower head and shoulders above any man in Nebuchadnezzar's army. *The blood of the giants must run in his veins*, he mused. Interesting. Everyone had heard the tales of the giants in Philistia, though it appeared as if the blood of the Nephilim was slowly being diluted.

Nebuchadnezzar waited until his men had settled themselves and then he addressed the prone man at his feet, his anger at the man evident to everyone. "Look upon me, king of Ashkelon. You may be defeated, but you are still a man, so look upon me and know your fate."

The tall man leveraged himself to his knees with great effort. Blood ran down his face, staining a gray beard. He wore only a loincloth, Nebuchadnezzar's men having stripped him of his more valuable clothing. His breathing came in wheezing gasps, and he held his side tightly with one arm. His dark eyes held glittering hatred when they finally looked up at the Chaldean prince. "I see you," he whispered in a hoarse, smoke-strained voice.

"Then know your fate. For defiance, I have razed your city and slaughtered your people, your wives, and your children. Your fields have been sowed with salt, and so your city will become a dunghill, a byword that all who behold it might know the price of defiance. As for you, you will be taken to Babylon where you will learn humility, a testament to my people of your weakness. This is your fate."

The captive's shoulders slumped, and great tears left trails through the soot staining his face. "I hear you, prince of Babylon," he rasped out bitterly. "I would seek mercy and ask that you slay me here with the edge of the sword. Let me die with my people."

Nebuchadnezzar shook his head, a surge of anger coloring his face even darker. "Nay, *your* price of defiance will be to live with this knowledge all the days of your life." He gestured to his men. "Secure him in the prisoner's carts. Give him no opportunity to slay himself or cause harm to another." His eyes narrowed. "Break his arms and fingers if you must."

His captains saluted with their weapons and dragged the tall king away. The man went silently, his eyes still locked on the crown prince of Babylon with such bitter hatred that Nebuchadnezzar could feel the force of it. It made him smile. Dismissing the defeated king from his mind, he turned back to watching the city burn.

After a time, Nebuzaradan spoke. "What now, my lord? The king of Egypt has fled across the sea. We cannot follow."

Nebuchadnezzar nodded slowly, choosing his words carefully and doing a mighty job of suppressing his irritation. Anger could lead to incaution here. "This I know. I would push on and corner the Egyptian rat in his hole and slay him there, but we must proceed with prudence. We are surrounded by enemies, and if we are cut off, we may perish between Egypt and the many cities here. They have all sworn to serve Egypt."

"Where to next then?"

Nebuchadnezzar glanced at his personal bodyguard. Standing a hand taller than Nebuchadnezzar himself, Nebuzaradan was the perfect Chaldean warrior. His body rippled with muscles and Nebuchadnezzar knew from experience that the captain was perhaps the most lethal fighter in the army. The man had never lost a fight and he had a tactical mind that made him even more dangerous. His piercing gray eyes didn't miss a thing. Underneath his helmet, he was bald. A little hair grew on the sides of his head, but he shaved it every chance he got. His dark beard, however, was weaved in the Chaldean fashion and cut square a handspan below his chin. Perhaps the most fascinating thing about Nebuzaradan was that he never got excited—unless it was about riches—never grew flustered, never grew angry, and never raised his voice. It was such a contrast to Nebuchadnezzar himself, who could go off like a brush fire during a hot, dry summer.

Nebuchadnezzar glanced at an attendant standing nearby. "Fetch Ashpenaz." After the man ran off, Nebuchadnezzar turned to his captain. "I would have the chief eunuch's counsel, for I have had a dream these last nights."

Nebuzaradan's eyes snapped to the prince's face, a tiny frown darkening the lines beneath his beard. "How many nights?"

"Since Hamath. The dream is always the same."

Both men knew that dreams contained visions of power and messages from the gods. They were not to be dismissed, and Nebuchadnezzar had no intention of doing so. They waited in companiable silence until Ashpenaz, huffing and wheezing like a herd of diseased swine, finally made it to the top of the hill. The fat eunuch's sweaty, cleanshaven face showed red despite his bronzed skin, and he collapsed to his knees, which would surely stain his expensive robes. A purple scar bridged his nose, and his very short hair stuck straight up, like thorns from a bramble bush.

"Here am I, my lord!" he said in a surprisingly high voice. "Many apologies for keeping the great prince waiting. I beg, scourge me, my prince, and strip the skin from my unworthy bones!"

"Stand," Nebuchadnezzar said, trying to hide a smile.

When Ashpenaz had been a young man, he'd been the perfect model of masculinity, and had been personally chosen by Nebuchadnezzar's mother to rule the palace eunuchs. Much wine and food had changed his appearance drastically, but the man retained one of the sharpest minds Nebuchadnezzar had ever known. And it was that mind he needed now.

After the eunuch had heaved himself upright, Nebuchadnezzar began. "Harken," he said to his two closest advisors, "for I have dreamed. I beheld from on high a walled city stretched upon two hills and a great temple to an unknown God sheathed in gold and flanked by two bronze pillars. A mighty altar, cold and empty, stands before the temple next to a sea set upon twelve oxen. And as I beheld, a voice spoke, the sound descending from the heavens as a mighty trumpet, saying, 'Arise Nebuchadnezzar, my servant,[1] and bring this city under your dominion, for I have given it and its inhabitants into your hand.' At the word of this command, I stretched forth my hand and the ground shook, and the gates of the city sprang open, and the inhabitants thereof cried aloud for mercy. This was my dream, a dream that befell me every night since the march from Hamath." Nebuchadnezzar regarded the captain and eunuch. "I would know its meaning." He paused before adding, "The priests of Ishtar and Marduk are silent. They claim only that the God of another people has spoken to me, and they whisper among themselves much like children forbidden some treat."

The chief eunuch sucked in a large breath, causing his chest to rise expansively. "O mighty prince, slay this one if his words do not please your ears, but your priests tell you truly. The dream is not of Ishtar or Marduk or any of the other gods of Babylon, for the city in your dream is none other than Jerusalem and the temple, the temple

---

[1] Jeremiah 25:9, 27:6.

of the Hebrew God. The voice, therefore, belongs to the Hebrew God, and it is He who bids you to take the city."

Nebuchadnezzar looked troubled. He'd already known that the city in the dream was Jerusalem; that much had been obvious. But why would the God of the Hebrews speak to him of this? "Does the God of the Hebrews despise His own people that I must do this?"

The eunuch bobbed his head, his version of a shrug. "Who knows the will of the gods, O prince? Not I. My lack of knowledge is an affront to your ears. I beg, therefore, cast me into a pit of vipers that I may learn wisdom."

Nebuchadnezzar smirked, regaining some of his humor. This was why he held Ashpenaz above many of his other counselors. "We will reserve that for later." He glanced at his captain. "What say you, Nebuzaradan?"

The captain turned and looked nearly due east. "Jerusalem lies there, no more than a two-day march. The city is strong and well-fortified." His eyes slid slyly to Nebuchadnezzar. "And did I not tell you of gold therein? Was not gold in your dream? My lord, I would not presume to speak for the gods, but already Marduk and Ishtar have blessed your steps, why not this God of the Hebrews? If He will deliver the city into your hands, then let us go hence and bring the inhabitants therein under your yoke. You have already decreed that it would not do well to leave enemies at our back as we push south."

This was all very much as Nebuchadnezzar had expected. He only needed verification from his two closest advisors. He despised the delay. More than anything, he wanted to pursue Necho. A seething anger burned in his breast against the man. But Jerusalem was a power in the region, and he would risk much by leaving them at his back. And now, with even the Hebrew God commanding him, he dare not bypass the city. "Then we will march upon Jerusalem and take it. Prepare the men. On the morrow, we march."

Nebuzaradan saluted by drawing his sword and bowing low. "As you command, O prince." He straightened, gestured to some of his subcommanders and began walking down the hill, barking orders in that deceptively calm voice of his as he went.

Nebuchadnezzar turned to Ashpenaz. "I would know more of this Hebrew God who would deliver His people into my hands."

The fat eunuch mopped sweat off his brow with a thick hand. "We know little, O prince—may you boil me in oil for my ignorance! This God appears fickle, sometimes blessing and sometimes cursing His people. He seeks no sacrifice of man, only that of sheep and oxen."

That surprised Nebuchadnezzar. "Truly? Is not the shedding of man's blood the highest form of worship? Tis little wonder that this Hebrew God would that I bring these irreverent people under dominion. They must put little worth in their God."

"This I know not, may you cut off my fingers, O prince, but there are tales of wonders done by this Hebrew God. He is most powerful, and we would do well to heed His words and obey His voice—rip out my tongue if you like not my words, my prince!"

Nebuchadnezzar fell silent as he thought it through. He didn't like being at the beck and call of a foreign God. Serving his own pantheon of gods was exhausting enough without having to worry about every stray god displeased with his people. But in truth, he had heard of the wonders done by the Hebrew God, so displeasing Him would not be wise. And since his own ambitions lined up with the dreams given him—well, mostly anyway—he saw no reason to rescind his orders to march on Jerusalem.

"You have spoken well, my servant," he told Ashpenaz, clapping the man on the shoulder and turning him about. "I shall not rip your tongue out this day." They began walking toward the encampment where Nebuchadnezzar's wives awaited his return.

"This humble servant is most grateful, O prince. Howbeit, if you decide otherwise, I will not gainsay you, but rip it out with my own hands."

Truer words were never spoken. Only, he needed his servant's tongue, but that would not prevent him from ripping out the tongue of others. They had already caught three Hebrew spies. Them maybe.

As they walked, Nebuchadnezzar thought on his dream and on Jerusalem. He hoped the campaign against the city would not take long. The more time he took to secure his flanks the more time that snake of an Egyptian, Necho, would be able to consolidate his armies, making conquering Egypt all that more difficult.

Still, if the stories of what the Hebrew God had done to the Egyptians in legend were true, then perhaps having obeyed His voice would gain Nebuchadnezzar favor. He would not mind such power being used on his behalf.

The chief eunuch cleared his throat. "If I may—roast me over a fire if I may not—but what will you do with the inhabitants of Jerusalem? How will you ensure they will not betray you?"

That was a good question. "I know not," the prince said at last. "I would that you think on it and offer what advice you may. You have two days."

"I will, O prince."

9

Ezekiel caught up to Jeremiah and the others an hour before midday. Being young, he retained much of his energy and so where Jeremiah might have found himself short of breath, his younger counterpart looked to be hardly breathing despite his long run. "You were correct," the young priest said in a way that could mean he was joyful or mired in panic. "We are being followed."

Jeremiah sighed. Somehow, he'd suspected as much. It was too much to ask that they would be able to escape Judah with the ark entirely unnoticed. "Know you them?" he asked.

"Nay. Their leader appears to be a priest. I counted a dozen men. At least six are soldiers."

The servants exchanged nervous glances. They knew Jeremiah and the others were up to something secret and likely dangerous. And any trouble that came upon the three priests and lone scribe would befall them too. Jeremiah forced out a smile to assure them, but based on the way they stepped back, he failed.

"How far?" he asked, deciding to ignore the servants.

"They are no more than two hours behind. They follow our trail and are moving faster than we. They will catch us by nightfall."

Jeremiah pulled at his beard, his wideset eyes flickering toward the sun to judge its position. Mount Nebo rose up before them, a sentinel that Moses had once stood upon to view the promised land.[1] The law stated that he had died upon that mount and was buried by God Himself in an unknown valley hereabouts.[2] It gave Jeremiah a chill, and he adjusted his long tunic self-consciously. They were close. Very close. He gritted his teeth. To be found out now! All he needed was a little more time.

To make matters worse, the sabbath began that night, and by law, he could not travel on that day. What must be done, must be done before the sabbath began. He turned toward his friends. "Harken," he said, stopping and facing them. The oxen pulling the cart shambled forward a half dozen feet and then came to a stop with no one to prod them forward. "From here, I must go on alone. It falls to you to delay our pursuers until I return." He gestured toward the sun. "The sabbath is nigh and we may not journey, so I must reach my destination before then."

Baruch frowned, squinting at his master. The young scribe saw better in candlelight than he did in sunlight. "Where is your destination, my lord?"

Jeremiah shook his head. "No man will know. The LORD God of Israel leads me." And it was true. The moment Jeremiah had set eyes on the mount, he knew where to go. He couldn't say exactly how he knew or what he would find, only that each step toward the mount lessened his uncertainty.

"Should we not mark the way?" Buzi asked. "So that we may fetch the ark again in an appointed time."

---

[1] Deuteronomy 32:49, 34:1.
[2] Deuteronomy 34:5-6.

"Do not," Jeremiah warned, his voice taking on a commanding tone unusual for him. "The place will be unknown until the time that God gathers His people again and receives them unto mercy."[3]

Ezekiel's father stiffened. "And when shall that be?"

"That is for the LORD to decide. We here must only obey His command." Perhaps Jeremiah had gained some of Ezekiel's vocal ability, for Buzi quieted and bowed to show his submission. Jeremiah continued, "Serve the LORD in this way: hinder those who follow. Let them not discover the way. Hide, I pray, the tracks left by the cart and let none follow after me."

Ezekiel nodded. "It shall be done as you command."

"Then it is well," Jeremiah said, turning away and beginning to prod the oxen forward.

Baruch ran up, his face stony. "Nay, it is not well," the scribe argued. "How will you hide the ark? It is not for one man alone to do!"

Jeremiah frowned. He hadn't actually considered that problem. Two strong men could carry the ark a short distance, but one man alone could not. But something burned in his heart. He couldn't stay. He *knew* this is what he must do. He shook his head. "The LORD will provide a way. Fear not."

Baruch's mouth hung open in clear distress. "My lord, I plead, allow one man to accompany you!"

"Nay, the LORD has bidden me to go alone. The matter is at an end." The words felt right.

The scribe managed to snap his jaw shut, but Jeremiah could see the displeasure in his friend's eyes under those awful protruding brows. He knew the scribe wasn't trying to discover where the ark would be hidden. No, he but feared something untoward would happen to Jeremiah if he attempted to move the ark alone. Jeremiah

---

[3] 2 Maccabees 2:7. I don't consider the Apocrypha books to be Scripture, but they are historical and, in this case, represent the oldest written possibility of what may have happened to the ark of the covenant.

appreciated his friend's concern. He placed a hand on his shoulder and squeezed.

"Have faith, my friend. All will be well."

Baruch bowed. "As you say. We will await your return."

Jeremiah nodded, knowing that Baruch would wait until he grew old and died if he must. Quickly, they pulled most of the water and supplies out of the wagon. Jeremiah wouldn't need much anyway, not with the sabbath nigh. Then prodding the oxen on, he left his friends and the servants behind so that they might hinder their pursuers.

It had indeed taken two days and much of a third to reach this point, but the end was in sight. Using a goad, he urged the oxen onward, praying that he could reach his destination before nightfall. Little grew in this region beyond the Jordan River to hinder the oxen as they plodded on. Low shrubs, an isolated tree, and dead grass constituted much of the landscape. And rock. Lots of rock. A few clumps of fir trees dotted the peak of Mount Nebo, but otherwise the mountain was windswept, providing shelter only for a clump or two of tenacious grass hidden between rocks.

Fortunately, Jeremiah's destination did not lie at the peak of the mount, but rather along one of the slopes. He'd know it when he found it. He urged the oxen to move faster, the nearest one throwing him a reproachful look.

Four hours later, Jeremiah found what he was looking for. The feeling of rightness had only grown stronger until it became a certainty that finally resolved into a narrow cave entrance mostly hidden by rocks near the base of the tall mount. Within was a chamber that would take the tent and ark together. It was perfect. Indeed, he would be able to squeeze the ark through the opening—barely.

But how to do it? He was one man alone and the oxen would be of little use now. He studied on the problem, working it out in his head. Glancing at the sky, he noted that the sun was descending in the west over Judah. He didn't have a lot of time. As soon as three stars were visible in the night sky, the sabbath would begin, and he would need everything finished before then.

First, he unhitched the oxen and tethered them nearby, letting them graze on dead grass. Then he set about tearing the cart apart, taking out the sides and forming a ramp and a sled. Not being a carpenter, he didn't have the necessary tools to do the job right, but he had plenty of rope and so was able to lash the planks together. This took him another hour and a half. Carefully, then, with many prayers, he tipped the cart and lowered the ark gently onto his makeshift sled. He then lashed the covered ark in place and took the tent of the tabernacle into the cave.

Inside, he paced off the space and found his initial guess to be right. The hollowed-out space was just large enough to set up the tent. The cave was almost perfectly round as if a giant had scooped it out with his hand. Minerals embedded in the wall glittered in the firelight, and the walls were so smooth that Jeremiah could hardly feel any texture when he ran his hand over one. Truly, the LORD had prepared this place. This would become holy ground, so after he erected the tent, he spent time kneeling and praying, confessing his sins, and preparing his heart for what must be done.

When all was in readiness, he left the cave and slipped into the harness he'd devised for the sled and pulled the ark toward the cave entrance. His muscles screamed at him as he dragged the sled over the rocky ground. He had to stop often and move rocks out of his way, but within the next hour, he was able to pull it into the cave where he collapsed, breathing heavily. He couldn't rest for long. The sun sat on the Judean mountains, nearly on top of Jerusalem itself. He had to work fast.

Regaining his feet, he pulled the ark the last few cubits to the center of the tent. Dim light spilled in from the cave entrance and only a small fire he had started cast light to see by, but it was enough. It took a bit, but Jeremiah succeeded in leveraging the ark off the sled, letting it rest upon the hard floor of the cave. The golden ark seemed to undulate in the glow of the dying fire.

JEREMIAH

Retrieving the altar of incense, he placed it just outside the tent entrance and within the cave entrance. Using the fire he'd already started, he burned the last of the incense before the LORD. He continued to pray and sing psalms until most of it had burned, filling the cave with a sweet aroma.

One last thing.

He exited the cave and looked at the sky. A single star was visible. Two more and the sabbath will have begun. Taking a deep breath, he scrambled up the slope to a large pile of rocks that sat precariously above the entrance. He hadn't been at all surprised to see the rocks when he'd first come upon the cave. It wouldn't take much to dislodge them and send the entire pile crashing down on the cave entrance, burying the ark, the tent, and the altar of incense until such a time as the LORD decided to reveal it again to Israel.

In fact, one particularly large boulder balanced above the others appeared to be the perfect catalyst. With a mighty shove, the boulder tipped and then crashed down onto the slope, gained momentum, and then slammed into the other rocks. With a deafening roar that sent shockwaves rebounding off the slope, the entire pile of boulders crashed over the cave entrance.

In the twilight, billowing dust rose like a cloud, slowly settling over everything. Both oxen rolled their eyes and stamped their feet in protest, but not a single rock made it to them. Jeremiah glanced at the sky. Three stars. The sabbath had come, and it was time to rest.

No one had come. Baruch and Ezekiel must've been successful in delaying those who followed. It was still concerning. There would be questions…too many questions. It bothered Jeremiah that soldiers had been dispatched to follow him. It implied that King Jehoiakim had taken an interest in his doings. Thinking of Urijah, Jeremiah didn't doubt that if the opportunity presented itself, his pursuers had instructions to kill him.

The ark was safe, even if he himself was not—well, the ark was *almost* safe. He would still need to mask the trail. The fresh rockslide might be too obvious a clue, but that wasn't something he need worry about until the sabbath had passed. Surely, Ezekiel could delay their pursuers on the holy day of rest.

Surely.

The law stated that he could not leave his place.[4] However, tradition said that one may travel two thousand cubits to worship the LORD on the Sabbath, for that was equal to the space given to the ark of the LORD in the wilderness between it and the Hebrew camps roundabout.[5] It was also the distance of the suburbs outside a city that would still be considered part of the city.[6] So traveling that far was believed not to have left one's place.

At daybreak then, he would travel two thousand cubits back toward where he had left the others. Perhaps then, when he was discovered, his pursuers would not think to look further.

It was the best plan he could come up with.

Sighing, his eyes drifted toward the top of Mount Nebo, and he grinned suddenly. Perhaps there was a better plan after all. There was a way to explain his purpose without revealing anything about the ark. But discovering Jeremiah's purpose in the land of Moab might not be his pursuers' ultimate goal. They might have been sent to simply kill him.

He fervently hoped not.

---

[4] Exodus 16:29.
[5] Joshua 3:4.
[6] Numbers 35:5.

10

When they found Jeremiah late the next afternoon atop the highest point of Mount Nebo, the prophet had completed a crude altar and sacrificed both oxen upon it to the LORD. With no cart and now no oxen, Jeremiah prayed it would seem obvious as to his purpose in coming to Mount Nebo. So, with the smoke of the sacrifice staining an otherwise clear sky, the sudden appearance of the group of men, violating the sabbath in at least a dozen different ways, didn't surprise the prophet at all.

Neither was he surprised by who led the soldiers.

"Ho, Pashur," Jeremiah called to the governor of the temple, adding a frown to his face to show his displeasure. With the man came the high priest's son, Seraiah, and behind them, Ezekiel, Buzi, and Baruch walked uncomfortably, their faces bruised and hands tied with stout cords. Of the servants that had come with Jeremiah, there were no sign. Testing out a sterner voice, he demanded, "What do you here away from the temple and your duties? Is not this the sabbath, a day most holy unto our God?"

Pashur's flushed face, likely from his exertion up the mountain, darkened. "You speak of profanity, false prophet, when it is your tongue which do spew forth lies to the people of the LORD. We are the priests of the LORD God of Israel, and our *duty* is to put an end to abomination and falsehood wherever it be found, even on the holy sabbath." Clearly satisfied with his justification, the priest looked at the altar and the sacrificed oxen. "What do *you* here?"

"The LORD bid me come here," Jeremiah replied simply. True enough, if not the whole truth.

The man looked around with equal parts suspicion and contempt. "Your companions said nothing of your purpose here. They have been deceived and will pay for this abomination." He gestured to the altar. "You built a high place to the LORD?"

"As have you," Jeremiah retorted, bristling at the implied accusation. "What of the high places in Jezreel and Hebron?"

"It is not your place to do this," the high priest's son snapped. He fairly quivered in indignation. "Your order does not serve the temple during this course, and you have not been ordained to the temple service!"

"The LORD chose me to speak His words," Jeremiah countered.

"So you say," Pashur said in a low voice, "howbeit there are others who come in the name of the LORD and who speak different words."

Jeremiah should have expected this, but hearing it nettled him. He stiffened. "Who presumes to speak in the name of the LORD?"

"Hananiah, son of Azur, of Gibeon, for one."[1] Seraiah said with a sneer. "The LORD has decreed deliverance through him!"

Jeremiah knew of the man, though he'd not encountered him afore. He met Seraiah's young eyes steadily. "I pray his words come to pass, but the LORD has spoken different words to me."

"You speak lies," Pashur said in a satisfied tone. "We will return to Jerusalem so that the truth might be learned of your purpose here.

---

[1] Jeremiah 28:1.

Word has come to me that you have fallen away to the Chaldeans and would betray Jerusalem into their hands."

Jeremiah stepped back. "That is a falsehood! The LORD has but told me that the Chaldeans come and that we must yield to their yoke or be destroyed. I have given warning, nothing more!"

"Out of your own mouth do you speak treason! You do fall away to the Chaldeans! The people must decide your fate." Pashur's lined face gave the lie to his words.

The people would have nothing to do with his fate. If Pashur had his way, Jeremiah would be dead already. That was as clear to the prophet as rain heralding the presence of clouds. The man had another agenda. No sooner had the thought crossed Jeremiah's mind than the governor gave voice to it.

"The LORD is merciful," Pashur said in a silky voice that gave life to the vanity in which he invoked the LORD's name, "and has given you the chance to speak the truth. Upon our return to Jerusalem, you will renounce your former words and preach deliverance to the people. You will give strength to their hearts and lighten their fears. Preach that the LORD will turn back the Chaldeans and will deliver the people, and you shall live and not die." The governor spread his hands. "See? Did I not say that the LORD is merciful?"

Jeremiah stilled as a shiver ran down his spine. He didn't want to die. In fact, he wasn't all that sure he even wanted to be a prophet. This business hadn't been his choice to begin with. The LORD had called him when he was but a lad, leaving him with little preference in the matter. It had worked out fine during King Josiah's reign, but the goodly king was now dead and his son, an evil man, sat on the throne. Jeremiah fervently wished the LORD would choose another. No one was heeding his words anyway, so why speak them?

Swallowing, he nodded slowly. "So be it. I will speak the truth."

Pashur's smooth smile slipped down into his beard. He studied the prophet with probing eyes full of suspicion. Deciding he liked what he saw, he gestured to the guards, "Then let it be done. Take him! We leave now."

The prophet's mouth fell open, momentarily stunned out of his fear. "This is a day of rest," he protested. "We may not travel this day!"

Seraiah snorted as two soldiers advanced on Jeremiah. "The law is not for the priests of the LORD, false one. We may do as we will, for we are holy even as the sabbath is holy."[2]

The blasphemy that fell so easily from the young man's lips stunned Jeremiah into silence. He stood still as the two soldiers grabbed him roughly, jerking him around and swiftly tying his hands behind his back with a stout cord. Tears gathered in Jeremiah's eyes. How had the priests of the LORD fallen so far?

He had been turned so that he faced the Jordan Valley. Sunlight glittered off the Salt Sea, but a dark cloud hung over where Jerusalem should be. How appropriate. Jeremiah idly wondered if he stood in the exact same spot as Moses had when looking down upon the promised land just before his death. It was good that the ancient prophet had not lived to see this day.

He was jerked back around and shoved toward the waiting men. He caught Baruch's eye. The scribe looked scared. And angry. In fact, Jeremiah could not recall a time he had ever seen the scribe so angry. Both Buzi and Ezekiel wore identical expressions that gave nothing away as to what they felt. He fell in among them and, as a group, began their descent down Mount Nebo. Jeremiah breathed a silent sigh of relief when they took a direction away from where the ark was hidden.

"Tell me, Baruch," Jeremiah whispered to his friend, "that you have not marked the way."

The scribe shook his head. "The LORD forgive me for desiring so, but I have done as you have commanded. The way is not marked."

---

[2] Jeremiah 5:31, 18:18; Ezekiel 22:26.

Jeremiah let his breath out slowly. If either Pashur or Seraiah thought any of them had been marking a trail, they would have surely known something more than a sacrifice had brought Jeremiah and the others to the land of Moab. He gave silent thanks to Jehovah that his friends had heeded his command.

It took some time to make their way off the mountain, and when they did, it was only to join up with another six men, two of whom were soldiers and the remaining four were porters who carried the bulk of the travel supplies.

Frowning, Jeremiah looked around. "Where are the servants who accompanied us?" he asked.

He hadn't meant to be overheard, but Pashur turned to face him with a predatory smile. "They were in league with the prince of the Chaldeans and so were put to death."

The prophet blinked, disbelieving his ears. "You slew them?"

"They were examined and found wanting," Pashur said with a shrug. "They were not Hebrews, but strangers who would betray us to the prince of Babylonia." The temple governor moved close, crowding Jeremiah. His voice dropped low so that only the prophet could hear the next words. "So is the fate of all those in league with the LORD's enemies."

The threat was not lost on Jeremiah. He wanted to say something right then about Nebuchadnezzar being the servant of the LORD, but those words would only earn him a swift death. Instead, he said nothing, looking away from Pashur and blinking to hold back tears. He had promised to reward those servants who had helped safeguard the ark. Instead, he had led them to their deaths.

It was not lost on Jeremiah that only five men remained who knew that Jeremiah had hidden the ark—six, if you counted Ahikam, the temple scribe—and only Jeremiah knew the exact location. One of the men who knew was Seraiah's father, the high priest. Jeremiah worried that if things turned ill, the high priest might try to buy his life with this knowledge. Despite the man's aid in the matter of the ark, he and Jeremiah had never been true friends.

It was something else to worry about.

And so began the march back to Jerusalem. On the way, Pashur made sure that Jeremiah beheld the bodies of the servants, each stabbed in the chest and their bodies already beginning to bloat. Carrion birds had begun to gather, their cawing and fighting over the decaying flesh mocked Jeremiah as he passed.

Fording the Jordan wasn't difficult this time of year, and they passed close to Jericho on their way to Jerusalem. The temple governor seemed to be in a hurry, so it was late the next day that they reached Jerusalem.

Which was only the start of Jeremiah's troubles.

Such woes had truly started with the LORD, Jeremiah's God. Knowing death awaited him in the city if he spoke true, Jeremiah argued with the LORD, crying out in his spirit, *O LORD, You have deceived me! You are stronger than I and have prevailed over me. I am in derision daily, and everyone mocks me. I did as You commanded and cried out to the people…I cried violence and spoil and none do heed!*[3] He waited for some indication that his pain was heard, that the LORD saw his tribulation. Nothing. Since King Jehoiakim had been made king by the pharaoh of Egypt, the Word of the LORD had become a reproach to Jeremiah as he was derided daily for his words.[4]

He had only done what the LORD had commanded him to do and now, unless he lied, he would be killed—and even if he did lie, he suspected Pashur and Seraiah would still have him killed. In a fit of depression, he wondered why he had come forth out of the womb only to see labor and sorrow. *My days are consumed with shame!*[5] he shouted silently to God. *Why?* he begged. *Why?* But once again, no answer came.

---

[3] Jeremiah 20:7-8.
[4] Jeremiah 20:8.
[5] Jeremiah 20:18.

JEREMIAH

"So be it," Jeremiah muttered under his breath as the walls of Jerusalem came into view, "I am finished. I will no longer make mention of Him or speak in His name!"[6]

He meant it too. He thought of Urijah and how he had died speaking the Word of the LORD. *Why should I die likewise? Nay, I will not. If they want me to speak falsely, then I will do so!*

But even as he thought it, something began to burn in his heart.[7]

---

[6] Jeremiah 20:9.
[7] Jeremiah 20:9.

11

Daniel watched his sister eat grapes with what he suspected was exaggerated relish. Daniel fidgeted, adjusting and then readjusting his legs under the low table. Despite its softness, the cushion he sat on felt like a stone as he waited for his sister's attention.

After several more minutes of uncomfortable silence, Nehushta finally sighed and set her cluster of grapes on the wooden table. "I see you are greatly troubled. There is more on your mind than supper, is there not?"

Daniel nodded, and then stalled by taking a plump fig and chewing on it. His sister waited patiently—much more patiently than he had. When he swallowed the last bit, he said, "I have heard ill tidings and would know if you have heard ought of them as well."

"What ill tidings?" His sister unconsciously adjusted the ruby tiara that held back her black locks. Her oval face, half shadowed in the light of the oil lamps on the table, appeared relaxed.

DANIEL

This amazed Daniel. He had never met anyone who could show such poise under even the most trying of conditions. His sister possessed a quiet and subtle intelligence that always surprised anyone who discovered it. She had set out from the beginning to become queen before Daniel had even been born, caught Jehoiakim's eye when he was but a young prince, and they were wed before Jehoiakim even understood he had been the prey and not the predator. When Jehoiakim's younger half-brother had been chosen by the people to be king instead of him,[1] it had been Nehushta who had prevented her husband from going off in a murderous rage. She had counselled him to bide his time, and when Pharaoh Necho took Jehoahaz captive, Jehoiakim was positioned perfectly to be the Pharaoh's choice as king of Judah.

Most of it had been orchestrated by Daniel's sister behind the scenes. Daniel even suspected that his sister could read and write, a rarity in the world they lived in. But despite that, Nehushta was not an ardent worshiper of Jehovah, the God of Israel. She, like many of the people in Judah these days, believed in many gods and worshiped whichever god most closely aligned with her needs or ambitions. In this, she had strayed from the teachings of her father and mother, influenced, Daniel suspected, by the lure of being queen.

An idol of the goddess Ishtar sat behind a small altar in the center of her room, and incense burned freely upon it, giving the air a sweet-sickly smell. The idol, among other things, had contributed to Daniel's discomfort. He needed to be careful around his sister. If he displeased her, she could make his life very uncomfortable. Already, her son, Jehoiachin, plotted against his life, and given the choice between a much younger brother and her own son, Daniel was under no delusions as to which one she would favor. He needed to speak his words with care.

"Come, Daniel, speak freely," Nehushta said.

Daniel let his eyes slide to the two eunuchs standing before her door. Three other girls, his sister's attendants, stood or sat around

---

[1] 2 Kings 23:30.

the edge of the room, ready at a moment's notice to do as their mistress commanded.

"They will say nothing of what happens here," she said with a light laugh. The sound held an innocent quality to it that seemed to be at odds with what Daniel knew of her cunning.

He vowed not to underestimate her as so many others had done. Bowing his head in acknowledgment, he began, "I have heard rumors that our father is no longer in favor at court." That seemed a safe topic to broach. Nehushta knew her position as the king's favorite wife would be tied to her father's position in her husband's court. And it would get her thinking in the right direction.

She frowned, fiddling with a golden goblet filled with wine. "What know you?"

"Only that there are some who believe that anyone who shows compassion to the prophet Jeremiah must be in league with the Chaldeans."

"Father is one such?"

"He fears only that the prophet's words are truly from the LORD God of Israel. If so, then our continuance will depend on the mercy of the king and prince of Chaldea. Babylon is in ascendance. Egypt is in descendance, and all do know that your husband, the king, was placed upon the throne by Egypt." He sat up straight and leaned over the table, lowering his voice. "What if our God is truly angry with us for our sins and has chosen to use the arm of this Nebuchadnezzar as His instrument of wrath against Judah?"

His sister didn't so much as change expression during this explanation. She stared into her goblet, swishing the wine from side to side. But Daniel knew Nehushta was thinking. After a moment, she sat the cup back on the table and locked eyes with Daniel. "There are other gods we may call upon," she said at last, her eyes flickering to the idol of Ishtar. "The hereditary God of Israel has not always fought for us. Was not King Josiah, a devoted servant of Jehovah, defeated by the Egyptian gods?"

Despite the heat of summer, Daniel felt a chill settle in his bones. "Our God is a jealous God, my sister.[2] You know this. You know that if we serve Him and Him alone, He will fight for us. But we have turned our backs upon Him, and we have called down His wrath upon us."

Nehushta shook her head, the jewels in her hair sparkling in the light, and for the first time, her countenance showed irritation. "Those words sound much like the words of Jeremiah. Is this also Father's words?"

Daniel leaned away. He was treading upon dangerous ground here. "When have the prophet's words not come to pass?"

"Yet there are other prophets of the God of Israel who speak other words." Nehushta tapped her chin with a long, slim finger. Her dimples stood out. "Wherefore should I put more faith in one over the other?"

Daniel chewed on his lower lip. He wasn't getting anywhere with this line of conversation. What he really wanted to know was if Jeconiah had confided in his sister his desire to kill Daniel and if the king himself condoned it. If the king wanted him dead, it would complicate matters immensely. "What thinks the king?"

She raised a suspicious eyebrow. "My husband makes offerings every day to Molech. With Molech's favor, he believes the Chaldeans will be turned back. He likes not the words of Jeremiah the prophet. Such words do hurt to the people's confidence and sow fear and discord in their hearts. Such words are treason."

"And if the king learns that Father may believe such words?"

Nehushta's lips pursed. "We must prevent the king from learning such," she said firmly. "The king will not look favorably upon our father if this is known." She looked Daniel square in the eyes. "Or you, my brother. Take care of what you say in ears beyond this room." She popped another grape casually into her mouth.

Daniel visibly relaxed. So, the king didn't know. If he did, and if he had condoned Daniel's murder, his sister would know. Her

---

[2] Exodus 20:5, 34:14.

power of influence, however, clearly did not extend to her son who had not confided in her. For Daniel felt certain his would-be murderer had been dispatched by Jeconiah and Mattaniah and then killed in turn after he had failed. But this was information he dared not impart to his sister. As intelligent and intuitive as she was, she was blind when it came to her own son. There, she saw only what she wanted to see.

Jeconiah was not the only son of King Jehoiakim. He might be the oldest and the most favored, but he wasn't the only one, and Daniel's sister would likely do whatever it took to keep *her* son in his position to become the next king of Judah.

He got up from the table and bowed. "I thank you, my sister, for the meal."

She looked at the food he'd hardly touched, a small smile playing across her lips. "You were most hungry indeed."

"With your leave, I will be off."

She waved a hand. "Go with my blessing, my brother."

Daniel didn't know how he felt about that. But he fixed a smile on his face and backed away, moving toward the door.

"Daniel," her soft voice called, freezing him in his tracks. "I had word before you came that the prophet Jeremiah has been found and is even now being brought to the outer court of the temple to give answer for his prophecies. Perhaps you should venture there and hear for yourself if he will stand by his former words."

Another chill raced up Daniel's spine. That she had withheld this news until this moment meant she had seen deeper than he'd wanted her to. He bowed again to her, wryly conceding the victory of their subtle duel. She was a worthy opponent indeed, and he could appreciate the finesse with which she had wielded her sharp wit. "I will heed your words," he said, turning away.

"See that you do," she replied in the same tone.

Grinning, he left. One of the eunuchs opened the door for him. Out in the hall, another man stood, waiting. Surprised, Daniel stopped when the man bowed to him as the door to Nehushta's quarters closed. Daniel knew this man. Ebedmelech was an Ethiopian eunuch, not the chief, but still highly placed in the king's palace.[3]

"My lord," the man said, keeping his bow, "forgive me for speaking, but I would give you warning."

Daniel shot a look around. The two were alone. He didn't think Ebedmelech would attempt to harm him. Dutiful, competent, and trusted, the Ethiopian had served as a eunuch to the king's wives since he was a lad. But if any could carry out an assassination attempt in the palace, it would be one of the eunuchs.

Just in case, Daniel shifted his feet in preparation. "Speak," he said. "I will harken."

The eunuch straightened, his long, cleanshaven face adding shadows to his dark skin. "Leave not by the palace gates, my lord. Your presence here is known, and men do lie in wait for you."

Daniel sucked in his breath. *So soon?* He hadn't expected another attempt so quickly. He'd underestimated Jeconiah and Mattaniah. That irked him. "Why do you tell me this?"

Ebedmelech bobbed another bow. "I too serve the LORD God of Israel and have from my youth."

Surprised all over again, Daniel reached out and grabbed the servant by the arm. "Yet you are a stranger in Israel."

A flicker of a smile touched the servant's thin lips. "I will say to them which were not My people, you are My people, and they shall say, 'You are my God.'"[4]

Daniel recognized the quote. "The prophet Hosea?"

"Aye."

Daniel had not lingered long on the words of the prophet Hosea, but he had never seen those words in quite such a light as the eunuch did. He would have liked to talk to him at length about it, but now was not the time. "Then I thank you. Know you another way out?"

---

[3] Jeremiah 38:7.
[4] Hosea 2:23.

"I will take you."

At Daniel's nod, they set out.

"And, my lord," Ebedmelech said softly as they walked, "beware of your sister. She is most cunning, and she may not be as blind as she causes others to believe."

Frowning, Daniel reflected on his options. Nehushta was as much part of the problem as anyone else in Judah. She had forsaken the God of Israel and followed after false gods. But she had still warned him and at the same time tasked him with keeping their father out from underneath the vengeful eyes of the king. She clearly was in no position to do so, so she was relying upon Daniel. This gave Daniel some leverage, something he knew his sister resented no matter what face she showed him. But if the eunuch's words were right, his sister had somehow deceived him. Only he could not see how.

She had deliberately waited to tell him of Jeremiah the prophet. He felt certain that meant something. Only he didn't know what. Layers upon layers. That was his sister.

After the prophet's disappearance, Daniel had assumed Jeremiah had escaped for his own safety. But if he had been found and brought back, then perhaps the LORD had truly bidden him to speak other words to undo his former ones. Could God change His own mind? That other gods were so fickle was taken as a matter of course, but traditionally, the God of Israel had always abided by His own word.

Daniel decided to heed his sister's advice and go hear the prophet. It would be instructive either way. With a prayer for protection, he followed the eunuch from the palace by way of a small postern gate used only by servants. He bid the Ethiopian farewell and skirted wide of the courtyards before the palace, lest he be seen. The men lying in wait could simply keep on waiting for eternity. The thought brought a smile to his lips.

On his way to the temple, he came upon Mishael hiding between two houses and staring at the palace through the narrow opening at the other end. Daniel threw a rock at the boy's feet. Mishael surely jumped ten cubits. He came down, whirled, and spotted Daniel. He darted out of his hiding spot, eyes glittering with eagerness and excitement. "There you are! How did you escape the palace? What did you discover? I wager your sister knew all about the assassination. Is she in league with the king? Does the king know? We will have to flee the city, will we not, Daniel? I saw men waiting near the palace entrance. They had an ill aspect about them. I liked them not and so hid. I tell you truly, Daniel, I—"

"Guard your tongue," Daniel snapped, glancing around. No one was too close, but there were several people looking their direction.

Mishael swallowed, his Adam's apple bobbing in his neck. "Forgive me," he whispered, looking contrite.

Daniel waved it away. "We must watch our words," he said harshly. Then his conscience was smitten. "Howbeit, we will not hide the words of the LORD our God. We will rise as the LORD commands and come what may."

Mishael's grin took up his whole face. "We will prevail?"

"Aye." He considered his own words for a moment. "Howbeit, if not, we will still stand. It is in the LORD's hands."

"What said your sister?"

"She knows nothing of a plot from the king."

"Then we must contend with Jeconiah and Mattaniah alone?"

Daniel snorted. "That is not enough for you?" He gestured toward the palace. "Who think you put men to lie in wait for me?"

The lad grinned even wider. Sometimes Daniel wondered if the lad truly understood the danger. Not like Daniel at all. *The innocence of youth,* he reflected ironically.

"Where go we?" Mishael asked.

"To the temple. They have found Jeremiah the prophet."

Mishael's grin slipped. "He is captured?"

"I know not. He is to speak to the people. This is all I know. We go to hear him."

"Then let us make haste!" Mishael took off, his curly, black hair bouncing atop his head like a goatherder atop a horse for the first time. Daniel ran after him.

They found a crowd gathering before the upper Benjamin gate that led directly to the temple mount. Daniel found this odd. There was much more room before the new gate between the lower and upper court of the temple mount. But here, below the temple and in the city proper, people had to line the streets or look down from the roofs of houses.

Neither Mishael nor Daniel had reached their full height yet, so they found it difficult to see over the heads of the crowd, mostly men, murmuring to each other and gesturing, sometimes angrily, toward the gate. The street sloped upward here, climbing what had once been the southern slope of Mount Moriah. This did help, and Daniel did catch glimpses of priests standing on the gate steps looking down at the people. He could probably back up to see better but then he wouldn't be able to hear.

Looking around, he found two houses where the walls did not adjoin directly but were separated by a few cubits. He squeezed between them and began to shimmy his way up. Mishael followed quickly. When they reached the top of the house, they found the roofs already occupied by men. One, likely the owner, glanced at the two lads, grimaced at the rudeness of the intrusion, but waved them over. Daniel and Mishael bowed their gratitude and squeezed into an empty corner of the flat roof to watch, looking down upon a sea of turbaned heads.

Someone was already speaking, his voice ringing out over the crowd. "...repented of the words he has spoken in the ears of all the people! The LORD God of Israel has chastised him and humbled him so that we may know the truth and our hearts may be uplifted in joy, knowing that our God will defend us on all sides, even from the Chaldeans!"

"Who speaks?" Mishael whispered not so softly. He earned a hard look from one of the nearby men.

"Pashur, governor of the temple this course," Daniel whispered back.

"Is that Jeremiah the prophet?" Mishael asked, pointing to the man standing beside the governor.

"Aye."

"Hold your tongues," a man hissed nearby.

The two lads fell silent, listening.

Jeremiah was thrust forward, nearly stumbling. He looked somewhat battered and disheveled, his outer mantel dirty and travel stained. His turban was missing, exposing his head to the sun, and his hair looked greasy and stringy. Wherever they had found the prophet, they had not allowed him to clean up.

The prophet stood there for a long moment, shoulders slumped and eyes blinking against the summer sun. *He appears defeated,* Daniel thought sadly. For all his life, he had heard of Jeremiah, the mighty prophet. The man looked anything but mighty.

Pashur prodded Jeremiah with the end of a staff. "Speak!" he shouted. "For once, let truth pass your lips! No evil shall come upon us, and neither shall we see sword nor famine. The words this man spoke are but wind! The word of the LORD was not in his voice. Now we shall hear the truth!"[5]

Daniel leaned forward over the low wall that circled the roof. Jeremiah glanced back at Pashur and two other men, one the high priest, standing in the shadows of the temple wall before the gate. Looking back over the crowd, something seemed to settle over Jeremiah. His stooped shoulders straightened, and he seemed to gain handspans in height. His eyes, shadowed and hollow, took on a new life as if a fire had been lit within. His face, sagging and dejected, firmed and the deep lines of his face melted away.

A blaze of anticipation suddenly burned in Daniel's breast, and he wondered if all felt the same, for the prophet was about to speak.

---

[5] Jeremiah 5:12-13.

And speak he did. As he lifted up his voice, a breeze sprung up from nowhere, carrying his words far out over the city of Zion, and Daniel heard each word as if the prophet stood directly before him.

"Thus says the LORD God of hosts!" Jeremiah cried, his voice ringing out and his attention focused upon Pashur. "'Because you speak this word of safety and deliverance, behold, I will make My words in your mouth *fire*, and this people wood, and it shall devour them!'" The prophet flung his hand out toward the north. "'Lo, I will bring a nation upon you from far, O house of Israel,' says the LORD. 'It is a mighty nation, it is an ancient nation, a nation whose language you know not, neither understand. Their quiver is as an open sepulcher, and they are all mighty men. And they will eat up your harvest, and your bread, which your sons and daughters would eat! They shall devour your flocks and herds, your vines and fig trees! They will impoverish your fenced cities with the sword in which you trust!'"[6]

Jeremiah's eyes blazed as he spoke, and Daniel felt his jaw drop. He knew without a shadow of doubt that God had spoken through the prophet. Only he didn't like the words, for Jeremiah had pronounced doom on Jerusalem and Judah. Daniel wasn't the only one.

"Nay!" Pashur shouted, his whole-body quivering. Like a snake, he lashed out, striking Jeremiah with his staff.[7] The blow caught the prophet across the head and neck, knocking him clean off his feet.

Jeremiah tumbled part way down the steps as a roar of rage erupted from the people who hissed and shook their fists at Jeremiah, cursing and threatening. The prophet picked himself up, blood running down his face and staining part of his neck.

He spoke again, his words somehow quieting the crowd. "Hear now this, O foolish people without understanding. You have eyes and see not! You have ears and hear not! 'Why fear you Me not?'

---

[6] Jeremiah 5:14-17.
[7] Jeremiah 20:1-2.

DANIEL

says the LORD. 'Will you not tremble at My presence?' But all this people have a revolting and a rebellious heart! They do not say in their heart, 'Let us now fear the LORD our God who gives rain in His season or reserves for us the appointed weeks of the harvest.' Nay! Your iniquities have turned away these things, and your sins have withheld good things from you!"[8] The prophet's glare seemed to take in the whole city. "'Shall I not visit these evils?' says the LORD. 'Shall not My soul be avenged on such a nation as this?'"[9]

"To the stocks with him," Pashur cried, still trembling in rage. "Give him neither bread nor water until he learns the errors of his ways!"

Several priests rushed down the steps to where Jeremiah stood, swaying under the beating sun. They dragged him back up to where the wooden stocks waited. Daniel realized they had intended this all along and was why they had commanded him to speak here instead of on the temple mount. Jeremiah was never going to be spared the stocks. They had fully intended to make an example of him before the people. Daniel itched to do something, but he could only stand and watch as they shoved the prophet inside and slammed the upper half down, locking it in place around his neck and wrists.[10]

Daniel had never felt the bite of the stocks before, but the contraption looked to make one incredibly uncomfortable. It was raised high enough off the ground that the prisoner had to partially stand to take the weight off his neck. Such prisoners found their legs trembling and shaking within hours of such a position, but they dared not relax. To do so put too much weight on one's neck. Those left overlong in the stocks were often crippled. Some never recovered.

Under the roar of the angry crowd, Daniel grabbed Mishael and whispered into his ear. "We must do something." Even as they watched, fat figs shot out from the crowd to smash into either the

---

[8] Jeremiah 5:21-25.
[9] Jeremiah 5:29.
[10] Jeremiah 20:2.

prophet's face or the wooden stocks, staining the man's beard with the dark juices. If things didn't calm down soon, those figs would turn into stones.

Mishael nodded, but even he understood that acting now would be the height of foolishness. Maybe under the cover of darkness they could help the prophet.

Then a ram's horn sounded from the tower of Meah at the northwestern corner of the temple mount. Everyone froze, shouts dying on lips, curses snatched away by the wind. An unnatural silence descended over Jerusalem. Then the horn sounded again, a deep reverberating sound that pierced bone and muscle and left a sense of dread. It was the warning trumpet.

An enemy approached the city.

As one, those on rooftops looked toward the northwest, the only logical approach to the city by an invading force. The rest of the city was built above steep slopes that overlooked valleys, so the main weakness of the city lay to the north. For this reason, years ago, King Hezekiah had destroyed many houses to use the stone in making the northern wall unusually thick and strong.[11]

Daniel and his friend already occupied that corner of their roof, so they had an unobstructed view over the western hill and beyond the wall. Banners, snapping in the air, crested the rise. From this distance he couldn't make out any detail, but he, like everyone else watching, already knew.

The Chaldeans had come.

---

[11] Isaiah 22:10. Parts of this wall, 23 feet thick, still exists in Jerusalem to this day.

12

A few torches placed in wall sconces near the gate cast the only light by which Jeremiah could see. The muscles in his legs and back screamed at him from trying to remain in a position that took pressure off his neck. He had nearly choked once already while trying to relax those muscles.

Mostly, he stared at the ground. The stocks didn't provide him much room to move. He could twist his head some, but lifting his head only caused him to smack the wood pinning his head. His trapped wrists didn't allow for any leverage to hold himself up, so he was forced to rely entirely on his legs and back. And he couldn't stand upright either. He could manage nothing more than a half crouch.

The prophet intensely regretted his words that had landed him in this position. The only thing it had accomplished was this torture. Nothing else. No one had given heed to his words, so he didn't see the point in speaking in the first place. In truth, in the beginning, he had vowed to remain silent and let Pashur make of it as he would.

But then he had been thrust before the people and commanded to lie, and something had sprung up in his heart, a burning flame that threatened to consume him unless he spoke.[1] So speak he did.

He wished now he hadn't.

He knew what was coming and he knew it was unavoidable. The wrath of the LORD would not be denied...delayed perhaps, but not denied. Tears of shame gathered in his eyes. Shame for himself, yes, but also shame for his people and for his beloved city of Jerusalem.

And the Chaldeans had come. He knew this even if no one had directly told him. It was likely the only reason he hadn't been stoned to death. The people had fled to the walls to watch over the invaders. The only consolation Jeremiah had was the fearful look cast at him by Pashur. The governor was wise enough to realize that much of his credibility had been destroyed at that first warning trumpet.

Seraiah, the high priest's son, had given him an entirely different look. One of pure hate. Well, he was young yet. But what burned in Jeremiah's mind the most was the look from the high priest. Azariah had only looked sad and resigned. Jeremiah knew how he felt.

"My lord prophet," a voice whispered out of the darkness, so close that Jeremiah jerked in startlement.

He banged the back of his head and fought hard to muffle a cry of pain. Squinting to see better, Jeremiah twisted around. "Who goes there?" he demanded hoarsely. Whoever had spoken had clearly meant him no harm, trying not to alert the guards. He saw little sense in spoiling his visitor's attempt at stealth.

"It is I, Daniel, son of Elnathan."

Jeremiah remembered him. The lad had told him of Urijah's death and had come to warn him that the king's wrath might be turned upon him. He was a God-fearing lad, a true son of Israel. A dark shape filtered around the edges of the torchlight, moving slowly toward the prophet.

---

[1] Jeremiah 20:9.

JEREMIAH

"I bring food and water," the lad whispered.

The mere mention of sustenance caused Jeremiah to salivate and his stomach to growl. He licked his parched lips. "Water first, I beg."

But first, a block of wood was thrust under the prophet's knees. He settled his weight on it, his back and legs quivering with pained relief. The boy had thought of everything. Only then was a bowl thrust beneath his face and held close. He had to lap it up like a dog, but it was the best water he had ever tasted. It was an effort to do it without making too much noise, but he managed to lap the entire contents up. He sighed. He felt better already.

A loaf of bread replaced the empty bowl, and he bit a chunk out of it and began to chew gratefully. Between bites, he asked, "What tidings? I heard the warning trumpet."

"The Chaldeans have come according to the word you did speak. Even now, they surround the city, and the city is shut up. The gates have been barred, and archers man the walls." There was a pause, and then the lad continued, "The Chaldeans bring a mighty army. They are like the sand of the sea and sow fear in the hearts of all men."

Jeremiah grunted. He hated being right about this. "What says the king?"

"The king is shut in the palace with his counselors. I have been forbidden entry this night, but the king will go forth in the morning and view the Chaldeans from the wall of the city."

The lad didn't sound so sure of his information, but it made sense. The king couldn't be seen to cower. The people would not stand for it. Curious, he asked, "What think you the king will do?"

Daniel was silent for a time. When he spoke, he did so with the confidence of one who had given the subject much thought and debate. "The king will seek aid from Egypt if he may, for he is beholden to the pharaoh. We have water and food and so may last for some months before famine strikes the city. He will place his hope in the Egyptians to deliver us."

Jeremiah was astonished at the lad's perception and understanding of the situation. For one so young to see so clearly was rare and a wonder. "And will Egypt deliver us?" the prophet asked.

"Nay," came back the immediate reply. "The LORD God of Israel has spoken through you, my lord. We know Egypt will not deliver us from the hand of the prince of Babylon. The king believes this not, but it matters little that he does. For Egypt has been defeated and Pharaoh Necho driven back to his cities and homeland. The Egyptians dare not bestir themselves to come north across the desert for at least a year. They will fortify their cities and see if Nebuchadnezzar comes to them."

Again, Jeremiah felt amazement. The lad had a clear grasp of the political situation of three nations. Knowing the answer, he still asked, "What advice would you give the king then?"

The lad sighed and sat down heavily in the shadows. The guards still hadn't noticed anything out of the ordinary and stood sleepily at their posts. Likely, they were worried more about the invading army than one lone prophet in the stocks whispering nonsense to himself.

"My heart does cry against it, but the king must yield to the Chaldean prince or be grounded to dust and his name blotted out from under heaven. Only then may the city continue to stand. I would advise the king to heed your words, my lord, to give ear to the God of Israel, and repent of our sins…which are many."

The lad fell silent. Only the heavy sound of his own breath reached Jeremiah's ears. He spoke, "You are wise beyond your years, young Daniel. The LORD has granted you this wisdom. In the days ahead, you must rely upon Jehovah to aid you in the coming darkness, for if you stay true to our God, He will keep you and protect you."

There was a slight motion from the shadows that might have been a nod. "I so swear to stay true, my lord."

"Then it is well. Now begone. You have aided me, but there is nothing more you can do, and you risk the governor's wrath if you

JEREMIAH

are caught here. Even a prince of Judah would do well to avoid his attention."

"What of you, my lord?"

"Fear not for me. With the prince of Babylon here, the king will call for me." He sighed. "Though I wish it not."

"I will beseech God on your behalf," Daniel whispered, standing.

"I give you thanks," the prophet whispered back. He hesitated. "Yet leave the wood for my knees."

"As you will, my lord."

Then the lad was gone, fading into the darker shadows outside the light of the torches. But morning was coming and with it, Jeremiah felt certain he would be freed. For a time. The LORD, it seemed, was not yet through with him.

Morning came, and as predicted, Pashur and a contingent of palace guards arrived at the upper Benjamin gate where Jeremiah had remained all night in the stocks.[2] The temple governor regarded Jeremiah with an unreadable expression, noting the block of wood under his knees that gave the prophet a measure of comfort from the stocks. Pashur's eyes narrowed, but he said nothing of it. Jeremiah detected a measure of apprehension in the other's bearing.

"Set him free," the governor ordered the guards.

The chains were loosened, and the top half of the stocks lifted off. Jeremiah immediately slumped to the ground, his muscles cramping so that he had to curl into a ball.

They gave him a moment, but then Pashur said, "Lift him up."

Two of the guards reached down and dragged the prophet to his feet. His muscles rebelled and he cried out in pain as they sought to return to a more normal position. Sweat gathered on his brow and stung as it seeped into blood-stained cuts. Pashur's eyes glinted in a perverse satisfaction at Jeremiah's plight, and his nose scrunched up against the odor.

---

[2] Jeremiah 20:3.

When the pain passed, Jeremiah watched the priest. The man had dark circles under his eyes. Jeremiah wasn't the only one who had gone without sleep that night. "What have you done with my companions and my servant?" the prophet demanded.

Pashur wouldn't look him directly in the eyes. "I set them free this morning. They are well. Fear not for them." A strange, almost painful expression had been stamped on the governor's face. It bespoke a worry that transcended one's own ambitions.

Jeremiah was about to comment on it, perhaps irk the priest a bit, when something came over him and he went rigid. The hair on his head felt as if it was floating for a moment and all pain vanished.

He looked upon Pashur and spoke with an authority not his own, "The LORD has not called your name Pashur, but Magormissabib.[3] For thus says the LORD, 'Behold, I will make you a terror to yourself and to all your friends, and they shall fall by the sword of their enemies, and your eyes shall behold it. I will give all Judah into the hand of the king of Babylon, and he shall carry them away captive and slay them with the sword. Moreover, I will deliver all the strength of this city, and all the labor thereof, and all the precious things thereof, and all the treasures of the kings of Judah will I give into the hand of their enemies, which shall spoil them, and take them, and carry them to Babylon. And *you*, Pashur, and all that dwell in *your* house shall go into captivity. You shall come to Babylon, and there you shall die and be buried—you and all your friends to whom you have prophesied lies.'"[4]

Pashur's face grew slack and his brown skin somehow grew pasty. He gaped at Jeremiah, his mouth working but no sound coming forth. The guards holding Jeremiah let go and stepped hastily away as if to deny they had ever touched the prophet. They would have fled if Jeremiah hadn't speared each of them to the ground with his gaze and burning eyes.

---

[3] *Magormissabib* means "terror on every side."
[4] Jeremiah 20:3-6.

JEREMIAH

"The king has called me to attend him, has he not?" Jeremiah said finally, breaking the spell.

The guards blinked and shifted their feet uncomfortably, most leaning away from the prophet. Pashur looked to be barely able to stand. The governor gripped his beard with both hands, tugging harshly. He'd rip his own beard out in the next moment.

"Then let us go see the king," Jeremiah said, answering his own question. "Though I must change my garments and wash afore I attend the king." He began walking down into the City of David. He left it for Pashur and the guards to follow.

A smile played along the battered prophet's lips. That had been fun.

13

"The city is besieged," Nebuzaradan announced as he approached Nebuchadnezzar. The two men stood between two raised banners on a rise that faced the walls of Jerusalem. One banner depicted a gold lion on a field of blue, the symbol of the goddess Ishtar. The other one had a golden dragon emblazoned across a similar field of blue, the symbol of the god Marduk. With the blessings of these two gods going before him, Nebuchadnezzar knew he would prevail over any obstacle.

It didn't hurt that the Hebrew God had also blessed this siege of Jerusalem.

"All the gates are blockaded and the walls watched," Nebuzaradan continued his report. "No man shall escape."

"That is well," Nebuchadnezzar agreed, only partially satisfied. It had taken the better part of two days to fully surround the city, and during that time, there had been no entreaties from the king of Judah. It seemed the man was content to wait and see what the Chaldean prince would do. Irritated, the prince studied the walls, planning an attack if it came to it. He didn't like what he saw. The northern wall was the most massive of the city. Other walls might be thinner, but they had the advantage of being built high on a steep slope, making an attack with siege engines nearly impossible. Only the north and west offered any opportunity to breach the walls if it came to an assault. "It will take many new moons to reduce these fortifications," he grumbled.

"Perhaps," Nebuzaradan said. "Howbeit, we came upon them unawares." He gestured to a line of captives kneeling in the dirt halfway to the city walls and well within sight of any watching atop the fortifications. "Not one Hebrew scout escaped us to bring word of our coming. The inhabitants had no time to prepare for a siege. Their supplies will run low within weeks."

"I chafe at such passing of time," Nebuchadnezzar snapped. "While we delay here, the Egyptians rally and make ready for our coming. I like it not. If we must build siege towers, we will not leave here before the harvest."

He looked at his bevy of counselors and battle commanders standing nearby, hoping they would offer good advice on how to force the city to surrender. Among them were several members of the priesthood of the Babylonian gods. They were there to interpret his dreams, for that was how the gods spoke to him. Yet, since he had heeded the Hebrew God's call to besiege the city, he had had no more dreams. The gods were silent. It made him uncomfortable. He wished Ashpenaz was here, but he had left his trusted eunuch with his wives to oversee their comfort and disposition safely away from the coming battle.

"What say you?" he asked his counselors.

An astrologer stepped to the forefront, a young man whom Nebuchadnezzar knew possessed tremendous ambition. The prince approved—though in truth, he recalled not the man's name. The astrologer bowed low and then fell to his knees, touching his head to the earth. "I would speak to the vessel of the gods!"

"Speak then," Nebuchadnezzar commanded.

The man rose, keeping his head bowed. "Your star is in ascendance, my lord. Show the Hebrews your might and resolution. Break their will and they will surrender."

Nebuchadnezzar found it strange that when the gods were silent, the stars spoke. He ran fingers through his braided beard, shifting his armor on his shoulders and thinking over the advice. There might be a way at that. He gestured to his herald. "Speak you the Hebrew tongue?"

The man, dressed in resplendent robes and possessing the most impressive voice Nebuchadnezzar had ever heard, bowed. "I do," he answered in his resonating voice that carried to every ear on the rise with no effort at all. The man could float his voice on the wind and be heard leagues away. "It is a vile tongue and sits ill in my mouth, but I know it."

"Come," Nebuchadnezzar ordered, striding forward. Both the herald and Nebuzaradan followed. After a moment, the battle commanders also followed, though the prince noted that the priests, magicians, and astrologers all elected to remain safely out of bowshot range from the city walls.

The captive Hebrew scouts all knelt in a line facing the walls of their city. To the east rose two towers from the highest part of the city. Nebuchadnezzar understood that to be the temple mount of the Hebrews. Indeed, the mighty temple rose above the walls enough to be seen. It glimmered in the sunlight, foretelling of many riches within. It had caused more than one Chaldean to salivate. But it was to the wall directly to his south that he cast his attention.

A banner had been raised on the wall near the midpoint. It too sported a lion—though Nebuchadnezzar doubted it had anything at all to do with the goddess Ishtar. But then with these Hebrews, one could never tell. The lion, blue on a white field, had been lifted high upon the wall an hour past. This then was the king of Judah, and it was to him that Nebuchadnezzar intended to make his demands.

They stopped before the prisoners, facing the wall. "Proclaim my words in the Hebrew tongue, herald. Speak naught else."

"As you command, my lord."

Nebuchadnezzar began speaking and the herald lifted up his voice and shouted to the men watching upon the wall. His voice indeed seemed to be carried by the wind. Its clarity rang like a bell over the defenders, and Nebuchadnezzar felt confident that all watching heard clearly.

"Thus says Nebuchadnezzar, prince of Babylon, the God of your people has spoken to me in a dream, saying, 'Come, take the city of Jerusalem and have dominion over My people.' Whereupon, I have obeyed the voice of your God and am come to chastise you for your many sins. Think not that the walls upon which you rely will keep my hand from your wives and your children. Behold the might of Babylon and the gods of Chaldea! Yield your necks to my yoke and I shall spare you, your wives, and your little ones. Resist and be utterly destroyed, your walls broken, your houses destroyed, your riches taken, your fields sown with salt, your city made a dunghill, your wives and daughters ravished, and your little ones spitted upon our spears. Wherefore do you trust in the broken reed of Egypt? Behold, the armies of Pharaoh Necho are no more. Seek not for succor among the Egyptians for they will not come to your aid. I alone am your help. Yield and you will not be utterly destroyed."

With a sharp gesture to his battle commanders, Nebuchadnezzar drew his sword and whirled. With one clean stroke, he beheaded the first prisoner. The man's body flopped to the ground, his head rolling away several cubits closer to the city. Blood stained the earth. His commanders also drew their swords and fell upon the prisoners in like manner. All were beheaded so quickly that not a man among them had time to even cry out in fear—not that they could have anyway. Nebuchadnezzar had already removed their tongues.

A cry of protest did rise up, but it came from the Jews standing on the walls.

"Gather the heads," the Babylonian prince ordered grimly to his men, "and throw them over the wall. Let their dead speak for us." He then turned to the herald. "Speak yet again these words: Tomorrow, when the sun reaches its zenith, I will hear the king of Judah's answer."

Turning his back on the walls of Jerusalem, he marched away, keeping a sedate pace and showing his contempt for the defenders. Hopefully, his little demonstration would strike fear in the king of Judah's heart. If beheading didn't work, he could resort to public flaying. Watching someone staked to the ground and then having their skin removed little by little often caught people's attention. He would also have his men begin construction of siege towers and battering rams in sight of the people watching from the wall. But he hoped the casual brutality of the beheadings would be sufficient. He didn't want to spend overlong here. Every day wasted was one where Pharaoh Necho strengthened his arm against him. Egypt was the true prize. Jerusalem was nothing more than a distraction.

A rich one, perhaps, but a distraction nonetheless. Nebuchadnezzar needed this to end soon. If the Jews persisted in defying him, he would indeed raze the city to the ground and fulfill each threat declared to the Jews.

That would be the price for irritating the crown prince of Babylon.

14

The court of the king was filled to capacity. Every prince, significant priest, scribe, and counselor had come to hear the decree of the king of Judah. The only women in attendance, Daniel noted absently, were a few of the king's wives, Daniel's sister among them. They stood in a corner, whispering among themselves or to the maids who followed in attendance. The king's youngest son clung to his mother's skirts.

Daniel noted that many of the sons of the princes were also present. He bowed in acknowledgment to Hananiah and Mishael, standing near with their father. Close behind Daniel was a tall lad by the name of Azariah, the son of Michaiah, one of the temple scribes, and the same age as Daniel. Daniel didn't know him all that well, knowing only that he was the youngest son and so shouldn't have been able to get this close in the assembly, but then there weren't many who would seek to make Azariah do anything. His thick chest and arms bristled with muscles, and despite its handsomeness, his face sought to match hardness for hardness with an anvil. He didn't fit Daniel's impression of a scribe.

The king swept into the room from an antechamber, followed closely by his son, Jeconiah, and younger brother, Mattaniah. He sat upon the resplendent throne that had been raised so that he could look down upon all standing. The moment he sat, the crowd hushed so that only the rustle of cloth was heard. Jeconiah and Mattaniah took up their places on the lower steps to either side of the throne.

The king's thin face stared at the crowd, but his cruel eyes wouldn't settle. They kept darting about the room as if he expected Nebuchadnezzar to personally walk into the room with his sword drawn. Daniel, along with many of the people in this room, had both seen and heard what the Chaldean prince had done the day before. So when the king spoke, it wasn't surprising that his voice sounded strained and higher pitched than normal. "The prince of Babylon has decreed that we bring word to him by noon of this day as to our decision. Shall we yield or resist?"

Voices erupted from all around, most shouting defiance at the notion of surrendering to the Chaldeans. The air stank with fear. Daniel could smell it, mingled with sweat and the fragrance of spices and incense.

One voice rose above the others, Seraiah, son of Azariah, the high priest. "We must trust in Egypt," he cried. The crowd quieted, looking at him. The young man stood next to his father at the forefront of the room. From where Daniel stood, he could see Seraiah's dark features and flat face. He wore his hair long, a custom of heathen priesthoods more than that of the Levitical priests. He folded his arms against the attention that fell upon him. "Ever since Pharaoh Necho slew King Josiah, we have given him a yearly tribute in gold and silver. We have purchased aid of the Egyptians. Send word to them and they will come. We must only hold until then."

It was Daniel's father who burst out into mocking laughter. "Pardon, my lord," he said to King Jehoiakim in his deep voice, while keeping one eye on the upstart young priest. "But how shall

DANIEL

we send word? The Chaldeans have surrounded the city. Did not Seraiah see what the prince of Babylon did to our scouts? Did not we all? Nay, we cannot trust in Egypt. The Egyptians have fallen to the Chaldeans already."

"That was but a part of Egypt's full might," the young priest argued. "The pharaoh will rally his people and march to destroy the Chaldeans. But if we betray our oaths to Necho, how then will the Egyptians deal with us? If we become a wall to the Chaldeans that the Egyptians may grind their bodies to dust upon, then will we be rewarded."

"You are deceived," Elnathan shot back. "The Egyptians will not come again while the Chaldeans remain in the land. They will fortify their own lands against them for, surely, Nebuchadnezzar seeks to take Egypt."

Elishama, the chief scribe of the King's Court, stepped forward. "Elnathan speaks with wisdom," said Hananiah's and Mishael's father. "We must not put our trust in Egypt. Even if, perchance, Egypt will come to our succor, it will not be for many months. The walls may hold against the Chaldeans, but our sustenance will not. Famine will overtake us before the Egyptians can come to our aid."

The king squirmed uncomfortably in this throne. "Your words carry no hope. You suggest surrender."

Elishama bowed low. "Nay, my king. I suggest only that we cannot put faith in Egypt."

"But then from where may salvation come?" the king demanded. "I have called upon the gods of Baal and Molech, yet they are silent. Their priests have no word from their gods. Does this Nebuchadnezzar have the right of it, that the LORD God of Israel has given us into the prince's hand?"

Daniel's father and the chief scribe exchanged a quick look while dark muttering suddenly filled the room. Elnathan bowed again. "What says the prophet Jeremiah? He speaks for Jehovah. Let us hear him that the king may know of a surety if our God is against us."

King Jehoiakim's scowl could have curdled milk. "We do know already what the prophet would say. Why hear more?"

In a corner of the throne room, several men, priests of Molech and Ishtar stirred, muttering aloud. Daniel's father shot them an angry look, but he lacked the power to expel them. One, a large man, bald and heavily tattooed, stood forward, drawing attention to himself. "The king's words are wise. The prophet of Jehovah is in league with the Babylonians and so would seek our downfall. What more need have we to hear his words? Give us time, O king, that we may beseech our gods. Surely they will speak yet and give counsel and deliverance! Only bend not your knees to the Chaldeans!"

The man was a priest of Molech, chief of those in Jerusalem. Daniel's fingers itched. He wanted nothing more than to take a sword and run the heathen through. Likely the man feared what Nebuchadnezzar would do if he took the city. The prince of Chaldea worshiped other gods and would put Molech in descendance.

"False one!" Daniel's father shouted. "You whisper lies into the ears of the king." He bowed to Jehoiakim. "Heed them not, my king. Let us hear the words of Jeremiah that we may know the will of *our* God. Ask him to call upon our God for mercy. Mayhap there be hope yet."

The high priest of Jehovah also bowed, ignoring his fuming son, and throwing the priests of Molech a dark look. "The words of Elnathan are wise, my lord, and Jeremiah awaits without. Allow me to bring him in, for I too would hear his words and see if our God will show mercy unto us."

The king glanced at his brother, Mattaniah. The young prince's eyes hadn't left Daniel's father. They were the eyes that weighed and calculated. The lad bent then to whisper something in his brother's ear.

The king listened and then nodded. He straightened. "So be it. Bring in the prophet. We will hear his words."

The priest of Molech began to protest, but at the king's furious look, he bowed and backed away, melting into the knot of fellow priests who stood as if besieged.

Moments later, Jeremiah strode into the King's Court followed by Baruch, two soldiers, and Pashur, the temple governor. The prophet looked haggard, but Daniel was glad to see that they'd given him a new white tunic and an outer robe made of stout wool. They'd even cleaned him up some. And despite looking haggard and tired, he walked with a firmness absent when Daniel had stolen a conversation with him the night before. Daniel couldn't prevent a smile from creeping onto his lips. The prophet had, at least for the moment, found an inner fire.

The battered prophet stopped before the king and bowed respectfully. "Here am I, my lord. What would you inquire of me?" His voice still sounded hoarse, but it carried a purposeful confidence.

The king rose to his feet and looked down upon the prophet. "Speak truly, Jeremiah. Is there yet hope? Will the LORD our God give us into the hands of the Chaldeans? Some say we must trust in Egypt. Others say that Egypt is a broken reed. What say you?"

Jeremiah regarded the king quietly and then let his eyes scan the crowd. They stopped briefly on Daniel, and the lad thought he saw the corners of the prophet's mouth rise ever so slightly. But then the eyes moved on and a flash of anger replaced the light within. "Harken to the word of the LORD," he proclaimed, finally stopping to lock eyes with the king. "The LORD bid me go to the potter's house and this I did. And there, I beheld as the potter wrought a work on the wheels. But the vessel he made of clay was marred in his hand, so he made it again another vessel as seemed good to the potter to make it. Then the word of the LORD came to me, saying, 'O house of Israel, cannot I do with you as this potter? Behold, as the clay is in the potter's hand, so are you in My hand, O house of Israel. Of a kingdom, I may pluck it up, pull it down, and destroy it. Howbeit, if that nation, against whom I have pronounced destruction, turn from their evil, I will repent of the evil that I thought to do unto them.'"[1] Jeremiah's head bowed. "There is yet hope, O king. Deliver yourself into the hands of the LORD and all this people and He may yet remake you into vessels of honor."

Dead silence followed that pronouncement, and Daniel held his breath. The words had stirred him like little else had. He wanted to be this vessel of the LORD, but at the same time, it brought confusion. Despite the parable of the potter, Daniel's mind was filled with the image of a smith's crucible, a vessel in which metal could be superheated and then reshaped. It brought to mind fiery trials and change that would reshape his life forever. He shivered. This last feeling, apparently, was shared by the king.

Jehoiakim flopped back onto his throne, his hands gripping his robes as if he meant to tear them. "How can we yet repent?" he demanded. "Will the LORD deliver us from the hand of Nebuchadnezzar? Speak forthrightly, prophet. If I humble myself before the LORD, will there be salvation?"

Jeremiah shook his head. "Nay, O king of Judah, for the Chaldeans are the potter's wheel upon which Jehovah will remake you. Give yourselves willingly to the king of Babylon and you may yet be remade. Only in this way will the city be spared and you find life for your wives and little ones, for the words of the prince of Babylon will come to pass if you stiffen your necks and refuse to bow before him."

"Treason!" Seraiah screamed, his face molted in rage. "This man seeks to weaken our hearts and deliver us captive to the Chaldeans that they may spoil us! He is worthy of death! How many will be slain if we deliver ourselves into their hands?"

Strangely, it was Pashur who placed a hand on the young man's arm to silence him. The young priest stared at the governor in shock as the older priest of the Immer order said, "Hold your tongue and speak no more. It is for the king to decide."

The king had buried his face in his hands. When he looked up at these words, he cried aloud and ripped a portion of his beard out

---

[1] Jeremiah 18:1-8.

of his face. Everyone jerked or gasped in shock and Daniel found himself taking a step back. In a wheezy voice, the king demanded. "How may I do this? Will not the prince of Babylon slay me if I deliver myself into his hands or take me captive into the land of Chaldea?"

Both options, Daniel knew, were distinct possibilities. Spies had already brought word of other prisoners taken by Nebuchadnezzar. Other kings had been ruthlessly killed in some of the most horrible ways imaginable. Daniel shot a quick, hard look at Mattaniah. This outcome would be to his benefit. Indeed, if the conversation Daniel had overheard was true, then Jehoiakim's captivity would be ideal for Mattaniah's plans.

Truly, the young prince wore a satisfied smile that he could not quite be rid of. Mattaniah covered it by speaking, "Let not the heart of the king be troubled. Harken to me, O king and princes of Judah. The prophet of the LORD has spoken truly. Let us deliver ourselves into the hands of the Chaldeans that we may live. Let not the king think that he will be slain. Has not the prince of Babylon spared those who have surrendered to him? Only those who have rebelled has he put to the sword."

Daniel shook his head in wonder. Even now, even in all the chaos, the wily prince was going forth with his plans. The young prince was saying all the correct words, but for the wrong reasons. After today, Mattaniah might be one step closer to the throne. Daniel vowed to stop it. He would enjoy being Mattaniah's enemy.

But should he speak up now? Warn the king of his brother's and son's treachery? But if he did, would King Jehoiakim refuse to yield to the Babylonians and thus bring about the destruction of the city as spoken by Jeremiah? Daniel shot a look at the prophet, but Jeremiah stood as if unconcerned. Of course, he might not know of the younger brother's plots.

The king slid out of his throne and fell heavily to his knees. He sucked in great lungfuls of air, his chest heaving. Finally, he looked upon the prophet. "I have much despite for you, O prophet. For the words you speak have stolen my strength and weakened my heart. Hear my decree, you who would speak for the LORD God of Israel. If I am slain, then you also will be slain by the sword in the very same hour." His bloody face contorted in emotional agony. "I will reach out from the grave and pull you down to hell with me, O Jeremiah the *prophet*." The last word was spat from the king's mouth like venom.

Jeremiah looked steadily at the king, his face strangely at peace, as if he had expected nothing less than those very words. In a soft voice, he inclined his head once, and said, "So be it."

Climbing heavily to his feet and leaving bloody strands of his beard on the stone steps of the throne, the king of Judah looked over the crowd of princes and priests. "Come then and let us deliver ourselves into the hand of the prince of Babylon and see if we may yet find mercy." Still breathing heavily, he whispered with a glance at his son, "For it may yet be the only way to save our children."

On his part, Jeconiah stared steadily back at his father without a hint of compassion or empathy. Daniel knew then that the lad wanted his father to fall, wanted him to be slain or taken captive so that he might take the crown in place of his father. But if that happened, then Jeremiah would be killed as well.

The king came down to the bottom of the steps and began moving toward the doors that led out of the palace. "All under the sound of my voice will attend me beyond the gates. We will surrender as one people." His eyes stayed locked on the stone floor as he walked. "Or we will die altogether as one people."

15

The sun hung high in the sky and only a few white clouds stained the blue expanse. A breeze flitted through the olive and fig trees of the hillside, some of which were laden down with fruit. *Truly*, Nebuchadnezzar mused, *this is land of milk and honey.* Wryly, he added to himself, *And a land of contradictions.* For not much beyond the mountains to the east lay a stark desert where even tufts of grass struggled to find nourishment and the most common sight was sand and rock.

He stood upon his chariot on the highest portion of the hill that overlooked Jerusalem. His army was arrayed behind him, banners snapping in the breeze, and the men restless as they watched the gates of the city in the northern wall. All the other gates were being watched too, but this is where events would take place—if they were to happen at all.

Noon.

And still the gates hadn't opened. The Chaldean prince scowled in dissatisfaction that quickly turned to a burning, simmering anger.

It looked as if he was going to have to assault the city, a prospect of weeks, perhaps even months. And by then, the window for campaigning against the Egyptians would have closed. He would be forced to return to Babylon before winter.

He glanced at the partially completed siegeworks. They would take another three days or so to complete. He didn't relish assaulting the walls without them, but perhaps a probing attack against Jerusalem's defenses would at least convince the inhabitants of the city that he would keep his promise and raze the city. And raze it to the ground he would. His anger demanded no less.

Nebuzaradan stood to his right and his other battle commanders were scattered throughout the army. They awaited his command. He drew his sword and raised it high, preparing to give the signal to begin the attack.

But then a horn sounded from the city, coming again, and then once more. Curious, Nebuchadnezzar lowered his sword and waited. The massive gate, situated in the center of the northern wall, cracked and then split as it was pushed open, and a man emerged dressed in royal robes. He was followed by a large procession of men and boys, all dressed as nobles of the land. Soldiers came also among them, but most of the latter hung back, protecting the gate. Interestingly, two of the Jewish warriors dragged out a somewhat disheveled looking man between them, a bound prisoner, but not a Chaldean—one of their own.

These Jews were most strange.

Gathering the reins, he slapped them across the backs of the horses hitched to his chariot. The four horses moved out at an even trot and the Chaldean army surged forward, not in an attack, but to hem in the approaching mass of people. The Babylonian warriors would let no treachery befall their prince. At the prince's side trotted his herald who would interpret for him.

Nebuchadnezzar studied the man at the fore of the Jews—clearly King Jehoiakim—noting the man's bloody chin and missing hair in his beard. This then, he realized, hadn't been an easy decision for the king of Judah. A grim smile found its way to Nebuchadnezzar's lips. The bloody chin was small compensation for irritating the prince of Babylon. Though certainly not nearly enough. Still, he felt gratitude toward the enemy king. The man's surrender meant he could get on with the important task of pursuing the Egyptians.

Nebuchadnezzar pulled his horses to a stop, and his army folded around him into a half circle that caught the Jewish nobility within it. Even if they wanted to, they could not run. They'd be cut down in moments.

The king of Judah bowed deeply and then as if thinking that not enough, fell to his knees and then bowed until his head touched the earth. As if that was a signal, the rest of the nobles followed their king's example, kneeling and touching foreheads to the earth—all except for the man held by the two guards. This man didn't even bow his head, but looked upon Nebuchadnezzar with clear, penetrating eyes.

Strangely, Nebuchadnezzar wasn't offended. The man had done something to incur the wrath of the Jews, so in his mind, that made the prisoner an ally of sorts. He refocused on the king of Judah. "Speak," he ordered through his translator.

King Jehoiakim rose to his knees. "O mighty prince," his herald translated, "I and these, my fellow kinsmen, nobles of Jerusalem, deliver ourselves into your hand and throw ourselves upon your mercy. The city is yours."

A cheer rose from the mouths of Nebuchadnezzar's army, and not a few took steps toward the city and the riches contained within. But they held rank, knowing that a breech in discipline here would see them flayed or staked out in the sun until their blood boiled.

Nebuchadnezzar had thought long and hard as to what he would do on the off chance the city did indeed surrender. Jerusalem and Judah had become a powerful force in the region. If he didn't bring them fully under subjugation, they could very easily rally, betray him, and then join with the Egyptians. Being caught between two armies was a tactical blunder he had no intention of making.

Ashpenaz, true to Nebuchadnezzar's command, had offered several solutions to prevent the inhabitants of Jerusalem from rebelling at some later date. One in particular had intrigued the prince.

He gestured to his men. "Bind the king of Judah in fetters," he ordered. "Tell the king that he will be taken to Babylon as hostage for his people's behavior. And as payment for my mercy, the riches of the city will be delivered to me and carried to my father, the king."

The men did as he said, binding the king in fetters of iron.[1] The man looked totally dejected and even his people raised no murmur against this judgment, staying one and all upon their faces before him.

Nebuchadnezzar continued, "Which of these is your son?"

The man stiffened and then began to tremble. "Have mercy, O Nebuchadnezzar! I beg! My son is yet tender of years, unable to resist the wolves who would devour him and steal his strength. If the prince of Babylon would allow, keep me as your vassal upon the throne of Judah. I will serve you and only you all the days of my life. What tribute you ask, I will pay. The armies of Judah will stand beside you against the Egyptians. But, I plead, leave me as your chosen vessel to do your will, for I fear that my son would soon fall prey to those who will not submit to your will."

By Ishtar's eyes, Ashpenaz had predicted this very outcome! He would have to reward the chief eunuch. Spies had already informed Nebuchadnezzar of the political reality within Jerusalem—though Jehoiakim's prisoner told him that he hadn't learned all. But he already knew that the Jewish king's son—presumably the boy at the king's side—was young and inexperienced, and as such, Nebuchadnezzar dared not leave such a one on the throne. He would be overthrown quickly by greedy and ambitious men and the region destabilized. At that point, having Jehoiakim as his hostage

---

[1] 2 Chronicles 36:6.

would be of no value at all, and he would be forced to conquer the city all over again. Besides, if the information he had gathered was any indication, Jehoiakim wasn't the most beloved king. Many would rejoice if Nebuchadnezzar took him captive to Babylon.

He turned to Nebuzaradan. "What think you?" This too was part of the act that Ashpenaz had suggested, for surely some within the ranks of Jews spoke the Chaldean tongue.

His bodyguard pursed his lips as he squinted at the prostrated Jews, doing his part. His face twisted in disgust. "There is wisdom in this, my lord. It is ill chance that his son is yet so young. My advice is this: take his son or others of the king's seed and of the seed of the nobles of the land for hostages against their obedience. Let the nobles of the land swear allegiance to you and to our gods on pain of the death of their sons. In such manner, we may ensure their fealty."

Nebuchadnezzar tried to look as if he was thinking the matter over. They'd already discussed why the benefits of taking the boys were much greater than as mere hostages. If he took the best and the brightest of the noble sons, they could be trained in the ways of Babylon, taught the Chaldean tongue, and prepared to serve as counsellors, astrologers, and administrators in the providences of the kingdom. And if they started young enough, they would only know the Chaldean way and so would be a powerful weapon that might tame these far western provinces under Babylonian rule.

Besides, Nebuchadnezzar hated to waste talent. If he could turn that cunning and intelligence to aid him, then when he became king one day, he'd have an army of the most intelligent people in the world to serve him. This, he knew, could be stronger than any armed force at his disposal. Here was a treasure far greater than any silver and gold that could be found within the city. He would spoil Judah of her most talented children and turn them into loyal servants.

Truly, his chief eunuch had a most devious mind.

"Fetch Ashpenaz," he ordered Nebuzaradan. "I will let him make the choices."

Nebuzaradan bowed and turned to a runner standing nearby, giving the fellow instructions. After the runner had departed, Nebuzaradan joined Nebuchadnezzar who had returned his attention to the kneeling king of Judah. Speaking to the herald, he ordered, "Tell the Jews to stand and face me."

The crowd of Hebrews stood, silent and watchful. Nebuchadnezzar saw fear among them, but he also saw anger and hatred. Not all agreed with the king of Judah's choice to surrender. So be it. Taking their sons should keep them placid enough. Still, he didn't remove Jehoiakim's chains. Not yet. Let the king think what he will. Instead, the Chaldean prince ordered his men to bring the Judean king along. While he waited for his chief eunuch, he wanted to satiate his curiosity.

He came to stand before the nervous Jewish guards holding their disheveled prisoner between them. Now that Nebuchadnezzar stood before the man, he realized the prisoner was younger than he first appeared, perhaps mid-thirties or early forties. Blood from a scalp wound stained part of his face. And unlike the rest of the Jews watching, he lacked any head protection. Ill-treated as he was, someone had made an attempt to clean the man up and put new clothes on him. Nebuchadnezzar didn't know if that was for his benefit or not.

The two guards immediately released their prisoner and fell flat on their faces before Nebuchadnezzar. He ignored them, noting again that the prisoner, though bowing respectfully, didn't seem the least bit worried.

"Understand you my words?" Nebuchadnezzar asked the man.

The prisoner glanced at the herald, but replied in Chaldean, "Some little. Know not large words."

Nebuchadnezzar grunted. The fellow likely meant he didn't know *many* words. Still, it was a far sight better than speaking the absurd Hebrew tongue. "What is your name?"

NEBUCHADNEZZAR

The man again glanced at the herald, but said, "I Jeremiah be, a God prophet." Jeremiah grimaced and repeated it again in his native tongue.

The herald translated. "The man claims to be a prophet of the Jewish God."

Interesting. "Ask him why he is a captive."

After a few moments of a rapid exchange, the herald cleared his throat and turned to Nebuchadnezzar, looking troubled. "This Jeremiah is a prophet of their God. For years, he has been prophesying your coming, that because of their sins and evil, their God has delivered them over to your hand. Forgive me, my lord, but their ways are strange. He says that you are the servant of his God and that he and the inhabitants of the city should serve you. I understand it not."

Nebuchadnezzar studied the prophet, trying to understand how this fellow might fit into his plans. His first instincts had been correct. The man was an ally—of sorts. "Why then is he in bonds?"

"His people liked not his words and so bound him. If you, my prince, had slain the Jewish king, then these men—" he gestured to the prostrate guards "—would have slain the prophet."

The Chaldean prince shook his head at the utter foolishness of the Jews...to slay one of their own who spoke the will of their God! How truly foolish. "Loose his bonds," Nebuchadnezzar commanded. "Give him sustenance. He has done us a great service, and it should not go unrewarded."

The two guards were driven away, and someone cut the rope binding the prophet's arms behind his back. Jeremiah rubbed his arms to restore circulation. He eyed the Chaldean prince with something close to admiration, but was probably closer to resignation, as if he stood on a bridge and had learned it was about to collapse. There was no escape, no matter how hard you ran, so the truly wise man resigned to the inevitable. This is what Nebuchadnezzar saw in the man.

Turning to the bound king of Judah, Nebuchadnezzar pointed to the prophet. "This man is not to be harmed. Surely, he has saved many lives this day for if you had not yielded to my hand, I would have razed your city and homes."

Once the translation reached the captive king's ears, the man twitched, and a flash of pure venom crossed his eyes as he looked upon Jeremiah. But then it was gone, and the man bowed to Nebuchadnezzar, chains clanking. "It will be done as you command, my lord."

Nebuchadnezzar ran his fingers through his braided beard. He didn't trust the Jewish king, not one bit. Jeremiah's life would yet be in danger. He mentally shrugged it aside. In truth, he cared little. If the Jews turned on each other, they would destroy themselves. One more problem solved.

Then Ashpenaz appeared, breathing heavily as he forced his corpulent body to obey the prince's summons. He fell upon his face, his breath creating a small cloud of dust to billow up from the ground. "I am here, O mighty prince. I beg forgiveness for my tardiness and request that my teeth be ripped from my mouth so that I may learn to hasten!"

"Nay, my faithful servant," Nebuchadnezzar said, once again stifling a smile. "I have a different task for you."

The man pushed himself up, his intelligent eyes regarding his prince eagerly. Of course, he already knew what was coming. "What task, my lord?"

"Harken then." Nebuchadnezzar motioned to the herald. "Speak to the princes and elders of Jewry my words." The man nodded and Nebuchadnezzar continued. "I will remove the bonds from King Jehoiakim and restore unto him the throne of Judah upon the following terms: That he swear allegiance to me and my father, the king of Babylon, breaking all ties with Egypt. That the kingdom of Judah becomes my vassal to do with as I will. That the marks of our gods be branded into his flesh so that all who look upon him will know that he is my servant." Jehoiakim flinched at this, his face growing slack in horror, but Nebuchadnezzar wasn't finished. "That some chosen of your children become my servants in Babylon, hostages to your vows of fealty and allegiance, children of the princes and of the king's seed."

This last condition caused a stir. The men of Judah protectively stepped in front of their sons, their eyes going flat in outrage and angry mutters springing up like weeds. Good. Very good. This deed would ensure the rebellious Jews' cooperation if not their loyalty.

With a casual gesture, his eyes never leaving King Jehoiakim's frightened face, he ordered, "Separate the sons of the princes and drive their fathers into the city." He paused for a moment as a thought struck him. "And separate also the sons of the scribes who may be able to stand before you." He fixed his gray eyes on Ashpenaz, the chief of his eunuchs. There was one thing he had not thought to ask, so he did now, "Speak you the tongue of these Jews?"

"Aye, my prince, may my skin boil for knowing such vile speech!"

Good. That was one problem solved. "Then bring certain of the children of Israel, and of the king's seed, and of the princes—children in whom is no blemish, but well favored, skillful in all wisdom, cunning in knowledge, understanding science, and such as has ability in them to stand in the king's palace." Nebuchadnezzar paused to make sure he had the chief eunuch's attention. He needn't have bothered. The man was fixated on him like dust on a traveler. "See to it that all whom you choose may learn the tongue of the Chaldeans."[2]

Nebuchadnezzar waited until the separation had begun, smiling at the cries of distress that rose from the men as their sons were pulled from their ranks. A few would die to be made an example of, but that was always the way of things.

Then, looking greedily at the temple that rose above the wall in the northeastern portion of the city, he ordered Nebuzaradan,

---

[2] Daniel 1:3-4.

"Bring a contingent of men. Let us view the treasure houses of this city."

16

Two hundred soldiers followed Nebuchadnezzar through the streets of Jerusalem. The inhabitants wisely stayed out of his way, melting into their houses and buildings like ice on a warm day. He allowed his men to kick in any door they wished and take what they wanted from the home as long as it didn't hinder him reaching his destination quickly. After the destruction of Ashkelon, his men had been robbed of much of the potential spoil. But not this time. This time, there was ample opportunity to take spoil, and Nebuchadnezzar would not deprive his men of the opportunity.

But such as they found was small treasure; the Chaldean prince wanted the greater prize.

Immediately behind him, and still in chains, came King Jehoiakim, pushed along roughly by Nebuzaradan. Nebuchadnezzar had decided to keep the other king bound until he left the city. Seeing their king in fetters would make it clear to the people of Judah who it was that truly ruled this land—a necessary point, the prince felt, given the Jews' history of rebellion. Along with the Jewish king came the high priest of the God of Israel and a knot of lesser priests. They would be witness to his spoiling of the treasure houses of their God.

When Nebuchadnezzar arrived at the outer court of the temple, he came to a stop to marvel at the sight. The temple rose high into the air, flanked by two pillars sheathed in bronze. The capitals of each pillar had been engraved in lilies.[1] It was magnificent—perhaps not as magnificent as the ziggurat in Babylon, but awe-inspiring, nevertheless. Even more impressive was the massive molten sea set upon twelve life-sized oxen. The engraving work was meticulous, and Nebuchadnezzar estimated that the sea could hold some two thousand baths of water.[2] Bronze glistened in the sun from every direction. He made note of the storehouses that had been built around the outside of the temple. Treasure lay within those walls; he could taste it from where he stood.

The tall, rearing altar was no less impressive, though it had clearly been created to sacrifice animals upon and not humans. Again, Nebuchadnezzar wondered about a God who would not demand human life as the highest form of worship and devotion. Did the God of Israel think so little of His people or did the Jews think so little of their God? It was most strange.

With covetous looks all around, he and Nebuzaradan headed right for the temple porch between the two pillars, his herald and translator following the pair respectfully. Nebuzaradan shoved the folding doors open and stepped inside. A priest standing there, looked momentarily startled and then tried to bar Nebuzaradan entrance. The mighty captain simply sent the man sprawling with an armored elbow. The man slid across floors of gold and came to a stop against walls of gold, his bloody face in sharp contrast to the gold that fairly glowed in the light of ten massive candlesticks.

Nebuchadnezzar paused to take it all in. Truly, this was a treasure house. He couldn't remember the last time he'd seen so

---

[1] 1 Kings 7:21-22.
[2] 1 Kings 7:23-26. It could hold between 16 and 20 thousand gallons of water and was at least 17 feet in diameter and 8 feet in depth.

much gold outside the treasure houses of his own gods in Babylon. But his eyes went immediately to the steps leading up to a blue and scarlet curtain drawn across the western wall of the temple. *There,* he thought. *That is where the true treasures will be.* There, he knew, would be the most sacred instruments dedicated to the Hebrew God.

Grinning like a lad about to do mischief, he marched toward that curtain. Behind him, the high priest and his bevy of followers all fell to their knees and began praying—even the king of Judah clanked to his knees and buried his face in his hands that he might not see. *Interesting.* Nebuchadnezzar paused to look at them, wondering. They sounded and looked scared as if praying for their very lives. One even had the audacity to cry out to him, "My lord prince of Chaldea, do not, I beg, enter into the presence of the LORD God of Israel lest He slay you!"

The translation caused Nebuchadnezzar to stop altogether. Did the foolish priests truly believe he would be killed for going into the next room? He gestured to Nebuzaradan. "Bring that man to me!"

Nebuzaradan jumped down the golden steps and hauled the speaker up from his knees and dragged him bodily across the floor. The other Chaldean soldiers took up position around the Jewish priests, waiting for word from their prince. Everyone's life hung in the balance at that moment.

Nebuchadnezzar regarded the priest being brought to him. His clothes proclaimed his office, but all defiance had drained from the man's face. He looked entirely frightened. Nebuchadnezzar glanced at the curtain again, considering.

The priest landed at Nebuchadnezzar's feet where Nebuzaradan had tossed the fellow. "Have mercy upon me," the man cried in a sobbing voice. Nebuchadnezzar didn't need a translator for that.

Nebuchadnezzar pointed to the curtain and looked at the herald. "Say thus to this man: you will precede us and make the way safe." The man began to tremble so badly that his knees began knocking. Sighing with growing irritation, the Chaldean prince motioned for Nebuzaradan. "Make him go before us."

Nebuzaradan yanked the priest up to his feet again and dragged the blubbering mad man up to the curtain where the captain shoved the heavy cloth aside to reveal another set of folding doors sheathed in gold and carved with pictures of seraphim, palm trees, and other ornate images. Strangely, there were no pictures of the likeness of their God, which again baffled Nebuchadnezzar. Why would these people not honor their God with a likeness? Did they have such little regard? Shaking his head, he drew his sword and pointed it at the cowering priest's face. "Herald, say thus: open the doors and go in or I will slay you here and now to appease your God with your own cowardly blood that I may enter. Decide now."

Perhaps it was Nebuchadnezzar's calm voice, devoid of passion and completely lacking any compassion or care that convinced the sobbing priest to act. It was all the same to the Chaldean prince. With the cry of a man going to his death, the man pushed open the doors and fell inside, landing solidly on the floor of gold within. The man gasped sharply, clutched once at his chest, and then lay still.

Nebuchadnezzar looked beyond the man to see what would so frighten the priests. Two massive statues of cherubims, also sheathed in gold, stretched their wings from one side to the other of the square room. But that was it. There was nothing else within the room. Nebuchadnezzar frowned, stepping over the prone priest and walking between the statues to see if something had been hidden behind them. Nothing. The room itself was a treasure, true, as there was enough gold here to make the venture to Jerusalem profitable, but he expected more, much more. Where were the true treasures dedicated to the God of Israel?

A dark suspicion formed in Nebuchadnezzar's mind. He turned to the prone priest who still hadn't moved. "Get you up," he roared. "Where are the treasures of your God?"

The translator repeated the words in the Jewish tongue, but the man didn't move.

Irritation turning to anger, Nebuchadnezzar marched over and kicked the man in the ribs. Still, the man didn't move, flinch, or otherwise acknowledge the blow that likely had cracked some of his ribs. Frowning, the prince prodded the man with the tip of his sword. Still no reaction. Nebuzaradan bent down and peeled the man's eyelids up. The eyes were glazed in death. Nebuzaradan looked up. "The man's heart has failed him. He is dead."

Nebuchadnezzar blinked in surprise. The man had literally scared himself to death. "The priest thought something lay within," he said to his captain. "He did not know it had been emptied." He turned to look out the doors and down to where the other priests continued their praying. "But there is someone who would know. Bring to me the high priest and his son."

Soon, the man named Azariah and his son Seraiah had been marched into the cubed room. The high priest looked serene, but Seraiah looked about fearfully as if expecting death to descend upon him at any moment. The younger man, Nebuchadnezzar decided, had never been in this room before. But his father…

"Speak in my voice, herald," he ordered his translator. "Where are the treasures of your God?" he demanded of the high priest.

The man turned partially to look back out of the inner sanctuary. "What is seen is all there is, prince of Chaldea. There be caldrons, snuffers, spoons, cups, bowels, and firepans—some in gold, some in silver, and some in brass. These are the treasures of the LORD God of Israel dedicated to His service."

"Yet there was something here," Nebuchadnezzar said, pointing to the spot beneath the cherubims' wings. "Something large rested there. Where is it?"

The high priest's eyes hardened, and his lips became firm. "I know not."

Nebuchadnezzar turned his attention to the son after hearing the translation. "Wherefore does your father keep secrets from me? Tell me what rested here."

The young priest glanced at his father and licked his lips. He then spoke rapidly, "The ark of the LORD did rest here, the seat of God."

Interesting. Nebuchadnezzar looked around. Did the priests of Israel believe that the very presence of their God lived in here, in this box? It *was* richly decorated. "Where then is it?"

"Truly, my lord, I know not!" The young man seemed on the verge of panicking. His father watched him with sad eyes. "The ark should lay within. It has *always* been within!" Seraiah's eyes swung back to his father. "Has the ark of the LORD been stolen? Tell me, my father!"

Azariah's eyes hardened further as the Chaldean prince listened to the translation. "Hold your tongue, my son. The ark of the LORD is safe, and not even I know where it is." He righted his shoulders and faced Nebuchadnezzar. "Do what you will to me but know that I cannot tell you where the ark of our God is hidden. It is beyond me and my son."

"Father," Seraiah cried, "you must tell. See you not that the prince of Chaldea means to slay you! Tell him!"

"Slay me, then, prince of Chaldea. But I know not where the ark is."

Once the translation caught up, Nebuchadnezzar nodded, acknowledging this truth. "Then who does?"

Azariah clamped his jaw shut, firm and unyielding. He, unlike the cowardly king of Judah, had found his courage. At length, the aging priest said, "I know not."

The man lied. Nebuchadnezzar could read it on his face without even hearing the translation. Frowning, he said, "Tell me, and I will not slay your son." He watched the priest carefully.

Seraiah gasped and began to tremble. "Father!"

"Forgive me, my son, but I may not speak this knowledge for the LORD has hidden it from me." Another lie, Nebuchadnezzar determined, watching the man. The high priest looked sadly at his son. "I pray for your soul, my son, for I do know that you have

NEBUCHADNEZZAR

turned from serving our God and have followed other gods. If you must be slain and I must be slain, then so be it."

The young man, quivering, fell to his knees and prostrated himself before Nebuchadnezzar. "Have mercy, prince of Chaldea! My father has betrayed us all. Surely you will not punish me for his transgressions! Spare me, and I will serve you and your gods!"

That got Nebuchadnezzar's attention. He studied the two men, thinking carefully about his next step. The treasure—the ark—was gone, and if the high priest truly knew where it was, he would surely have revealed it to save his son, despite his words. The king of Judah would not know either. Nebuchadnezzar sensed a lack of trust between the priesthood and the crown, and if Jehoiakim truly knew, the craven man would divulge it in a heartbeat to gain Nebuchadnezzar's favor. There were some who knew, surely, but it would take much too long to root out the conspirators and compel them to reveal this treasure's location. But surely, its value did not exceed the riches already here. Except for the importance placed upon it by the people of Judah, it was but a small thing. Nebuchadnezzar didn't have time to run down this mystery.

But such brazen hubris could not go unpunished. They should have never hidden this treasure from him. An example needed to be made. "I believe your words," Nebuchadnezzar said to the high priest. "Know, therefore, that I will ordain your son to be high priest in your place."

Azariah looked at the prince of Chaldea sharply, his eyes widening as realization dawned on him. He managed to take a single step back before Nebuchadnezzar's sword plunged through the jeweled breastplate of his office and into his chest all the way to the hilt. The blade burst out his back, spraying blood down the steps that led up to the inner sanctuary.

The Chaldean prince turned to look at Seraiah who, still kneeling, goggled at his dying father. Blood pooled on the floor, staining Seraiah's robes. Jerking the sword out, Nebuchadnezzar then turned and flung the high priest into the inner sanctuary where he collapsed on the same spot that the ark had once rested. The pool of blood that spread outward was a satisfactory gift to the God of Israel and would, hopefully, appease His wrath for killing His high priest.

Nebuchadnezzar looked down on the gaping son. "Harken to me, Seraiah, son of Azariah, high priest of the LORD God of Israel." The priest looked up, his body trembling as he listened to the translation. "The God of your father has bidden me to come here and have dominion over all the inhabitants of Judah. This is His will. Serve me and you will be spared. Defy me and you will scream for death a thousand times a thousand before I grant you the mercy of endless sleep. Pledge your vows to me."

Seraiah prostrated himself in the blood of his father. "I will serve you, and your gods, O prince of Chaldea! I swear this upon the God of my forefathers that have come before me."

Nebuchadnezzar knew this would be true for a time. But if left to himself, he felt certain the man would rebel. They all would. That was why taking many of the sons of the nobility was so important. He considered taking some of the priests too but doubted the effectiveness of such an action. The priests would be next to useless in Babylon. Hopefully, the captives would be enough to quell the rebellion that lay in the hearts of the Jews.

Striding away from the prostrate priest and stepping over the dead one whose heart had failed him, he walked down the steps into the outer sanctuary. "Take some of the treasures in this house," he commanded his men."

"Not all, my prince?" Nebuzaradan asked, following him down.

"Nay, if we take all, wherewith will they pay tribute? Leave two in three as a reminder of my mercy upon those that follow me faithfully."[3]

Nebuzaradan sighed, his disappointment palpable. But Nebuchadnezzar knew that this gesture might also be instrumental

---

[3] Daniel 1:2.

in keeping the Jews subjugated. If he took everything they had, then they would have nothing to lose. Letting them keep some of their precious treasures would make it harder to rebel, lest they lose them too. It was a calculated risk.

But that didn't mean Nebuchadnezzar couldn't humble them and give them a constant reminder of who they now served. He came to stand in front of the kneeling king of Judah. The king's thin face had grown slack, and his eyes stared right through Nebuchadnezzar, as if he could still see the high priest's body lying in the inner sanctuary.

"It is time, king of Judah, to make your vows to my gods."

Jehoiakim jerked and then stared up at Nebuchadnezzar in stupefied befuddlement upon hearing the translation.

The Chaldean prince grinned, watching the eyes of the captive king carefully. He wanted to see the reaction to his next words. "Shave him, and then mark his skin with his devotion to our gods so that it may be a testament forever to all who look upon him."[4] The man's face fell at that, but Nebuchadnezzar wasn't finished. His anger at being denied the true treasure of the Hebrew temple needed to be appeased, so he added, "And discover where his wives are and despoil them. All of them."

Jehoiakim's confusion turned to horror, and Nebuchadnezzar reveled in it.

---

[4] 2 Chronicles 36:8. Some scholars believe the phrase "abominations found in him" refers to images of false gods tattooed on his skin.

17

The boys had all fallen gravely silent. Other than nervous shifting of sandaled feet, they stood in ranks before the man called Ashpenaz, chief eunuch in service to the truly terrifying prince of Chaldea…though Ashpenaz himself didn't appear in any way terrifying to Daniel's mind. The fat eunuch's clean, round face and small eyes held a cheery aspect that somehow managed to set Daniel and the rest of the boys at ease—well, mostly at ease. Nothing could dispel their apprehension completely, for they all knew what was happening.

Some two hundred boys and lads stood in the open beyond the walls of Jerusalem and hemmed in by Nebuchadnezzar's army. Foremost among them was Jeconiah, the king's son, and Mattaniah, the king's brother. As brother-in-law to the king, Daniel stood just behind the only other son of the king, a boy of about six years of age. Daniel's friends, Hananiah and Mishael, stood nearby, though further back in the crowd of captive lads. Daniel wished they could join him—or he them—but the Chaldean eunuch had organized the boys according to rank.

Near the northern gates, the princes and fathers had been pinned against the walls while Nebuchadnezzar was within despoiling the city. The separating of the sons of the princes had not gone easily. At least three men had been killed and a dozen others beaten within a hairsbreadth of death. The bodies of the dead lay forgotten in the dust and dirt between the boys and the wall, a grim reminder of the price of disobedience.

Daniel had lost sight of his own father and wished desperately that he could push his way through the crowd and run to him. But the two boys who had attempted just that had been met with spear butts and maces. One stood near Daniel, blood dripping from his fingers as blood ran down his arm from a long gash in his shoulder. About eight years of age, he did not cry aloud, though his eyes blinked rapidly and his chest heaved with silent sobs.

Of all the men of the city, only the prophet Jeremiah stood nearby, though separate from both boys and men. The Chaldean soldiers gave him room, an island of isolation as he watched the proceedings. Still, his presence brought Daniel some comfort.

"Harken, sons of Judah," Ashpenaz cried from his position in front of the boys. That had been a surprise. The eunuch could speak the Hebrew tongue fluently. "From this day forth, think not of yourselves as Jews but as Chaldeans, the noblest tribe on earth. From henceforth, you will be remade, and for those able, you shall stand before the king of Babylon and serve him." His smile disappeared in a flash, replaced by a deep scowl. "For those of you not able, death awaits."

No one responded. The boys watched the eunuch much like a shepherd would a wolf that had suddenly emerged from the trees near his flock. Whatever ease the eunuch had first offered had vanished as quickly as snow in summer.

Ashpenaz adjusted his costly robes, his grin coming back as if it had always been there. Daniel knew not what to make of the man.

"Each of you will be examined. Fear not and answer truthfully and all will be well. Answer falsely and..." The eunuch cleared his throat and one of the soldiers presented his mace, smashing it harshly against his shield. The message was clear. "Wait in turn and speak not until spoken to."

The chief eunuch looked over the crowd of boys with a discerning eye and then pointed to Jeconiah, the king's son and said something in his native tongue. A solider stepped forward and grabbed the Judean prince by the arm and dragged him before the eunuch. The two then began a conversation in Hebrew that Daniel could not hear. After some minutes, the eunuch gestured off to one side and Jeconiah was moved to a spot by himself. The lad stood there trembling, his eyes locked on the eunuch with more fear than Daniel had ever seen in his nephew before.

Mattaniah was next. After his examination, he joined the younger prince off to the side. Then the youngest son of King Jehoiakim was examined, but he was sent to the opposite side of Ashpenaz, separated from Jeconiah and Mattaniah. This caused no small stir among the boys waiting their turn. Was one group found worthy and the other not? Would those in one group be put to death and if so, which? Fear, like feral leprosy, shot through the waiting boys, and the bowels of more than one child were loosened, adding a rancid smell to the air.

Daniel licked his lips, looking first at one group and then the other. Moments ago, his stomach had rumbled in hunger, but that had vanished the moment he realized that the chief eunuch was separating the sons of the princes into two distinct groups. Daniel wanted to be in the group with Jeconiah and Mattaniah. Surely, they would be taken to Babylon as hostages and not put to death. Their value as being close kin to the king was great. Jeconiah stood to be king after his father, and if something happened to him, Mattaniah might be king since the remaining son of King Jehoiakim was only six years of age.

Then the eunuch's fat finger pointed at Daniel, and a soldier, dressed in Assyrian style battle armor prodded Daniel forward with his spear. The man wasn't gentle, but Daniel refused to show the man any pain. Outside of fingering the blue thread on the fringe of his tunic, Daniel stared steadily at the eunuch, reminding himself that his God was superior to the false gods of Babylon. It brought some comfort.

"What is your name, lad?" the eunuch asked in his high-pitched voice, walking around him and examining Daniel from head to toe as one might a horse he meant to purchase. Daniel felt a bit violated at the close scrutiny. The eunuch even reached out and squeezed his arm.

"I am Daniel, son of Elnathan, a prince of Judah." Daniel kept his tone even, refusing to allow his voice to break in fear.

"Well spoken, lad. Tell me, know you how to read and write?"

An interesting question. *What purpose lay behind it?* Daniel glanced sideways at Jeconiah and Mattaniah. He knew that both could read and write the Hebrew tongue. The other son of the king was too young to have been taught fully. Was that the deciding factor? "I do, my lord. I can read and write Hebrew and speak the Egyptian tongue as well."

The small, gray eyes of the eunuch narrowed some. "Is this so?" He switched to Egyptian and asked, "Know you my words?"

Daniel nodded and replied in the Egyptian tongue, "I do, my lord."

Switching back to Hebrew, Ashpenaz gestured to the sky. "What think you of the stars? Do the gods speak to us in signs and wonders?"

Daniel frowned. "Israel's fate is not determined by the stars," he said firmly. "It is our God who created heaven and earth and all that are in them."

"Then the stars have no import? Your God does not speak to you in signs within the heavens?"

Daniel thought of the book of the law. "Perhaps. In the days that God created the heavens, He set the sun, moon, and stars to divide the day and night and to be for signs,[1] but our God speaks to us by the mouths of His prophets."

"But know you of the stars." It wasn't a question. "Where, therefore, are the wandering stars in this season?"

Daniel pointed into the sky. "One nears Orion and another passes through Arcturus. Both are low in the sky, near the setting sun."[2]

The fat eunuch rubbed his hands together in pleasure, though Daniel could not tell if the man was relishing his answers or his coming death. "What sciences know you?"

"I know the secret of iron and bronze and have been trained in the making of wine. I can read the wind in its season and divine the coming storm."

"What know you of numbers?"

Daniel answered slowly. He didn't understand where these questions were going or if his answers pleased the eunuch. "My father is father-in-law to the king and is often tasked with oversight of the treasury and the dealings with merchants. I know how to keep numbers."

"Will the prince of Babylon prevail over the Egyptians?"

Daniel blinked. The question had been shot at him from nowhere. This, he believed, was the true crux of the examination. It would be simple to say that the prince would be victorious, for surely those words would be most pleasant in the Chaldeans' ears, but Daniel wasn't one to avoid conflict, and the truth mattered much to him. With a shiver of energy, knowing that his life hung in the balance with his answer, he said, "Perhaps in time, my lord. Egypt, though defeated by your lord in the north is not an adversary who can be taken lightly. Egypt has allies to call upon that Nebuchadnezzar knows not, armies he has not yet faced. The

---

[1] Genesis 1:14.
[2] Job 9:9. These are constellations.

Egyptian homeland will not lightly be invaded, and your lord will be far from Babylon, forced to live off the land and plunder from his victories. Time is not Nebuchadnezzar's ally. A single defeat could be his end, whereas Pharaoh Necho may suffer many defeats as he retreats farther into the heart of his homeland and the seat of his true power, moving from one fortification to another. Entrapments will wear upon your lord's warriors, and many will wish to return home and leave alone the Egyptians as they yearn for their families and trades."

Ashpenaz studied Daniel with his gray eyes, his thick lips tightly compressed. The man had subtly shifted during Daniel's explanation, standing straighter and his grin slipping until it had virtually disappeared. Daniel worried that he had given offence, but the eunuch's next words surprised Daniel. "What is your age, Daniel, son of Elnathan?"

"I am fourteen years of age, my lord."

The man sighed and shook his head in wonder. "So young." He pointed to where the youngest son of King Jehoiakim waited, shivering alone in fear. "Wait there, son of Elnathan."

Slowly, wondering if death would come to him before the day was out, Daniel moved over to stand with the small boy. The boy immediately crowded close to him, his fear palpable. *He senses it too,* Daniel thought. He swallowed. If death was coming, he would face it without fear. The lie felt heavy in Daniel's mind.

As he turned to face everyone, he spotted the dark looks thrown at him from Mattaniah. Daniel had never proven that the king's brother had been behind the assassination attempt on his life, but all the signs were there. Strangely, even if he was to die, Daniel was grateful that he had not been assigned to stand with Jeconiah and Mattaniah. Despite his earlier hope and now that he had been examined, the last thing he wanted was to be associated in any way with the two conniving, evil princes.

And so the examinations continued and the two groups of boys grew as Ashpenaz directed each lad to one side of him or the other.

The process baffled Daniel. At times, a boy would be looked up and down and simply directed to stand with Jeconiah and Mattaniah without ever being asked a question. Sometimes, the examination went long. It hardly made sense.

The prophet Jeremiah continued to watch the proceedings closely, his feet seemingly anchored to the spot on which he stood. No one bothered him or denied him.

Hananiah's examination went quickly, the eldest son of the chief scribe joining Daniel after the briefest of conversations. Mishael's lasted longer, but when the two lapsed into the Chaldean tongue, the lad was sent to join his brother and Daniel. Daniel remembered that Mishael was already learning the Chaldean tongue well before Nebuchadnezzar had arrived in the north to punish the Egyptians.

Night had fallen and fires lit to provide light by the time the last lad was brought forward to be examined. The two groups had swollen in size, Daniel's being the smaller of the two with roughly seventy-five boys. The last examinee was Azariah, the son of Michaiah. Of all the sons of the princes and scribes, he looked the most imposing and even two of the Chaldean soldiers moved forward, hands fingering their spears as the tall lad was pushed to stand in front of the chief eunuch. His examination lasted the longest. Azariah answered each question succinctly and with a permanent scowl plastered on his face, visible in the light of three fires built around the eunuch.

This Azariah looked as if he was spoiling for a fight. Daniel wondered if this was because he was the youngest son in his family. The lad surely knew it would be his older brothers who would stand in the place of his father one day, not him. In fact, his brothers, those who were of young enough age, had already been examined and were standing in Jeconiah's group.

So it said something that the chief eunuch finally pointed toward Daniel's group. Without a change of expression, Azariah stomped over to stand before Daniel. They exchanged nods, and the large young man spun back around to take in the entire Chaldean army with his scowl. He now stood in the vanguard of the group as if he meant to defend each boy with his life if need be.

Ashpenaz looked both groups of boys over, and then addressing Jeconiah's group, he said, "Return to the city and to your fathers' houses. Remain there until such a time as the prince of Babylon has departed."

A wave of exhaled relief rippled across the group of young lads so singled out. Slowly at first and then in a rush, the boys raced toward the city through the parted ranks of Chaldean warriors. One or two of the boys took a spear butt in the side and was chased on by harsh laughter, but they all made it safely enough, melting into the ranks of the men, their fathers, watching from near the city gate.

Only then did the reality of the situation strike Daniel. He had been so concerned about dying—they all had—that he hadn't even thought on what it might mean to be chosen to be a hostage in Babylon. And to suddenly realize that the other group would remain home while his would be led away captive was like a knife to the stomach. His knees grew weak, and he stumbled, barely catching himself. All feeling in his body fled, and his tongue grew thick. He was to be taken many months journey away from his family, away from his city, away from his people, to be a slave in Babylon. Everything he'd ever known was being taken away. He didn't understand. How could this be?

The same dawning realization came upon the rest of those in Daniel's group and a wail of anguish rose up to strike the starry sky and echo off the city walls. Several darted away in a desperate attempt to join those returning home, but soldiers casually swept their feet out from under them and pinned them to the ground with their spears. Their mocking laughter taunted the boys, forcing the others to cringe together into a tightening knot.

Ashpenaz waited for a bit, but when it became obvious that the wailing would not die down, he cried aloud, "Weep not, children of Judah. You have been chosen as the most favored of the king's seed, able one day to stand before the king of Babylon and serve him." His eyes glittered in the firelight. "You have all been chosen for greatness. Weep not. Rather rejoice!"

The man sounded as if he meant it. But it had little impact on the boys grouped close together. Tears stained dirty faces and sobs rose into the night sky. Daniel, alone among them, fell to his knees and began praying, beseeching the LORD God of Israel to grant him mercy and bring deliverance.

But then a weathered hand, pulled Daniel to his feet. Blinking away his tears, he found the prophet Jeremiah looking deep into his eyes. "This is not the end," the prophet said in a husky, emotion-filled voice, and though he spoke to everyone, Daniel felt the words were meant for him alone. "Hear you the Word of the LORD. Your captivity may be long, but it is not the end. Learn not the way of the heathen and be not dismayed at the signs of heaven, for the heathen are dismayed at them and their customs are vain. But the LORD is the true God, He is the living God, and an everlasting king. At His wrath, the earth shall tremble, and the nations shall not be able to abide His indignation."[3] Jeremiah squeezed Daniel's shoulders tightly. "But fear not, O my servant Jacob, and be not dismayed, O Israel. 'For, behold,' says the LORD, 'I will save you from afar off, and your *seed* from the land of their captivity. Jacob shall return, and be in rest and at ease, and none shall make him afraid. Fear not, for I am with you and will make a full end of all the nations whither I have driven you, but I will not make a full end of *you*.'"[4]

Daniel found strength returning to his limbs. He took a long shuddering breath and cleared his mind. If God would not forsake him in the land of his captivity, then he would abide and wait for the salvation of the LORD.

But the next words he heard almost undid him. "Bind the captives in chains," Ashpenaz ordered, his high voice carrying easily to everyone watching. "We leave on the morrow."

---

[3] Jeremiah 10:1-3, 10.
[4] Jeremiah 46:27-28.

18

"Is this all you have chosen?" Nebuchadnezzar demanded of Ashpenaz, surveying the chained boys. Not one was older than sixteen and the youngest was six, the king of Judah's youngest son, or so he had been told. Altogether, only little more than seventy boys had been selected by his chief eunuch to be taken back to Babylon. Nebuchadnezzar had expected more.

"May my flesh be devoured by rats, O prince, if my choices have displeased you. Blind my eyes with coals of fire that I might learn wisdom, my lord!" The fat man prostrated himself before Nebuchadnezzar.

Grunting sourly, the Chaldean prince said, "Rise, Ashpenaz, and give an account of your decision."

The eunuch heaved himself upright. "I did as you commanded, O mighty prince. I examined each in turn. Of all that stood before me, only these show the potential you seek and are without blemish. Only these may one day stand before the king, your father, and you, O prince."

"Only these?" Nebuchadnezzar blinked in amazement.

"Aye, my lord. Of the others, they lacked the wit and wisdom required or they were not well favored. Some few I turned away were cunning and well favored, but deceitful. They would not serve well."

Nebuchadnezzar nodded slowly, accepting his chief eunuch's choices. The man was keen, an able interrogator, and quite possibly the most intelligent man the prince had ever met. If these were the only boys who met his criteria, then he would be a fool to challenge it. He picked out a young man chained and kneeling in the forefront of the captives. "That one," he said pointing, "tell me of him."

Along with his intelligence, Ashpenaz never forgot a single thing—ever. He could, verbatim, recite a conversation that had occurred by chance twenty years ago.

The chief eunuch gestured to a guard and the boy was pulled to his feet. Iron fetters cut cruelly into the boy's bare ankles, the skin beneath already bruising. Nebuchadnezzar strode over to stand before the lad. The boy was dressed in a fine tunic of white linen, his hair bound in a matching turban. Although fine, his clothes were not ostentatious. His sandals looked well used, but sturdy, and his belt was made of oxen leather. The lad bowed respectfully to Nebuchadnezzar, though his brown eyes weighed the Chaldean prince on some internal scale. *Interesting, I wonder what he sees.* A strong jaw foretold of a strong character, he determined of the lad, and the chin sported a hint of whiskers. A reddish birthmark glowed lightly upon the nape of the boy's neck in the sun but did not detract from the lad's obvious well-favored countenance. And every tooth in his mouth was perfectly aligned, a rarity in Nebuchadnezzar's experience.

Ashpenaz made the introduction, "This is Daniel, my prince, son of Elnathan, a prince of Judah. He is wise in knowledge and cunning in science. He understands the world of kings and princes and has accurately predicted the obstacles to your victory over the Egyptians."

"Truly?" Nebuchadnezzar studied the lad more carefully. The boy couldn't be above fifteen years of age, but he had clearly impressed Ashpenaz—no easy task. "And what of his predictions?"

"Similar to our own discussions, my prince. He has gleaned the challenges you face and has peered into the character of Pharaoh Necho, your adversary. He missed several key points, but that is likely due to ignorance and not foolishness. I doubt not that his God has granted him a measure of wisdom. He will be valuable one day."

Nebuchadnezzar ran a hand through his square beard. "We shall see. I doubt not your words, my faithful servant, but mayhap you have overestimated this one's talent. It will remain to be seen."

"You are wise to question this one's wisdom, my lord. I beg, let your tormentors feast on my flesh with their instruments of cruelty and break my bones until I learn to quiet my tongue!"

Nebuchadnezzar only half listened to his chief eunuch's protestations. His attention had already wandered to the Jewish prophet standing nearby. The man was an enigma to the Chaldean prince. On one hand, the prophet had been most vocal in favor of the Babylonians, but he watched Nebuchadnezzar and his army as one would an unwelcome snake into one's home. "And you, prophet of the God of Israel, what say you? Have I obeyed the voice of your God to satisfaction?"

Jeremiah bowed in a respectful but reserved manner. "Can know any?" he said in broken Chaldean. "Be sorry, prince, and no be deceive of magicians and astrologers whom speak God wrong. Stay servitude pray."

Nebuchadnezzar's brows furrowed, but Ashpenaz came to his rescue after listening to the prophet speak in his native tongue. "The prophet warns you to be wary of your counsellors who speak against his God. He will pray for you that you remain in service to the Hebrew God."

"Ah." Addressing the prophet, the Chaldean prince said, "There are many gods, prophet, and I am the servant first of Marduk and Ishtar. As long as your God interferes not with the will of my gods, I will not be inattentive. This I swear."

Jeremiah bowed his head. In the distance, the Chaldean prince could see the walls of Jerusalem rising into the sky. It would be the last thing of the city that the captives ever saw. He had forbidden the Jews from coming near or speaking to the captives—except for the prophet. A clean break was best. The captive boys needed to begin thinking of themselves as Chaldeans as quickly as possible.

"Now," Nebuchadnezzar said, moving toward his chariot and mounting the vehicle. The captain of his guard followed close behind. "Marshal the army, Nebuzaradan, and prepare to march for Egypt. Ashpenaz, the disposition and care of the captives is in your hands. I would not that they be treated poorly for, one day, I might have need of them, but do not allow them to grow lax and delay my march." He considered. "Once we are suitably at a distance from Jerusalem, you may remove their fetters."

Ashpenaz bowed deeply. "It will be done as you command, my prince, or may the gods slay me."

A trumpet blew and the army of Chaldea prepared to march. They were leaving six men in Jerusalem, advisors to the king of Judah—spies would be a more appropriate role, but openly. Everyone knew why they were being left behind. All was in readiness. The plunder taken from the city treasure houses, including that of the temple and palace, had been loaded onto wagons and would proceed with Nebuchadnezzar's harem and the newly captive sons of the Judean princes. Food and other supplies had been stripped from the city in support of the army. The king of Egypt awaited. Nebuchadnezzar eagerly looked forward to seeing his adversary cast down and bearing his severed head to Nebuchadnezzar's father as a victorious banner.

The crown prince of Babylon made it no more than a thousand cubits when another trumpet blared out a warning and suddenly four chariots crested a hill from the north. Each bore the flag of Ishtar, proclaiming their allegiance to Babylon. Nebuchadnezzar had established a line of communication with Babylon that consisted of a series of chariot relays. He felt it important that he be kept abreast of the situation back home and to give the king, his father, news of his victories. But why *four* chariots when one would suffice?

Unless they bore ill news.

He pulled up and waited impatiently. The chariots thundered along the rutted road and came to a creaking, snorting halt not fifteen cubits from the prince. The drivers, vaulted over the sides and fell to their knees before him, touching forehead to earth.

"Rise," Nebuchadnezzar commanded, "what tidings do you bring?"

The nearest wore the armor of an officer. He rose first, saluted, and kept his head bowed. "My prince, ill tidings have come from Babylon. Your father, the king, is dead!"

Nebuchadnezzar stared, shocked into silence. Nabopolassar was aging, true, but he was yet in his fifties with many more years ahead—or should have. It took long minutes before Nebuchadnezzar could find his voice. "How died he?"

"In his sleep, my lord. He lay down and did not awake. His food and drink were inspected, my lord, and no evidence of poison was found."

"Who then sent word to me?"

"Your brother, Nabushumlishir, sent word, my prince. He bids you return to Babylon with all haste."

"My brother..." Nebuchadnezzar trailed off, thinking hard. He felt a small measure of sadness at his father's passing. Nabopolassar had been a mighty warrior, freeing Babylon from the Assyrians, conquering Nineveh, and driving the Assyrian remnants far from their former seat of power. Nabopolassar would be long remembered for the vengeance he brought down upon his enemies. In his latter years, he had yearned to rebuild Babylon into a city without peer. Already, mighty walls were being erected and the Esagil, the second temple dedicated to Marduk, was being restored. The great ziggurat of Marduk, rebuilt by his father, even now dominated the skyline of the city of Babylon. The city would become a wonder of the world.

Nebuchadnezzar turned his mind to his brother. Nabushumlishir was perhaps only a year younger and was considered by many to be Nebuchadnezzar's equal in cunning and intelligence. Of his brothers, Nabushumlishir was the only one who had the chance to take the throne for himself. And *he* was at Babylon while Nebuchadnezzar languished in the Levant, far from the seat of power.

And Nabushumlishir was ambitious—in a subtle way, having an imagination and vision equal to that of Nebuchadnezzar's.

"Nebuzaradan!" Nebuchadnezzar shouted, turning around.

"Here am I, my king."

My king. So, the captain had overheard the conversation. "What make you of these tidings and that my brother does send word to recall me back to Babylon? Has he taken the throne of my father?"

Nebuzaradan shook his head, his face beneath his conical helmet tightening. "I know not."

"What know you, messenger?" Nebuchadnezzar asked the officer who'd brought the news.

"The message has been relayed through many hands, my lord. I know nothing of what passes in Babylon."

He wouldn't. None of the messengers would. Turning back to Nebuzaradan, he said, "Ready fifty men in chariots. I will return to Babylon at once."

Nebuzaradan held up a warning hand, which he turned into a hasty bow. "Be not overly hasty, my lord. Pardon my words, but what, perchance, if the summons is a trap? You may need the army to secure the throne."

"Lend me your advice then."

"Let all the army return with my lord. None will rest until Babylon is reached and the throne secured."

"What of my wives and the captives?" Everyone understood they wouldn't be able to travel nearly as fast as Nebuchadnezzar needed.

"They will be pushed, my lord, to come along quickly. Your wives may ride in chariots or the baggage wagons, and we may remove the chains on the captives so they may walk unimpeded. The little ones may ride when their legs do tire, and once near unto Babylon and it is safe, you may ride ahead with the army, leaving some few to safeguard your wives and shepherd the captives."

"And what of Pharaoh Necho? Am I to leave him his head attached to his body?"

"You must decide, my lord. Your father is dead, and your brother holds Babylon—and your sons. On the other side of the scales is Pharaoh Necho, who is doubtlessly licking his wounds and trembling at your coming. Which weighs heaviest, my lord?"

As usual, his captain had the right of it. "You are wise, your advice is as the voice of the gods." Nebuchadnezzar sighed, looking south regretfully. Egypt could wait. Babylon could not. He had left wives and sons in Babylon—and a kingdom to claim. "Prepare the men. We march to Babylon. We march home."

19

Jeremiah paced the dirt floor of the house he hid within. He counted it a true miracle that he had not been arrested immediately upon his return to the city after Nebuchadnezzar's departure. But the king truly did have other things to worry about than one obstinate prophet. The one look he had of King Jehoiakim had been burned forever into his brain.

Every hair had been shaved off the king's head and symbols and images of heathen gods had been tattooed over every finger width of visible skin, including a truly profane image of Inanna, the Babylonian goddess of fertility. The tattooists had not been gentle, and the king's long face hung open at the mouth as if breathing through his nose was painful. To add to the king's pain, every one of his wives had been ravished by common soldiers a dozen times at least until the women were broken, shattered illusions of their former selves. This insult had forced the king to put away his wives, and each had returned to the houses of their fathers to live in shame until the day of their deaths. It would be unsurprising if not a few of the women were found to be with child in the coming days.

And the youngest of the king's sons had been taken captive.

Thus the king of Judah was bereft, a shell of the man he had been, but where ambition had once dominated his thoughts, anger now consumed him. Jeremiah could see it in his eyes, a poor substitute for the peace of Jehovah, but vengeance being the only purpose left to which he would cling. Jeremiah rightly divined that once Jehoiakim could think straight, he would begin to plot against his oppressors, and Jeremiah was doubtlessly included in that group—for his words had been in support of the Chaldeans who had shamed the king of Judah to the very heart of his soul.

"Peace, my lord prophet," came a melodious voice from the corner, "your much walking brings no harmony to the mind."

Jeremiah froze and looked askance at the dark corner. A woman sat within the shadows upon a stool. Little could be seen, but that was the intent. The woman within wore shame around her like a cloak. "I beg your pardon, my lady. I did not mean to bring offense."

The woman sighed and shifted gingerly. "It is I who must beg your pardon. My own darkness weighs heavily upon me."

A man stirred from the table and rose. His lips trembled as he walked to the woman. "My daughter, would you not rather rest upon a bed?"

"Nay, father, my fleshly vessel has been profaned by the Chaldeans. I am shamed and in some pain, but I would yet hear the prophet's thoughts. Perhaps I might add some knowledge hidden from your minds." She hesitated and sighed. "I was once a queen and privy to much." Iron seeped into her voice. "Perhaps I shall yet be again."

Elnathan, the woman's father, retreated to his position near the table and slumped back to his spot on the floor. He clearly didn't have the heart to order her away. Nehushta, once favorite wife of King Jehoiakim, mother to crown prince Jeconiah, and sister to the intriguing young man, Daniel, bowed in gratitude to her father. The other wives of Jehoiakim might be shattered, but this one was merely broken—cracked, perhaps. There existed iron in her veins.

Jeremiah cleared his throat, trying to redirect his thoughts. "I thank you again, Elnathan, for hiding me beneath your roof."

The broken man waved the thanks away. "It is nothing. The king will not look for you here."

True enough. He would not come near any house wherein lived one of his former wives. The women were unclean, and no one would expect a priest of the LORD to abide near such a woman. But a single thought from the LORD had put Jeremiah's mind at ease in this matter: *I have seen your adulteries, the lewdness of your whoredom, and your abominations. Woe unto you, O Jerusalem! Will you not be made clean? When shall it once be?*[1]

If the LORD God of Israel thought Jerusalem could be made clean, then so too could a woman be made whole from the vileness cruelly inflicted upon her. It was this same hope that had compelled Jeremiah to speak to Daniel before the lad was taken away and give him words of comfort. Indeed, this was not the end. The LORD could cleanse any filth and stain from a soul. And Nehushta seemed willing. This was good enough for Jeremiah.

"Nevertheless, I am most grateful." To ease Nehushta's mind, Jeremiah also found a place around the table and sat upon a rug, leaning against a pillow. A bowl of half-ripe figs sat uneaten in front of him. Few had much of an appetite these days anyway, and the Chaldeans had taken the vast majority of the edible food for their army. There was enough to last until the harvest, but it was pitifully small in comparison.

"Baruch should have been here by now," the prophet finished lamely by way of excuse.

"He will come," Elnathan said softly without looking up. In one day, his daughter's virtue had been stolen and his only son had been taken captive to Babylon, likely never to return. It had

---

[1] Jeremiah 13:27.

destroyed his wife who even now lay abed in mourning. Normally, Hebrew homes were enlivened by song, but few had a song on their lips these days.

"Aye," Jeremiah agreed, not sure what else to say or how to comfort the man. He had already shared with the man his parting words to Daniel. That had given him only a small comfort. How could anything comfort such loss?

They all lapsed into silence as no one knew what else to say.

Sometime later, a surreptitious knock sounded on the door. Elnathan rose quickly and went to see who had come, while Jeremiah tried to make himself as small as possible. No one believed the king would find him here, but his shoulder blades itched all the same and he jumped at the slightest unexpected sound.

"It is Baruch," Elnathan announced softly.

The door opened and closed quickly and there stood Baruch, blinking against the sudden dim light. In his arms, he carried a long roll parchment, a pen, and a clay pot full of ink. Jeremiah half rose from the table. "You fool! What you carry is a sign to any who look upon you! They will know that I am within!"

The scribe looked confused for a moment and then he began stuttering an apology and looking back at the door in fear. Jeremiah swallowed, poised between running and lashing out at the thoughtless scribe.

Elnathan intervened. "Fear not," he said, cutting into Jeremiah's thoughts. "He was not followed, and the king does not yet seek for you. You are safe here."

Trembling, Jeremiah collapsed back into a sitting position, breathing hard. Elnathan was right…he had to be right. He had to be. "Hide your intent in the future, Baruch," he said finally. "A bag would have been wisely used to hide your instruments within."

"Forgive me; I have failed!"

"Nay, you have not failed. Though, I beg you, be wary in the future. That is all."

"As you command, my lord." Baruch staggered over to the table and practically dropped his writing instruments on top, sagging down and wiping sweat from his brow. "I was careless and thoughtless," he muttered.

"As the LORD wills," Jeremiah said, half apologetically. His own reaction shamed him. "It is not the king only who would seek to apprehend me."

"You speak of Seraiah, son of Azariah, the high priest," Elnathan agreed.

The young priest now wore the ephod and was anointed to the office of high priest not two days gone. The day *after* Nebuchadnezzar had left Jerusalem. Strangely, the prince of Chaldea had gone north, not south as most had predicted. They were forsaking Egypt and returning home. With haste. No one understood why, but rumors abounded.

Nehushta spoke from her corner, startling Baruch who hadn't seen her, "Seraiah made great haste in this. He mourned not for his father."

"Aye," Jeremiah agreed, "he has long coveted the high priest's office. I think he had little love for his father."

"And they say that the ark of the LORD is missing," Nehushta added in a thoughtful tone. "Did Azariah hide the ark as some do say? Think you that his son does know where it be?"

Jeremiah and Baruch exchanged a warded look. Jeremiah said, "I doubt me very much that Seraiah knows where the ark is. If he has knowledge of it, he would have delivered it into the hands of the Chaldeans."

"I would not be so certain, my lord prophet," she said softly. "The son of Azariah has much ambition."

True. Heaving a sigh, Jeremiah shook his head. "It is of no import. If Seraiah knows of the ark's fate or not, he will not give us this knowledge."

Elnathan nodded. "This is so. He seeks favor in the court with King Jehoiakim and sees all else as obstacles to his power—this is especially true of you, Jeremiah. You must be wary around him. He has no love for your words, and it may be only the prince of Chaldea's admonition not to harm you that has held back his hand thus far. Yet, I fear, he will soon permit the priests of Molech to offer their abominations upon the holy hill of the LORD God of Israel. I see not how we may avert the coming wrath."

Jeremiah's lips quivered in emotional anguish. He knew this better than anyone else. He looked at Baruch. "This is why I called you, my friend. The LORD has commanded me to write in a book all the words that He has spoken against Israel and against Judah from the day His Word first came to me—even from the days of King Josiah."[2]

The scribe's fingers twitched as if he wanted to grab a pen and begin that instant. Instead, he asked a question, "For what purpose, my lord? I understand not."

"It may be that the house of Judah will hear all the evil which the LORD has purposed to do unto us, and in so hearing, they may return every man from his evil way. Only then will the LORD forgive their iniquity and their sin."[3] Jeremiah rubbed his eyes tiredly. He couldn't recall the last time he had gotten any real sleep. "It is the only way to avoid the wrath to come. We must do this and read it in the ears of the people."

Baruch settled himself at the table, arranging his instruments of writing. "You will not speak yourself?"

"I am shut up,"[4] Jeremiah replied blandly, looking around at Elnathan's house. "I cannot go unto the house of the LORD for I will be taken." Jeremiah looked steadily at his friend. "*You* must read it in the ears of all the people."

Baruch actually paled, his skin looking waxy in the lamplight. "Me, my lord?"

---

[2] Jeremiah 36:1-2.
[3] Jeremiah 36:3.
[4] Jeremiah 36:5.

"A fast day has been called for the ninth month,"[5] the prophet said, glancing at Elnathan for verification, "to beseech the LORD for the deliverance of our children taken captive by the Chaldeans. At noon on that day, read the scroll in the ears of all the people gathered upon the temple mount, for many will come out of their cities to fast—though not all will do so before the LORD only. I fear the false gods of the heathen have captured the hearts of many. Howbeit, there will be no better time to reach the ears of the people."[6] Jeremiah's voice dropped to barely a whisper. "It may be that they will present their supplication before the LORD and turn from their evil ways, for great is the anger and the fury that the LORD has pronounced against this people."[7]

"Will they not take me?" Baruch said just as softly. Worry saturated his eyes.

Elnathan put a hand on the scribe's shoulder. "Fear not. The words will be the prophet's, not yours. I will ensure your safety. Know you Michaiah, son of Gemariah?"

Jeremiah looked sharply at Elnathan. He knew the man. A prince of Judah and a temple scribe who was built like a wall and possessed the fiery temper of a nest of vipers. In times past, the man had been opposed to Jeremiah's words. Baruch looked equally discomfited. "I know of him."

"He has many sons, but his youngest, Azariah, was taken captive along with my son," Elnathan went on quickly, sensing the sudden tension. "He would see his son returned if he may." Glancing at Jeremiah's concerned face, he added, "He has come to me in sincerity and secrecy, wishing to hear more of how we may avoid the fierce anger of the LORD God of Israel." Pain flashed across the leathery face of the prince of Judah at having mentioned the loss of his son. But he recovered, taking a shuddering breath. "He will

---

[5] Jeremiah 36:9. The ninth month of the Hebrew calendar corresponds to our November-December.
[6] Jeremiah 36:6.
[7] Jeremiah 36:7.

vouchsafe you, Baruch. He will bring the book of the prophet to the princes, and we will take it to the king."

Nehushta added, "And we may yet have allies within the King's Court. Ebedmelech, a eunuch and an Ethiopian, served me well while in the house of the king. He will come to our aid if we call."

Jeremiah pulled at his beard. He'd seen the Ethiopian around but had never spoken to him. The man served King Jehoiakim by protecting the king's wives—though, now, he supposed, the king would choose new wives. But Ebedmelech was indeed a highly placed servant in the palace. His aid would be invaluable. "And there yet be some among the priesthood who will lend you aid. I think of Ezekiel, son of Buzi, foremost. But even with such allies, think you this will work?"

It was Nehushta who answered. "My husband, the king, will heed the words of the book," she said confidently. "If all the princes of Judah do join together and are of one mind in this. The king's mind will be persuaded. It is our only hope."

The three men looked at the former queen silently, taking heart in her words. Yet in Jeremiah's mind, he knew how unlikely it was that the king would repent and turn back to the LORD God of his fathers. The word of the LORD continued to burn in Jeremiah's heart, and in those words, he sensed the vast depth of Jehovah's wrath as it was turned toward Judah. Too many abominations, too much innocent blood had been shed for the LORD to repent of the evil He thought to do to Jerusalem and its people.

But Nehushta had the right of it. Hope yet remained. The LORD was merciful and could be persuaded to spare Judah. Much of it, he knew, depended upon King Jehoiakim's response to the book he and Baruch would write.

"Then it is decided," he said at last. He nodded to Baruch's writing instruments. "Let us begin. Write only what the LORD bids me to say."

The scribe, after a searching look at the other two men, nodded and spread the roll of parchment out upon the table. Picking up his pen, he looked expectantly at Jeremiah.

This would be a lengthy task, but they had more than three months to accomplish it. The prophet straightened his shoulders and *remembered*. When he spoke, his words rang with the authority of heaven. "The words of Jeremiah, the son of Hilkiah, of the priests that were in Anathoth in the land of Benjamin, to whom the Word of the LORD came in the days of Josiah the son of Amon king of Judah, in the thirteenth year of his reign…"[8]

Only the sound of a pen scratching against parchment accompanied Jeremiah's words.

---

[8] Jeremiah 1:1-2.

POSSIBLE ROUTE TO BABYLON

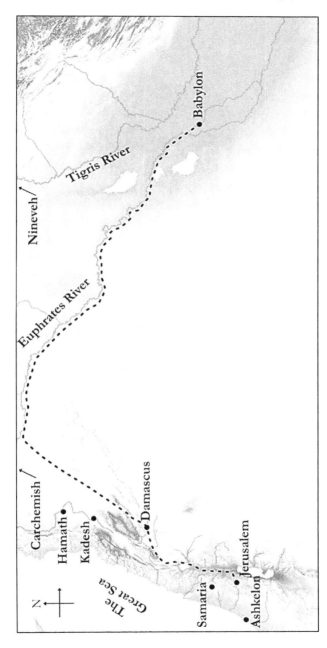

20

Mishael nudged Daniel and pointed with his chin to the captive king of Ashkelon. "I give odds he will not live to see Babylon." Daniel agreed with the assessment. The former king of the neighboring city to Jerusalem stumbled along behind the wagon he was chained to. Blood dripped freely from the iron fetters around his wrists with new lacerations added anytime the wagon lurched unexpectedly, jerking the man forward by his bound hands. Twice, Daniel had watched him being dragged along for dozens of cubits before the Chaldeans decided to toss him into the back of the wagon. Long stringy hair, greasy and dirty, hung down, hiding his face. The man never looked up and saw nothing but the ground immediately before the next step of his bare, bleeding feet.

Clearly, the exceedingly tall man wanted to die. But the eunuch watching him from the back of the wagon intervened on occasion, forcing the former king to drink and to eat and even binding some of the more serious wounds, and when the man could go no farther, he was made to ride in the wagon until he regained enough strength to walk again. Simply watching it was painful. Daniel didn't know how much more a human could take.

Tiredly, he looked away and dry swallowed. It had been hours since their captors had last allowed them water and hours more before they would be given an opportunity. Unlike the hapless king of Ashkelon, none of the Hebrew boys were in chains. But the forced march north over the last week had taken a dreadful toll on all of them. Daniel had lost weight and his sandals had been nearly worn through. If he didn't get a new pair soon, he would be as barefoot as the former king. He'd left with but the one tunic and that was now filthy and ripped in several places.

Most distressing of all was that they'd marched right through the sabbath. Daniel had attempted to pray the morning of the sabbath, but Ashpenaz, the chief eunuch, had personally pulled Daniel to his feet and pushed him forward. The other Hebrew lads had already begun to move.

"Pray as you walk," the eunuch had said in his high voice, adding a disarming grin to complete the odd effect. "You Jews do not make graven images of your God. Is this not because your God is in every place? He can hear your supplication on the road." Ashpenaz had glanced sideways at the soldiers surrounding the captives when he said it.

The message was clear. Walk or be dragged. With little choice, Daniel had prayed while he walked, often turning when he could to face Jerusalem, and once walked backward for a hundred paces, praying. This had sparked a round of mockery from the soldiers, and Daniel had been given many dark looks from his fellow captives who felt the sting as those remarks fell on their ears as much as they did on Daniel's.

It wasn't as if they were treated badly—not like the man chained to the wagon—it was only that the prince of Chaldea was in a mighty hurry to return to Babylon and so set a punishing pace. Even the soldiers in the army grumbled about the haste, and most of them carried their armor, weapons, and a pack so they had more cause for complaint. Daniel and the rest of the captives, at least, had no burden to bear other than their own selves.

"I wish to return home," Mishael muttered when no one responded to his quip about the chained man.

His brother, walking along side, nodded, his gaze looking off into the distance. "As do I," he said softly.

"Remember the prophet's words," Daniel reminded them. "This is not the end. We must endure."

Azariah, the son of Michaiah, grunted. "We can escape," he insisted again for the hundredth time, his eyes flickering to the soldiers walking all around them. "The Chaldeans are lax. At night, we may flee and return home."

Daniel was tempted to try it. More than tempted. He desperately wanted to try it, but it wasn't as easy as Azariah made it out. The son of Michaiah might be a muscular lad with the endurance of a team of horses and the stamina of the ocean tide, but the rest of them were often too exhausted by nightfall to even think about escape. Azariah marched all day, slept soundly at night as if on his bed back home, and didn't complain at the little food. He did, however, glare with a seething anger and hatred at every Chaldean who came near. Daniel feared it would get his new friend in trouble one day.

"Are we alone in thinking of escape?" Daniel asked in a low voice, looking around at the other captive boys walking around them. Some, the youngest, rode in wagons, but for the most part, they walked…long into each day and sometimes into the night.

"We are not," Hananiah said, with a sidelong glance back at a specific knot of boys walking at the back of the captive Hebrews.

Four lads around Daniel's age had formed a conspiratorial alliance that shunned most of their fellow captives. The oldest was Jokim at sixteen years of age. The others were no younger than fourteen, consisting of Naam, Ziph, and Ishi. The latter two were brothers, but all four had been among those who had conspired with Mattaniah's schemes and ambitions. Daniel would not have found it surprising if all four had been involved in the assassination attempt on his life, even if they had acted as unwitting messengers between the king's brother and the assassin. It would be worrisome if not for the fact that they had seemed to have forgotten entirely that Daniel even existed. They were consumed with their own problems.

Hananiah continued, "I have overheard their words at night. They too seek escape, and they have little patience. They will try this night. They have stolen water and bread from the other boys to keep up their strength."

A surge of anger at the injustice built in Daniel's breast, but he suppressed it. It wasn't as if he could do anything here. Not yet anyway. Azariah, however, looked speculative as he digested Hananiah's words. "They will provide distraction then. Perchance this will be our opportunity to escape as well?"

Daniel, gnawed on his lower lip, feeling the beginnings of a soft, growing beard hidden behind the dirt and grime. His tired body plodded along, his feet more shuffling than walking. Still, to escape and return home...he dry-swallowed again and cleared his throat as best he could. "Tell me more."

They discussed it in depth, careful not to let anyone overhear their plans. Already, due to Nebuchadnezzar's haste, the boys had traveled farther than any of them had ever gone away from Jerusalem. They had left the lands of Judah behind within the first two days, traveling steadily north. The Euphrates River was the present goal, and from there, they would follow the river southeast—more east than south—all the way to Babylon. To head directly east, across the desert, though shorter, would be the height of desperation and foolishness.

The best time to escape would be now, before they reached the river. After that, even if they could escape, there was only one route they could take to return home, and the Chaldeans would overtake them quickly. But here, they had a number of escape routes available to them, greatly increasing the odds of confusing the Babylonians. Daniel estimated that another three or four days of this pace would bring them to the river. They had to act now, while they still had the strength and opportunity.

"Damascus is but a two day walk south," Azariah put in. "We could hide therein if we must. Surely the Chaldeans are in too much of a haste to look for us."

And that, of course, was their biggest advantage. Daniel nodded slowly, forcing his tired mind to think it through. "The Chaldean prince is most anxious to return home. If we are well away, they will not look overlong for us." He hoped.

But they would have to move swiftly and at night. Since passing Damascus, the land had undergone a drastic shift. Gone were the lush forests and hills of Dan north of the Sea of Chinnereth.[1] The land reminded Daniel of the desert that lay between Jerusalem and the Jordan River, bleak, blasted, and barren. Hiding out here would be difficult. Kadesh lay off to the west somewhere and Daniel could see a line of tantalizing green on the horizon that hinted of water and places to hide. If they could make it there, they might have a chance.

It was a measure of Nebuchadnezzar's haste that he risked cutting through even this much of the desert, and if it wasn't for the supplies plundered from Jerusalem and Damascus, the Babylonian prince would have been forced to cut west and then north, adding days to the journey.

"Know you of Jokim's plans?" Daniel asked Hananiah, referring to the leader of the other boys who were planning an escape.

"Nay," his friend said, shaking his head. "Only that they will make the attempt during the second watch of the night."

"We must be vigilant then," Daniel said, looking around. "They will not leave without notice or noise. They will surely be seen. It will give us the chance we seek."

The other three lads nodded.

And with that, Daniel ran out of words, concentrating on putting one foot in front of the other. A torn toenail sported dried

---

[1] The Sea of Galilee. Numbers 34:11; Joshua 13:27.

blood under what remained of the nail, making it look black. He found it suddenly fascinating, an effect of his exhaustion no doubt. The sandal immediately in front of that toe had been split, the leather frayed, the tear running directly to the toe. Likely, that had been the culprit, allowing a sharp rock to catch his toenail and rip it half off. The pain even held a hypnotic effect for him. It throbbed with every step, keeping rhythm with his pace and becoming a comforting counterpoint to his misery. How odd.

Time passed with no more words exchanged. Each of the lads waited for nightfall and the opportunity to rest, eat, and quench their thirst. The late summer sun beat down upon their heads. Daniel had lost his turban somewhere—he couldn't remember when, and the brightness of the sun hurt his eyes—so he studied his feet or rather that injured toe.

"Daniel," Mishael's voice said, cutting through the mental fog that had become all of Daniel's life. "Daniel!"

Daniel stumbled to a stop, blinking. He looked up. At some point, darkness had crept up on Daniel and he hadn't even noticed. Everyone had stopped moving, and already men were finding suitable places to make camp for the night. A majestic tent was being offloaded from several wagons. That would be where the crown prince would sleep with his wives. From experience, Daniel knew that lesser tents would be erected around it, quarters for Nebuchadnezzar's battle commanders and trusted counselors. The men in the army would make do on the ground wherever they may.

So would the captive Hebrew boys.

Daniel slumped to the ground right there as a wave of exhaustion overcame him. "I must sleep," he said to the others. "I can go no farther."

Mishael and Hananiah collapsed beside him. "I as well, Daniel," Hananiah muttered. "How will we wake for the second watch of the night?"

Azariah, looking hardly bothered by the forced march, shrugged. "I will keep watch and wake you when it is time."

"But you will sleep not," Mishael said, looking at the older boy in something close to awe. "Can you do this?"

"I am tired," the large youth admitted, "but if I must remain awake to escape, then that is what I shall do."

Mishael nodded as if the lad had said something profound. "Ho! Look!"

Daniel did, seeing a troop of eunuchs, bearing bread and waterskins and under the watchful eye of Ashpenaz, begin moving through the captive boys. When a silent eunuch reached him, Daniel snatched the waterskin and drank greedily, careful not to let any of the water spill. He'd seen more than one boy receive a bruise for being careless with the water. A half loaf of bread was placed in his lap. It was hard and stale, but he ate at it determinedly. He would need his strength if he was to escape this night.

The others finished eating and then curled up next to each other to share body heat. With the setting of the sun, the desert shed heat like wool on a sheared sheep. It would grow uncomfortably cold, and only their shared heat would allow any of them to rest that night.

"I shall keep watch," Azariah said, sitting down with his back up against Daniel's. "I will wake you at the beginning of the second watch."

Daniel hardly heard the words. He was already drifting off into sleep. A second later, a hand shook him out of a deep sleep.

"Daniel, the second watch is upon us. We must be ready."

The words made no sense. The only thing he needed to do was sleep for the next year or ten. He rolled over to get away from the offending hand. But it followed him.

"Awake, Daniel, our escape is nigh."

The voice would not leave him alone. Daniel finally sat up, blinking. The cloudless sky shone with innumerable stars. Sure enough, based on the stars' position, the second watch of the night was nigh.

Escape.

DANIEL

Memory flooded back. Casting a furtive look around, he saw that only a few fires had been lit. Most everyone slept. A few tired guards roamed around the perimeter, but surely not enough to stop them from escaping. Once beyond the light of the campfires, they could lose themselves in the darkness. By morning, they would be well away and, with Jehovah's favor, be too far to pursue. Azariah moved on to wake Hananiah and the lad's younger brother. Once everyone was fully awake and alert, they waited.

Daniel could see where Jokim and his conspirators had bedded down for the night. Looking carefully, he thought he saw movement among the shadows. He glanced at his companions. "Be ready," he whispered. "It will be soon. Lie down and appear as if we still sleep."

They followed Daniel's lead, lying down so that the guards would think them asleep, but keeping a close eye on the shadows where Jokim and the others waited. It should be soon. They had decided to move in a different direction than Jokim and his companions took. Only they didn't know for sure which direction they would take. Daniel hoped they would simply go south. He wanted to go west, toward Kadesh and all that green he had seen earlier on the horizon.

Daniel saw more movement and he tensed, his heart thumping and driving away the last remains of his exhaustion. Then suddenly one of the campfires was blotted out to Daniel's left as a shape moved between Daniel and the fire. The apparition grew as it came toward them, the edges glowing where light from the campfire leaked around it. Daniel sucked in his breath, his heart pounding even harder. Had Jokim decided to escape by coming Daniel's way?

But the shadow resolved itself into a cleanshaven, fat man wearing costly robes. The man stood over the four young boys, looking down. Daniel shut his eyes and pretended to be sleeping. He knew that shape. Ashpenaz. *Away with you!* he half prayed half shouted in the vaults of his mind.

"You deceive me not, young ones," the high-pitched voice said in Hebrew. "Sit. We will talk."

Warily, Daniel opened his eyes and looked. Ashpenaz sat down just outside the circle of his friends, arranging his robes carefully around him. Faint light reflected off his round face, enough for Daniel to see a smile of amusement playing on the man's lips.

There would be no escape this night.

Sighing, he sat up as did the three other lads. They all faced the chief eunuch. "We harken," Daniel said glumly. He noticed that Azariah's fists clenched and unclenched as if he wanted to attack the eunuch. Daniel put a stilling hand on the boy's arm. It would not do to act in haste.

Ashpenaz noticed and nodded. "You are wise, Daniel, son of Elnathan. I am not your enemy this night, for I am here to preserve your lives."

This got the boys' attention. They stilled and looked at the chief eunuch as if the danger came from him, despite his words. "We are in jeopardy?" Daniel asked.

"Aye, from your own foolishness. You have been watched, and I know of a surety that you seek to escape this night." The chief eunuch held up a hand to silence their coming protests. "Do not attempt to deceive me—or yourselves. You are not the first captives taken to Babylon. We have learned the ways of those taken from their homeland."

The eunuch's knowing look sunk Daniel's heart. They never had a chance. He glanced to where Jokim and his companions lay, wondering if they too had been found out. "Forgive me, my lord, but why have you spoken of this to us?"

The fat man's smile took up his whole face. "You have found favor in my eyes, young Daniel."[2] Ashpenaz gestured to the sleeping boys around them. "Each of you has been chosen to serve Babylon and its king. In a few weeks, Nebuchadnezzar, son of Nabopolassar, will be crowned king. He it is who you must serve well, and he it is who you must please. It is my task to see that you are ready to stand before him one day. You will learn the Chaldean tongue and be

---

[2] Daniel 1:9.

trained in our ways. The gods have chosen this fate for you and there is no escape."

The boys each cast sidelong looks at each other, confused as to where this was going.

The eunuch noticed. "You must accept your lot, Hebrew children. Judah is your home no longer. You must become of the Chaldean tribe, children of Babylon, and serve our gods. This must be so in your own eyes, or you will die."

All four boys tensed at this, but the fat man only grinned broader.

"Aye, there is no escape. Only acceptance. For even your Hebrew God has ordained this to be. But an example must be made so that you might learn this truth."

Daniel's eyes narrowed and his heart decided to miss a beat. That had sounded like a threat. He glanced around, wondering if he shouldn't try to make a dash for freedom. The fat eunuch would be unable to stop him, and before the guards could be alerted, he would be out into the night. The army lay all around them, but surely they were as tired as he and would be slow to react.

Before he could decide, Ashpenaz said, "What I do, I do for your good." He heaved himself up with effort and gestured with one hand.

Daniel and his friends instinctively shied away from him, even as a dozen soldiers suddenly converged on the sleeping Hebrew children, shouting, and delivering kicks to any who did not move quickly enough. Fires suddenly burst to life, casting enough light to see by.

Into this chaos, a young man was dragged by the arms of two Chaldean warriors. Jokim, face bloody and bruised, hung like a limp weed in their grasp. Daniel felt his mouth go dry. Jokim had already been caught, likely before he had ever had a chance to even attempt his escape. Behind the beaten lad came other warriors, dragging his confederates, Naam, Ziph, and Ishi.

When the shouting finally died down, Ashpenaz looked over the cowering boys much as a fox might over a covey of trapped quail. "Harken, children of Judah, for your lives hang in the balance. This night has sedition and deception been discovered among you. This cannot be. Any who seeks to flee will fail and such evil must be dealt with harshly. Behold your fellow captive, one Jokim, son of Mishma." He swept a finger at the battered young man held tightly by hard-eyed soldiers. All eyes followed that finger. "He has whispered false words into your ears, saying that you might escape the Chaldeans and return to your homes. This may not be. Nebuchadnezzar, prince of the Chaldeans, has purchased your lives. You and all that you are belong to him, and there is a price to be paid for defiance. Behold!"

The chief eunuch made another gesture, and a soldier brandished an iron knife and quite casually and quite slowly cut Jokim's throat from ear to ear. Jokim thrashed violently for a moment, trying to scream, but it was to no avail. In moments, he hung limply, a dark pool of blood staining the ground at his feet.

"Behold the fate of any who defy Nebuchadnezzar."

At another gesture, the soldiers tossed Jokim's body atop his own blood and walked away, their duty done. Jokim's companions were all shoved into the midst of the captive Hebrew children, their bodies shaking in absolute terror. And no wonder.

Ashpenaz surveyed the captives, his eyes lingering on Daniel before he grinned again and said, "Sleep well. Tomorrow we march on." He left then, leaving the shocked Hebrew boys staring at the body of Jokim lying in a pool of his own blood.

No one would get any more sleep this night.

Perhaps Daniel should have been frightened into subjugation. Perhaps he should have surrendered to the inevitable. Instead, a burning resolve seethed in Daniel's heart. Instinctively, he fingered the blue thread that hung from his tunic fringe. It was as frayed as the rest of his clothing, but it reminded him of who he truly was. He would not ever be a child of Babylon. He was a Hebrew, a child of

Israel, and for him there could only ever be one true God. No matter what the Chaldeans declared for him, he would never serve their gods even if it meant his death.

He turned to Mishael who's eyes looked like they were going to bug right out of his head. "Mishael, teach me the Chaldean tongue." He looked at Hananiah and Azariah, his eyes flashing with determination. "Teach us all that we may understand their speech. This is not the end. The LORD our God will not forget us but will remember us in our distress. But in knowing their speech, may we find a haven among them that we might worship our God and become His vessels in a foreign land and survive this crucible."

His words settled over his friends, pulling their eyes away from the body of Jokim. Shoulders straightened, backs stiffened, and faces shed their fear. They would all likely end up like Jokim, but if that was their fate, the path that Jehovah would have them walk, then they would walk it.

And if Daniel had to walk that path alone, he would.

21

Four days later, the Chaldean army reached the Euphrates River. Somewhere near here, Daniel knew, was where Nebuchadnezzar had defeated the Egyptians and Assyrians at Carchemish. Nebuchadnezzar, riding in a chariot in the vanguard of the army, wasted no time in turning east and a bit south, following a well-worn caravan route that might have once been walked by Abraham on his journey to Haran.

Daniel and his fellow captives were ordered to refill the water casks lashed to the backs of wagons. It was exhausting work, trying to refill the cask and then catch back up with the wagons that rambled along the ancient road without pausing. But plunging his head into the cool waters and getting rid of some of the grime that had coated every span of his skin nearly made up for any inconvenience.

Blisters had begun to develop on his feet where his worn sandals no longer protected him. Every Hebrew boy could walk all day barefoot but doing so day after day without end wore down even

DANIEL

the hardiest of walkers. Every step was its own source of agony, and Daniel longed to rest for a bit longer than a night. A year would do just fine.

"Say it again," he muttered to Mishael, trying to distract himself from his screaming blisters.

Mishael repeated the unfamiliar Chaldean word, which according to him meant "city." Daniel formed the word in his mouth, repeating it several times until Mishael nodded enthusiastically. "You have the right of it now, Daniel. You have a natural ear for tongues."

Daniel nodded his gratitude. He already knew Egyptian, which was vastly different than Hebrew, but fortunately, this Chaldean tongue held many similarities to his native tongue, hinting at a common origin.[1] Again, it spoke of Abraham who had once traveled this route from Ur, also a city along the Euphrates River.[2] Perhaps this was the source of the common ancestry of the languages. Regardless, he was picking it up quickly in the four days he and his friends had been letting Mishael teach them what he knew. It was very similar to what the Assyrians spoke, though with a slightly different dialect. Already, he was picking up bits of conversation spoken by the soldiers and servants.

Azariah, bearing a water cask balanced precariously on his shoulders grunted. "I like this little, Daniel. Learning their heathen tongue is much like a surrender in my eyes."

Daniel had already covered this, but he explained his reasoning yet again. "We must know their words, Azariah. Only then can we negotiate our freedom. You heard Ashpenaz. They will make us into their image, erasing our God from our minds. But if we know their words, then we know their minds. It is there that we may become free to worship our God in the stead of the Chaldean gods."

---

[1] By Nebuchadnezzar's reign, Aramaic had become the everyday tongue in Mesopotamia. It is a Semitic language with similar roots to Hebrew. Parts of the book of Daniel are written in Aramaic.

[2] Genesis 11:27-31.

Azariah looked around warily at the mention of the chief eunuch. Daniel knew why. The man had an uncanny ability to turn up when he was least expected, having discerned things he should not. Within a day of beginning to learn the Chaldean tongue, the wily eunuch had discovered it and had shown his pleasure, even suggesting that Mishael teach some of the other Hebrew children.

It wasn't a bad idea, but it wasn't as if they had time. Daniel brought the subject up again as they reached the wagon and dropped their loads onto the bed. "We need to teach the others," he said to Azariah. "We must need find time."

"How?" The large lad gestured at the line of wagons and soldiers marching down the road. "We are given no time."

"We must be united," he explained even as Hananiah caught up and offloaded his water casket. The lad's face had turned an unnatural red from the exertion. They held onto the back of the wagon, letting it help pull them forward. "The prophet warned us not to learn the ways of the heathen. We must not forget who we are. For this task, we will need all of us."

Hananiah snorted. "Is not learning their tongue learning their ways?"

Daniel shook his head in denial. Secretly, he'd wondered the same thing. "Nay, if we are to be vessels of our God, then it is for us to show the heathen His power and majesty. There is no God but Jehovah, but though I would use Hebrew words, the heathen know them not. For this, we must use their own tongue." Daniel frowned and looked toward the head of the column where the Chaldean prince rode. "In the end, Nebuchadnezzar must be made to see this truth. Only then will we be given leave to follow the ways of our God and not the gods of the heathen."

"Your words are most persuasive," Hananiah said tiredly, "but nothing in them will be done quickly. You hint at a matter of years."

"Aye. The prophet said our captivity will be long. I know not if this means a year or ten, but whatever it is, we must endure, and we must not forget the LORD our God."

Mishael, who had remained unnaturally quiet during all this, spoke up excitedly, "We may have yet the chance. I spy Ziph, son of Jucal, coming."

Daniel looked up. Sure enough, Ziph, his brother Ishi, and Naam had slowed down from where they had been walking at the forefront of the Hebrew captives. Soon, Daniel and his friends would overtake them. It had to be deliberate. Strangely, Naam and Ishi left enough space around Ziph to make it seem as if the eldest son of Jucal stood on an island alone.

"The LORD is with us," Mishael blurted out, grinning all around. "Did I not say so? Did I not?" His shoulders squared as if he had personally arranged the coming meeting. "Perhaps they heard of the favor we have found in the eyes of Ashpenaz. I wager my sandals that this is so—by Jacob's beard!"

Azariah had shoved Mishael aside, nearly causing the younger lad to fall in the dirt. Mishael turned a thunderous glare at the bigger lad. He never lacked for courage. But Azariah ignored him, his eyes fixed on the three lads who had fallen back enough to join Daniel and his companions.

For a moment, no one said a word, each looking studiously around to ensure that they could not be overheard. Only the wagon driver, who walked at the head of the oxen, was in earshot and the boys knew from experience that he could barely speak his own language let alone the Hebrew tongue.

At length, Ziph turned the full force of his brown, hard eyes on Daniel. "I would know your mind, Daniel, son of Elnathan," he said bluntly.

Daniel frowned. Something warned him to keep his tongue in check. "Very well. What would you know?"

Ziph stood perhaps two finger widths taller than Daniel. He lacked Azariah's size, but he made up for it in sheer cruelty. But despite that, Daniel hoped to win him over. Ziph was a natural leader and many of the other boys would follow him.

"Is it not true that you preach the words of the prophet Jeremiah?" His words fell off his tongue roughly, like bark over stone.

"Have not his words come to pass?" Daniel asked blandly. "Why would I not preach his words if they be true?"

Naam, a squat young man with a full growth of beard at fifteen, barked a mocking laugh. "The God of our fathers has left us to die at the hands of the Chaldeans. That is the truth. Why then should we serve Him?"

Daniel's mouth nearly dropped. "It is not the LORD who has forsaken us but we the LORD. It is because of our sins that this evil has befallen us. We must endure it and turn back to our God. Only then may He have mercy upon us and return us to our people."

Ziph snarled, looking at his two companions with an air of superiority. "Did I not tell you that his words would be so? He has turned against his people and would have us be slaves to the Chaldeans."

"I would not have us be slaves," Daniel protested.

"Yet you preach endurance, that only by turning to the LORD may we be delivered—in time, a time long removed from now. You will see us all dead."

"Then what propose you?" Azariah demanded, bulling his way into the conversation. "How would you be free of the Chaldeans? Would you follow Jokim's foolishness?"

Naam, though quite a bit smaller than Azariah, looked ready to pounce upon him anyway. Naam and Jokim had been friends their entire lives. With marvelous restraint for one who bore foolishness with pride, he snapped, "Hold your tongue! You are but the youngest son of a lowly scribe and are unworthy to speak to me!"

Azariah's eyes went flat, his lighter skin tone revealing his taut and corded muscles.

Daniel intervened. "He has spoken wisdom," he argued, turning to Ziph. "What would you have us do?"

DANIEL

Ziph's thin lips compressed, and his brow furrowed. "To escape and return to our people, we must turn to the gods of the Chaldeans."

Mishael blurted, "You would further sin against the LORD?"

"Be gone, you dog. I like not the sound of your voice."

Rather than be angry, Mishael shrugged. "I would still know how sinning further against the LORD will deliver us from the hands of the Chaldeans."

The third lad in the other group, Ishi, Ziph's younger brother, had yet to speak. At these words, he turned questioning eyes upon his older brother who noted it and growled, "The gods of the Chaldeans are stronger than Jehovah. If escape is to be had, it will be through finding favor in the eyes of Ishtar and Marduk."

The wagon wheel hit a rut and jarred so sharply that it dislodged Daniel's grip on the wood, leaving a nasty splinter in his right thumb. He took the time the distraction gave him to think furiously as he dug the splinter out. Nothing came to mind, no way to salvage the situation and convince Ziph that the only solution was to return with a whole heart to the LORD God of Israel. Daniel could hear the disdain in the other's voice, and so knew the lad had made his decision. So be it. Time to cast the spear and see where it fell.

He looked squarely at the other boy. "Then we are at odds, Ziph, son of Jucal, and Naam, son of Shephatiah. You follow the way of folly and seek after false gods who have not eyes to see with or ears to hear with. I would not be near you when the LORD turns His eyes upon your abominations."

Ziph's eyes smoldered under his thick brows. When he spoke, he did so for Daniel's ears alone. "You have made an enemy this day, Daniel, son of Elnathan. Look well to your life, for as the life of Jeremiah is forfeit, so too is yours. The king's brother has already decreed this to be."

He then turned and stormed off. Naam followed just as angry, but Ishi glanced back at Daniel with a speculative frown on his face.

He gave Daniel a small nod of respect before hurrying after his brother and friend.

Daniel realized he was holding his breath. He let it out explosively.

"By Abraham's soiled foot," Mishael breathed. "Did I hear him aright?"

Hananiah crowded close. "What said he? He spoke too softly for my ears."

It made sense that Mishael had heard. "Mattaniah, son of Josiah, has decreed my death, and Ziph would see it done."

Azariah hadn't taken his eyes off the retreating backs of their enemies. "He will find it no easy task," he declared.

Daniel appreciated the words. He would not face whatever was to come alone. But a sadness filled him. Most of the other Hebrew boys would follow Ziph's lead now that Jokim was dead. Only a few would agree with Daniel, for none wanted their captivity to be long. All wanted to return home as soon as possible. It was no longer only the Chaldeans Daniel needed to worry about. Now, he must be wary of his own people.

Three days later, while making camp for the night along the Euphrates, Daniel discovered just how right he was.

22

Ashpenaz looked over the Hebrew children much like a mother over a brood of boisterous children. Daniel found the look to be unsettling. There was a possessiveness in the chief eunuch that Daniel thought boded ill for him and the other boys. He glanced uneasily at his friends, but they had their eyes riveted on the eunuch.

All the boys sat, massaging throbbing feet and aching muscles. Food and water were being dispensed through their ranks, consisting again mostly of bread and a few figs or dates. Daniel ate his share woodenly, wondering why the prince of the eunuchs had gathered them together.

Two other men stood with Ashpenaz. One, a whip-thin man in a conical hat and wide robes watched the boys with a look of disgust stamped upon his face. He had the look of a man who had swallowed something sour and knew he had to do it again. The other, a broad-shouldered man whose muscles had long gone to fat, possessed narrow, slanted eyes with which he looked upon the

Hebrew children. Despite that the man was also cleanshaven, Daniel could not read the man's expression.

Strangely, a bullock munched contentedly on a patch of grass behind the trio. It, more than the men, caused Daniel to wonder.

Ashpenaz raised his voice to be heard by the sixty remaining boys—there had been loses along the way—and spoke in Hebrew, "Harken, children of Israel, for Nebuchadnezzar has this day decreed your fate." He lifted a thick finger and pointed back the way they came. "Judah lies beyond your reach. Even now, we have entered lands long ruled by Babylon, and outposts along the river are always on the lookout for escaped slaves. Escape is death. Life may be found only in following the path now set before you."

The prince of the eunuchs paused to let his words settle in. The Hebrew boys stirred uneasily. Most had seen the outposts and patrols of soldiers on both sides of the riverbank. Most had already come to a similar conclusion. Ashpenaz continued, "Word has come that Babylon stands ready to receive her prince. On the morrow, Nebuchadnezzar, prince of Babylon, will take the swiftest among the army and press onward and claim the throne whereupon he will be crowned king. As for us, we will lessen our pace to a small degree so that you may find your strength and be ready upon entering Babylon to present yourselves to the king."

An appreciative murmur rose from the boys. A slower pace lifted their spirits immensely.

"But I would not have you to be ignorant of what lay before you," Ashpenaz continued, glancing about. "I have had a dream wherein the gods spoke to me. I spoke my dream to Nebuchadnezzar, and he called for the magicians to interpret it." He bowed to the skinny man to his right. "In my dream, I saw newborn sheep led by a mighty lion. The lion ate not the sheep but led them beside still waters and green pastures. In time, the sheep grew, becoming mighty rams that stood in defense of the lion when evil was determined upon all the lion's domain, and the rams delivered the lion from many hurts. This was the dream upon my bed this night past."

The thin man stepped forward, crowding past the eunuch as if the latter didn't exist. In a deep voice, he spoke in Chaldean. Daniel caught snatches of the words and gleaned some of the meaning, but the bulk of what the man said was still lost to him.

When he finished, Ashpenaz translated, "The watchers in the night have spoken. You, children of Israel, are the sheep and the lion is the mighty prince, Nebuchadnezzar. The prince has sheltered you, protected you from harm so that you may one day be a defense to the kingdom and a refuge to the prince. It has therefore been decreed that each of you will become eunuchs in the palace of the king of Babylon!"[1]

The Hebrew children knew exactly what that meant. A cry of protest rose from the lips of nearly all the children, including Daniel. He half rose to his feet, his mind going numb. Such mutilation meant not a single one of the boys would ever pass their seed on. There would be no children. Their bloodline would die with them. Would the LORD God of Israel permit this? A chill settled in his breast. He couldn't help it; tears gathered in his eyes and then spilled out, staining his cheeks.

The prince of the eunuchs was not deterred by this display. He spoke over the wails. "Only in this way may you stand before the king as wise men, magicians, astrologers, and counsellors." His round, normally jovial face, hardened. "All other paths lead to death. May I die a thousand deaths if I have spoken falsely to you. Harken, children of Judah, for a covenant is required of you this day, one made before Marduk, who will then grant you dreams and visions whereby you might bring counsel to the throne of Babylon."

The other, silent eunuch pulled the hapless bullock forward whereupon the astrologer—or priest, Daniel wasn't sure which—produced a knife and slit the beast's throat. The bullock continued to chew for a moment as if the pain of its slit throat hadn't yet

---

[1] 2 Kings 20:18; Isaiah 39:7.

penetrated to its brain. When it did, the beast tried to jerk away, but it was too late. Too much of its life's blood had spilled out. The bullock collapsed to the ground and lay still.

In short order, the knife-wielding priest had divided the bullock into two parts, separating them so that a narrow pathway led between the two bloody parts. Ashpenaz nodded in satisfaction and then addressed the Hebrew boys, "By entering into covenant with Marduk, you will be given a place of honor among the servants of Nebuchadnezzar and find favor in his eyes. You will see dreams and visions and be guided by our gods. Each of you who passes through the bullock will vow to serve our gods and to defend the kingdom against all enemies." His eyes glittered. "Know that your fate is set. Eunuchs you will be, but power and favor may be had by those who submit to this destiny. I, who am a eunuch from my twelfth year of life, do testify of this. Join me, children of Judah, and let us make a covenant!" With a grin, he added the last bit of lure, gesturing to the divided bullock. "And together, we will feast on the flesh of the covenant and eat no more bread but meat!"

Most of the boys had risen to their feet by now, staring apprehensively at Ashpenaz and the divided bullock. This type of covenant making was not new to them. Indeed, Abraham had made such a covenant with God,[2] but such a thing hadn't been done with the God of Israel since before Moses had led Israel out of Egypt. These days, such covenants were frequently initiated by the priests of false gods, especially since King Josiah's death.[3] To Daniel, such things were abominations. He'd rather die than enter such an unholy covenant.

But the tantalizing promises of meat to eat and power could not be ignored by these desperate children, and despite Daniel's resolution, he *was* tempted—if not for the dreams and visions, but for the meat. His mouth watered at the very idea after so long living on bread and little else. But this meat would be tainted, offered to a

---

[2] Genesis 15:9-17.
[3] Jeremiah 34:18-19.

false god to broker an unholy covenant. The feeling turned to ash in Daniel's mouth. No. He would not—could not.

But others would. The first one to come forward was Ziph, son of Jucal—though Naam was only a moment behind. Ziph paused before the divided bullock, standing on an island of isolation. Daniel had noted how the young man hated anyone being too close to him and that he despised being touched by any. This likely explained why Naam crouched several cubits away, giving his leader room.

"I, Ziph, son of Jucal, will make this covenant with Marduk, god of the sky," he announced clearly. He glared about him, daring anyone to dissent. He spared his most vile glare for Daniel, though. "I enter into covenant to serve the king of Babylon and defend the Chaldean kingdom from all enemies. This I do swear, and if I fail in this vow, may my flesh be divided as this bullock has been divided." He then strode arrogantly between the two pieces of the bullock. On the other side, he turned and faced his fellow captives, folding his arms across his chest, his chin lowered as he waited.

Naam's grin thrown at Daniel had all the subtly of a hungry wolf who finds itself in the middle of a herd of sheep. "I Naam, son of Shephatiah, do make this covenant with Marduk, chief god of the Chaldeans, to serve Nebuchadnezzar, the king of Babylon, and defend the Chaldean kingdom as I may. This I do swear, and may my flesh be divided as this bullock has been divided if I fail in this vow."

Naam, too, then walked between the two pieces of the bullock, skirting around Ziph—careful not to get too close—and taking up a position behind him. Daniel and Naam locked eyes. The latter fully expected Daniel to refuse and in so doing to be killed. Clearly, the bearded lad was looking forward to it.

One by one, the Hebrew boys passed between the bullock, entering into a covenant with Marduk. All but nine boys stood on the other side of the divided bullock, Daniel and his three friends, among those who had not passed through. Two things surprised Daniel. First, Azariah had not so much as budged. Daniel had only really gotten to know the young man since their captivity. He didn't know why Azariah had decided to follow him, but he felt strangely elated that his new friend had decided to stand with Daniel and his other two friends. The other surprise was Ishi. The young man looked first at Daniel and then at his brother, and when the last boy had passed through, he glanced nervously at his brother.

He clearly didn't want to make this vow, but Ziph's glare bespoke of much pain. Daniel watched the boy wrestle with his decision, and silently cheered him to stand firm, to defy his brother.

But then the lad slowly walked to the bullock. With a look at Daniel that seemed to express regret, he said the words and passed through the divided flesh. This greatly disappointed Daniel, though he didn't understand why.

Ashpenaz studied Daniel. "And what of you, Daniel, son of Elnathan? Will you not enter into covenant with Marduk so that he may impart wisdom to you in dreams and visions?"

Prepared for this, Daniel bowed deeply to the prince of the eunuchs, but when he straightened, he squared his shoulders and looked steadily into the eyes of the eunuch. He expected to be killed in the next hour for what he did here. "I may not," he said simply. "I serve the God of Israel, and it is He who has commanded us not to enter into any covenant with any other god." He took a deep breath, casting lots and flinging himself upon God's mercy. "To safeguard the king's life, I must stay true to my God. Was it not the God of Israel who commanded Nebuchadnezzar to take dominion over Judah? How then can the king be without counsel from Jehovah's people? O prince of the eunuchs, harken to me if you please. The God of my fathers has brought me to this place. I may not break my covenant with Him. Indeed, to serve the king of Babylon true, I dare not."

Daniel's friends said nothing, but they stood beside him in mutual agreement.

The magician-priest barked something at Ashpenaz who bowed and replied in a subservient voice. The priest of Marduk cast an angry glare at the eunuch and then one at the remaining Hebrew boys who hadn't participated in the covenant. He turned on his heel and walked away, throwing his knife into the dirt.

The chief eunuch picked up the knife and handed it to Ziph. "Give portions of the meat to all who vowed to serve Marduk," he ordered. "Let them all share in the bounty."

Ziph took the knife and stared at it. Daniel would have given much to know what passed through the young man's mind at that moment. Whatever it was, Daniel doubted he would gain any pleasure from it.

Then Ashpenaz and the other eunuch stood before Daniel and his companions. Here it was. They were going to kill him and his friends. Daniel unconsciously tensed, but there was nowhere to flee, nowhere to go. But instead of ordering the soldiers standing nearby to kill Daniel, the prince of the eunuchs gestured to his companion. "This is the Melzar,[4] my steward," he introduced. "I foresee much trouble with you and your friends, Daniel. However, your words were to my liking—though not to Baltasar, who wished you to be slain for your refusal to bow to Marduk. But it is I who have the charge over you, not the priest of Marduk. It is I who will decide your fate. It is true that my prince, Nebuchadnezzar, will need guidance from all sources of wisdom, even from your God. I would not anger the God of Israel who did speak to my lord, the king of Babylon. But I fear me that you have made an enemy this day, Daniel, son of Elnathan. Baltasar will not lightly forget what you have done, so I must be extra vigilant in preserving your lives. Therefore, the Melzar will have oversight of you so that I may know that you will be able to stand before the lord, my king, in the appointed day. He will be a bulwark between you and the wrath of Baltasar."

---

[4] Daniel 1:11. Most scholars agree that Melzar is not a name but a title that means, mostly, steward.

Melzar—Daniel mentally dropped the "the" before the title—bowed before him and his three friends, an odd gesture given to captives.

Ashpenaz continued, "The Melzar lacks a tongue, as it was taken from him as a child. He is of the Assyrian blood but has served me faithfully. He understands the Hebrew tongue, but from this moment on, he will only respond to the Chaldean tongue, so learn it well. And understand, that from this day forth, you must be better than all the other children of Judah in all things. You must not give occasion to Baltasar to have you slain. You must exceed where others fail, for the priest of Marduk will be watching for any reason to have you slain." The prince of the eunuchs regarded Daniel intently and then changed the subject so swiftly that it took Daniel a moment to reorient his mind. "Would you then protect my lord, the king, from all harm as you have said?"

Daniel nodded quickly. "The LORD my God has sent me into this land. Until my people repent of their sin and He releases us from our captivity, I am come and will serve faithfully."

"This is well. It is for this reason that I have delivered you from the hands of Baltasar. Know, therefore, that I cannot change the decree that all the Hebrew captives must be even as I am, a eunuch, but if your words be true and you be true men, then I may yet offer you a chance—a small chance—of surviving." The chief eunuch glanced at the eight boys who had refused to make the covenant with Marduk. "You will all be in great danger from this moment forth. Any hand that slays you will not be punished for the deed. Harken well to the Melzar and do as he bids you, and you may yet live."

Daniel swallowed hard. He'd known death was near and had accepted it. This, however, spoke of constant vigilance and a slim chance of survival. Such hope could bring about more tribulation than a swift death. He eyed the other Hebrew boys as they carved hunks of meat from the bullock and roasted their prizes over a fire. Snapping his eyes back to Ashpenaz, he said, "I have no wish for death, my lord, but neither will I break my vows to my God—even if it means my death."

"This I told Baltasar and is the only reason you yet live. I must now add further protection to you."

Daniel looked quizzical. "My lord?"

"Your Hebrew names are odious to our ears and uplifts your God above ours. This must not be. As long as you are called by such, you will be looked upon with suspicion, and Baltasar needs not much reason to slay you. But with names that bring honor to our gods, his hand will hesitate. Therefore, Daniel, to you I give the name Belteshazzar, meaning Bel will protect, as you have vowed to protect the king." He turned to Daniel's friends. "You, Hananiah, son of Elishama the scribe, are studious and deft with a pen. Think not that I have not seen your writings in the morning dust when we depart. To you, I name Shadrach, meaning the great scribe of the sun, whom we worship."

"What of me, my lord?" Mishael interjected, clearly fascinated by the renaming. Daniel gave him a hard look and the boy glanced down, looking shamed.

"To you, Mishael, also son of Elishama, I name Meshach, meaning belonging to the goddess Shach, who is known for her beauty and passionate nature."

Mishael looked dejected, and well he should. Daniel did not much care for his own new name. Bel was another name for Marduk.

Ashpenaz turned to Azariah. "To you, Azariah, son of Michaiah, I have seen the fire in your eyes and how you make your countenance as iron. Thus, I name you Abednego, meaning servant of Nego, the god of fire."[5]

Azariah didn't so much as blink at this but stared resolutely into the prince of the eunuch's eyes, who allowed a grin to spread across his face as if the large lad had only validated his naming.

The eunuch then regarded the four young men, noting their looks of dismay and anger. He grinned all the more. "Know that no

---

[5] Daniel 1:7.

Chaldean will call you by your former names. Only by your new names may you be called. This is the decree of Nebuchadnezzar. It is law. Understand you what I say?"

These last few words cracked at them like a bolt of lightning. Daniel glanced at his friends and then back at the prince of the eunuchs. He bowed, trying to cover his dismay. "It will be as you command, my lord."

"Then it is well." The chief eunuch turned to go. "The Melzar will come around later to see that you get a portion of the meat that remains."

"That is not necessary," Daniel said quickly. "We are full of the bread given earlier."

Ashpenaz didn't look convinced, but he moved off anyway, waving a hand casually at them. "As you wish." Melzar followed without a backwards glance.

Daniel watched them go, trying to work loose the knot that had formed in the pit of his stomach.

Mishael grumbled under his breath, "I was a hungered for the meat."

Daniel ignored him, thinking. *Belteshazzar.* No! He might be forced to use the name in public, but in secret, with his friends, Daniel, which meant the LORD is my judge, would be his name. Never the other.

And in a few days, they would all be made eunuchs, forever slaves in the palace of the king of Babylon. Still feeling numb, he began to pray fervently.

BABYLON
In the Time of Daniel

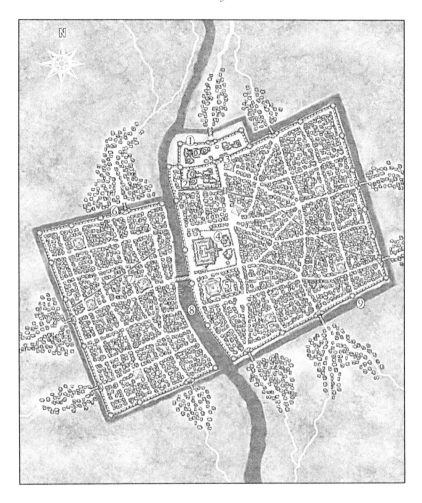

1 – Northern Fortress
2 – Southern Fortress
3 – The Ishtar Gate
4 – The Etemenanki Ziggurat
5 – The Esagila Temple
6 – The Enlil Gate
7 – An Enlil Temple
8 – The Euphrates River
9 – The Moat

23

A thousand men followed Nebuchadnezzar as he rode across the bridge spanning the moat—the first line of defense for the city of Babylon. The moat was more of a channel cut to allow the waters of the Euphrates River to run along the entire perimeter of the outer wall. It effectively made scaling ladders, siege towers, and battering rams irrelevant. His chariot, pulled by four of the strongest horses found in all of Babylon, rode quickly over the bridge and through the Enlil Gate. The fact that the gate stood opened and unbarred to his entry bode well for what he would find when he met his brother, Nabushumlishir, at the palace.

More than thirty guards, lining the tunnel through the wall, saluted and fell to their knees as he passed. He ignored them. Immediately behind him came Nebuzaradan and his other battle commanders—each and every one of them prepared for a fight.

"My lord," shouted Nebuzaradan, "beware of ambush!"

Nebuchadnezzar reluctantly pulled up, slowing the horses. He allowed his bodyguard to catch up, whereupon Nebuzaradan detailed a squad of men to run ahead of the prince.

Nebuchadnezzar asked, "Think you that Nabushumlishir will attack me in the city?"

"We know not," Nebuzaradan explained, pulling up alongside as they rode slowly down the road that ran straight as an arrow due south into the heart of the city.

Nebuchadnezzar glanced over his shoulder at the tall, forbidding wall that loomed up behind him. Archers stood poised on the battlements, but one and all, they had their bows raised in a salute, a cheer erupting from their lips. A good sign.

Nebuchadnezzar's weary army marched into the city behind him—not the bulk of the army, of course, he had left the foot soldiers with his harem and captives taken from the Levant. They would all be along in another week or so. But the numbers he did have with him would be a significant show of force in case his brother did challenge him for power.

"If not here, where would Nabushumlishir make his stand against me?" Nebuchadnezzar asked.

Nebuzaradan considered. "T'was best to stop you beyond the walls, my prince. That he has not may mean he intends to take you at the bridge."

The bridge, Nebuchadnezzar echoed in his mind.

The Euphrates River bisected the city of Babylon into east and west. Nebuchadnezzar had entered the city on the west side of the river, which meant he had to cross the only bridge that connected the two halves of the city—a bridge his father, Nabopolassar, had built. Thinking of his father, dead now, hardened Nebuchadnezzar's resolve. If Nabushumlishir indeed intended to make his stand on the bridge, there would be little room for battle. It was a choke point with the higher wall and stout gate on the east bank of the river. From there, archers could sweep the bridge clean of men without much effort. Nebuchadnezzar would be at a severe disadvantage.

They passed a temple dedicated to Ishtar—one of several in the city—and continued south toward the Enlil temple and the road that led to the bridge.

Nebuchadnezzar glanced over at Nebuzaradan, whose eyes constantly scanned the road for any threat. People had begun to line the street as word preceded him, bowing and cheering as Nebuchadnezzar rode by. Again, he ignored them all. "You fear assassination, do you not?" he asked.

Nebuzaradan, without taking his eyes from his surroundings, said, "Aye. If Nabushumlishir will not confront you directly, then a cowardly arrow shot from the shadows might be the quickest way to the throne for him. He knows you are beloved by the people."

"Howbeit, so is he," Nebuchadnezzar said, suddenly eying askance the people lining the street. If anyone was a match for Nebuchadnezzar, it would be without a doubt Nabushumlishir. The man was brilliant, an able commander, and an accomplished administrator and builder. His brother had overseen the construction of the moats that surrounded the outer walls of the entire city. Under their father's orders, he had begun restoration of the palace and raised the Etemenanki ziggurat to new heights.

Thinking of the ziggurat caused Nebuchadnezzar to look to the east. The mammoth temple to Marduk rose high into the sky, towering above the walls and any other building in Babylon.[1] Directly to the south of the ziggurat, lay the Esagil, the earthly home of Marduk. Though not nearly as tall, the Esagil was still a spectacular building, a true honor to the patron god of Babylon.

"Think you that Nabushumlishir would be so cowardly to slay me in the streets with an arrow to the back?" Nebuchadnezzar asked his captain. "I would not have thought him so."

"I too," Nebuzaradan replied. "Howbeit, the lust of power has created strange behavior in a man afore. He will have no better chance than now." He paused and then added, "And he may yet use your wives and sons as hostage."

---

[1] The height of the Etemenanki ziggurat is disputed by scholars, but was likely between 216 and 300 feet high, including the temple at the top. This is roughly equivalent to a 20 to 30 story tall building.

Nebuchadnezzar fell silent, thinking it over and hoping it wouldn't come to a battle. He'd risk it, even if it cost him the wives and sons he'd left in the city, but civil war was never a pleasant outcome. It depleted needed resources and wasted lives. And if Amytis, his favored wife, was slain in the heat of the struggle, it might spark a war with the Medes. Her father, the king of Media, would not look favorably upon her death.

Forcing away such thoughts, he studied Babylon. He felt a burning desire to make her the greatest city in the whole earth. During the journey back, he had formed many plans to accomplish just that. He wanted to build a new palace, rebuild the gates of Ishtar, and create a processional way that led right to the Etemenanki and Esagil.

And then there was his wife, Amytis of Media, and her longing for the lush vegetation of her homeland. Nebuchadnezzar envisioned gardens, suspended in the air and with cascading waterfalls. He would do that for her—if she yet lived. There was no knowing what Nabushumlishir had done in Nebuchadnezzar's absence.

They reached the bridge road and turned west, heading back toward the Euphrates River and the Etemenanki ziggurat. Nebuzaradan had detailed scouts to run on ahead to make sure the way was both clear and safe. One came running back.

"My lord," he said, falling to his knees and bowing, "I have tidings!"

"Speak," Nebuchadnezzar commanded, pulling up. He didn't want to stop, but if danger lay ahead, he needed to know it.

"Prince Nabushumlishir stands upon the bridge against your arrival, my prince!"

Nebuchadnezzar felt a chill slither its way up his spine. "With force?"

"Nay, alone. None else is with him."

The crown prince turned to Nebuzaradan. "What is this?"

His commander looked troubled. "I know not, my prince."

Nebuchadnezzar only considered the matter for a moment. Finally, he slapped the reins against the horses' backs, forcing them forward. The scout had to jump out of the way or be trampled. "It is no matter," he said. "The gods' will must be done. I will face my brother and hear his words."

"It might be a deception," Nebuzaradan said, moving his own chariot up alongside.

People continued to line the way, and a wave of bowing humanity followed him as he proceeded. What bothered Nebuchadnezzar the most, however, was that not a single priest for any god had come out to greet him. It was troubling.

"It may be as you say," Nebuchadnezzar agreed. "Yet I will hear his words."

They reached the bridge soon after. The stone span arched across the river to a massive open gate beneath equally impressive walls that followed the course of the river. Glazed bricks of various colors lined the bridge, showing images of lions and dragons. The bridge was wide enough to ride six chariots across side by side.

And upon the center of the bridge stood a man of dark complexion. A blue hat covered his head, and his square, braided beard looked immaculate even from this distance. His robes of office hung off wide shoulders. Golden lions had been woven into the cloth around the collar and sleeves. He bore no weapon that Nebuchadnezzar could see.

"Wait here," Nebuchadnezzar ordered, stepping down from his chariot and handing the reins to a soldier standing near.

"My lord?" Nebuzaradan said, the doubt in his voice clear.

"Do as I command. I would speak with my brother alone."

Not looking to see if his commands were being carried out, Nebuchadnezzar strode onto the bridge in full battle armor, sword slapping at his thigh as he walked. An entire army of archers could appear on the battlements above and turn him into a porcupine in an instant. At this distance, his iron armor would only deflect some of the missiles. He'd left his shield behind in the chariot.

NEBUCHADNEZZAR

But no attack came, and his brother stood placidly enough on the bridge, waiting for Nebuchadnezzar to reach him. For a moment, Nebuchadnezzar wondered if his brother would challenge him to single combat—no, that would be foolish. Of the two, Nebuchadnezzar was by far the greater warrior. His brother possessed other skills.

The two brothers met in the center of the bridge. For a long moment, Nabushumlishir said nothing, looking Nebuchadnezzar over. Finally, he dropped to his knees and bowed, forehead to the bridge stones. "The king, our father, is dead," he intoned in a ritualistic voice, "and Babylon has no king. Would you, Nebuchadnezzar, son of Nabopolassar, sit upon the throne of the whole world under the light of Marduk and in favor with Ishtar?"

Of everything that had gone through Nebuchadnezzar's mind, this hadn't been it. Yet of all possibilities, this was by far the most preferred. "I would," he said after finding his voice. "I would restore Babylon to her former glory and strength. By the grace of Nabu and by right of ascension as eldest son of Nabopolassar, I will bear the crown."

He'd said it loudly, his voice carrying over the waters to both sides of the river. An explosive cheer rang out from both sides.

The soon to be king, pulled his brother up. "Rise, brother, for I would greet you."

Of equal height, the two brothers embraced. When Nabushumlishir pulled back, he said solemnly, "I have kept Babylon for my lord, the king. Our father rests in state, embalmed after the Egyptian style. Now that you have returned, we must bury him with all honor."

"This is well spoken, my brother," Nebuchadnezzar said. "In truth, I feared you had sought the throne for yourself."

Nabushumlishir blinked and then looked surprised. "Not I! Our father named you heir. I would only continue the construction of the city entrusted to me as afore—by your leave, of course."

Nebuchadnezzar laughed. "You have it! And we have much to discuss for I have thought long on what must be done. I would have your counsel and advice on it. And—" he gestured toward the northwest "—treasures come which will help in the construction."

"You have much plunder?"

"Some, not nearly enough, but enough to fund much."

Nabushumlishir's eyes lit up. "Praise be to Marduk! Tell me, what found you in the Levant? We only had word of your victory over the Egyptians. Word reached us of captives from Judah, but what else?"

Nebuchadnezzar gestured for his men to begin crossing the bridge. "Aye. I have captives, brother, young men—boys—who are full of wisdom and cunning. They will become eunuchs and serve us well—once they have been properly trained and prepared. The journey here was difficult, and in my haste some few were lost." Nebuchadnezzar sighed. "I wished for it not, but when word reached me of the king's death—"

"I understand, brother," Nabushumlishir said softly.

"I will appoint the Jewish captives meat from my table and wine from my stores[2] that they may stand before me in time."

"You have a keen eye for talent, my brother. This may be a greater treasure than gold."

"Aye, and think not that I will forget you in this. Some of these captives may be cunning craftsmen that may aid you in your construction."

"I will welcome such," Nabushumlishir said as Nebuchadnezzar's chariot finally arrived. Together, they stepped into the vehicle. "Howbeit, such is not done in a day and these captives are young, are they not?"

"Aye, that they are." Nebuchadnezzar paused, musing. "What think you?"

---

[2] Daniel 1:5.

"Three years," Nabushumlishir said without missing a beat. "Grant them three years nourishment[3] at the least before they stand before you and are tested. No more than five."

Nebuchadnezzar nodded slowly. "That is well spoken." He then frowned and looked about, noting who was not present with his brother to greet the returning prince. "Where be the priests?"

"The priests and your other counselors await you at the palace to anoint you king. I must warn you, there is some dissension among their ranks."

That chill returned, and Nebuchadnezzar's shoulders stiffened as the chill turned to a white-hot flash of rage. If the priests resisted his ascension to the throne, he would be in for a battle that could draw in every citizen of Babylon. There were no fewer than forty-three temples in Babylon dedicated to over thirty of the gods. In their eternal conflict, the gods waxed and waned in power and authority. Right now, according to the priesthoods, Marduk, Ishtar, and Nabu were in ascendance largely thanks to the numbers of worshipers they had gathered—a direct result of Nebuchadnezzar's father's resistance to the Assyrians and their gods.

But if the priests defied his god-granted right to the throne, he would butcher each and every one of them, their wives, their children, and turn their houses into dung hills.

"What manner of dissension?" he demanded of his brother. He flicked the reins, and the brothers began moving across the bridge to the open gate beyond. Below them, the Euphrates River rolled sedately along, uncaring of the deeds and doings of kings and gods.

"They have had dreams," Nabushumlishir said, raising his voice to be heard over the noise of hooves on stone. "The gods have spoken, but the priests are at odds as to the interpretation."

The gods had often spoken to Nebuchadnezzar in dreams, but interpretation was left to the magicians and priests—often one and the same—to give Nebuchadnezzar clear direction as to the will of the gods. And if truth be known, the gods were, at times, at odds

---

[3] Daniel 1:5.

with one another. To have this happen now was the absolute worst of timings.

"Why this reluctance? Tell me."

Nabushumlishir bowed, no doubt noting the quality of Nebuchadnezzar's voice. He knew better than anyone how dangerous it was to provoke the eldest Chaldean prince to wrath. "It concerns the city of the foreign God of Israel, Jerusalem, and the captives you have brought. The dreams, they say, have been troubling. Some are of the thought that you should slay all the inhabitants of that rebellious city, every man, woman, and child, and remove their remembrance from under heaven. Their God has caused problems in times past and must not be allowed to have a place among our gods."

"They wish me to slay them all?"

"That is the thought of some," Nabushumlishir conceded. "They say it is the will of Marduk."

That struck a resonating chord in Nebuchadnezzar's heart. He relied much upon the gods and their wisdom. They had freed Babylon from Assyria and guided both his hand and his father's hand in their many victories since. He would defy the gods at his peril. "Very well, I shall lend an ear to their claims. And if I must, I will slay them all." He left it intentionally vague if he meant either the Jews or the priests.

In his heart, he was willing to do both.

24

With his brother in the chariot beside him, Nebuchadnezzar wasted no time in racing to the palace. Nebuzaradan and a score of other chariots rumbled along behind in escort. Along the way, Nabushumlishir caught Nebuchadnezzar up on the news of the city and the progress of the various building projects their father had begun but hadn't quite finished before he died. They also discussed the manner of his death.

"We have found no evidence of mischief," Nabushumlishir said. "The gods took him in his sleep."

Pulling at his square beard, Nebuchadnezzar kept a firm grip on the reins with his other hand. He hardly saw the ziggurat as they clattered past. "I had no wish for him to die. He was truly a mighty king."

"This is so," his brother agreed. "But perchance he foresaw his end. Did he not uplift you to rule alongside of him these two years past? He always intended you to rule beside him and succeed him upon the throne after his death."

The whole city knew this. Two years before, their father had announced the joint rulership and succession. Perhaps even then he knew his end was nigh. Still though, despite that Nebuchadnezzar did indeed want to be king, he had not wanted to succeed his father this soon. He had wanted to present a conquered Egypt to his father—and the pharaoh's detached head as a trophy.

And then there was no more time to reminisce. The chariots arrived at the palace courtyard in a clatter of hooves and shouting men. Servants lined the roadway leading to the main gates of the palace. Reconstruction of the palace was well under way, but incomplete. A massive slave labor force of mixed races had been brought in by Nebuchadnezzar's father, and many of these now lay prostrate on the hot stones as the crown prince descended from his chariot and strode toward the gates of the palace.

Over one hundred rooms existed in the palace, and with the reconstruction, half that again would be added. But there was only one room Nebuchadnezzar sought. The palace itself was a fortification of its own. If the city walls were ever breached, an enemy force would discover another set of stout walls surrounding the palace, prepared and able to defend those within.

Nebuchadnezzar entered another courtyard and turned left. The doors to the throne room stood open, and within, he could see the glazed bricks that showed brilliant decorations in shades of blue, white, and yellow. Directly across from the open doors in a niche built for that purpose sat a golden throne on a rectangular, raised platform. To either side, rows of priests, magicians, and wise ones of the city had gathered.

The throne room wasn't the grandest room, built more for utility than to bring honor to the king. That would change, Nebuchadnezzar vowed. As the voice and hands of the gods, the palace had but one essential function: to bring him honor and glory.

His entrance, still in battle armor, cut off conversation much like an arrow to the heart would. Looking neither to the left nor to the right, Nebuchadnezzar strode across the room and mounted the steps to the throne. There, he paused, looking at the empty seat where his father had sat. In another room nearby, his father would be laid out in state, his body embalmed in the Egyptian style, awaiting burial. He bowed his head and offered silent tribute to the man who had brought greatness back to Babylon and initiated Marduk's revenge upon the Assyrians. In the line of great Babylonian kings beginning with Hammurabi, Nabopolassar had brought Marduk back to preeminence in the world.

Finally, he turned to sweep his hard gaze across the men gathered in his throne room. Lifting his voice, he said, "I, Nebuchadnezzar, second by that name, have returned. As it was the will of the gods that my father, descendant of those kings of times past, ascend to the throne of Babylon, so too do I stand ready to take upon me this mantel of kingship and continue the will of the gods. Is there any here who would say me nay?"

The high priest of Marduk, a willowy fellow with white hair and deep lines running down his face stepped forward from the crowd and came to face the king directly. In his hands he held a golden crown. The last time Nebuchadnezzar had seen that crown, it had rested upon the brow of his father. The priest bowed and spoke in a sonorous voice, "It is not in us, O king, to say you nay. The gods have spoken, and you are our king, the vessel of the gods upon earth!" He strode forward, mounted the steps, and knelt before Nebuchadnezzar, holding up the crown.

Carefully, reverently, Nebuchadnezzar reached out with hands strong enough to crush the crown if he desired and took hold of it, setting it upon his head. A perfect fit. It didn't even feel heavy. Adjusting his sword, he sat upon the throne in a clank of iron armor.

"Bow to your king," he ordered softly. The throne room had been constructed to carry his voice to every corner. As the last syllable left his mouth, musicians hidden in the recesses of the room struck up a triumphant chord with their musical instruments. A symphony of sound washed over the room, and as one, every man in the room prostrated themselves before him, foreheads touching the stone floor.

Nebuchadnezzar nodded, satisfied. That part had been painless, at least. Now for the hard part. He let the music play on for a time and then raised a hand to silence the musicians. "Rise and lend me your wisdom, magicians and priests of Babylon, for I have heard of dissension among you, and I like it not." He leaned forward as the wise men rose back to their feet, casting apprehensive looks at one another. "What say the gods of the captives from Judah?"

The high priest of Marduk frowned. "It is not the captives we fear, O king, but their God. The records regarding the God of Israel are clear. He may bring us much trouble. It would be best, O king, to raze the city, destroy His people all, and blot out the remembrance of the God of Israel from under heaven. Only then may we be secure from His wrath."

"And yet," Nebuchadnezzar said, his voice lowering dangerously, "the God of Israel has given into my hand His people to have dominion over them. This came to me in dreams. I was to be His vessel in this matter." His eyes narrowed. "To bring a crucible upon this people."

This started up shocked murmuring among the many priests in attendance.

"The God of Israel has spoken to you?" the high priest of Marduk snapped in an incredulous tone of voice, momentarily forgetting himself. He bowed again. "Forgive me, my king, I am astounded."

Nebuchadnezzar could afford to be magnanimous. "Forgiven. But know that I have dominion of all Israel and its people. They will serve us and our gods, for they have forsaken their God and blasphemed His name. Therefore, fear not the God of Israel. Let all here instead rejoice for I have taken hostages of their children, boys who are cunning in wisdom and science who may yet stand before me and serve me, bringing prosperity to our kingdom. This is the will of the gods."

The priest bowed his head in acknowledgment. "This may be so, O king, yet the Jews are a stiff-necked people. How long until they rebel?"

Nebuchadnezzar's voice hardened. "In that day, they will know my wrath, and we will bring ruin down upon their heads." He stood then, causing everyone to prostrate again. "Now is not the time for such talk. Today, I have ascended to the throne of my father. Let this day be the first day of the first month of the year. Let there be a mighty feast to Ishtar and Marduk. Let the people rejoice and be merry. For tomorrow will be a day of mourning. Tomorrow, we bury my father, the king."

This had been anticipated. Messengers ran from the throne room to begin spreading word and start the festival. Horns would sound throughout the city, announcing Nebuchadnezzar's ascendancy to the throne of Babylon. There was a lot to do, a lot that must yet be done. Egypt still waited, like an injured lion, for his return. And with the projects he had in mind, he would need more slaves—and wealth. A new palace needed to be built, a new wall, and new gardens.

And soon, the Jewish boys from Israel would arrive and begin their true education. A picture of one young man in particular stood out to Nebuchadnezzar. He didn't recall his name, but it didn't matter. By now, Ashpenaz would have given each of the Jews a Babylonian name to honor Chaldean gods. But that boy...something about him had stuck out to Nebuchadnezzar. The prince of the eunuchs had high hopes for the lad, and Nebuchadnezzar expected the eunuch's faith to be rewarded. He would use up such talent, drain it dry in the construction of his kingdom if he must. The boy's God had given him into Nebuchadnezzar's hand, and he would use him until there was nothing left to be used. For *that* was the will of the gods.

"Fetch me my sons and wives," he commanded, dismissing the Jewish captives from his mind. "Let the festival begin!"

25

When Babylon at last came into view, Daniel stopped, staring in wonder. He had never imagined a city could be so large. Rising out of swampy terrain, Babylon shone like a jewel, gleaming against the flat landscape. Even the river that bisected the city looked dull in comparison. A tower, one that might even sit upon the same spot as the Tower of Babel once had, rose into the sky, taller than any manmade construction Daniel had ever seen.

"This cannot be," Hananiah breathed out in astonishment next to Daniel. "The city must rival Jerusalem by ten times at the least!"

Ashpenaz and Melzar, walking nearby, looked over, grinning. "Say again in Chaldean, young one."

Haltingly, Hananiah repeated himself, this time in the tongue of the Chaldeans.

Ashpenaz answered, "Nay, young one," the chief eunuch said, "by sixteen times at the least. I have beheld your city, and though grand it may be, it pales in the shadow of Babylon."

Daniel had to bite back an angry retort. Anything that outshone Jerusalem must be an abomination.

Mishael, hopping up and down to see better, pointed toward the city. "What manner of tower is that?"

Every eye within earshot fastened on the massive tower that jutted into the sky. "That is the stairway to heaven, young Meshach," explained Ashpenaz. "It is named Etemenanki, meaning the foundation of heaven and earth. It is so that our prayers and sacrifices may be closer to heaven where the gods reside. Perhaps, one day, you will ascend its steps and offer tribute to Ishtar, the Queen of Heaven."

That caused most of Mishael's enthusiasm to fade away much as the desert soaks up a drop of water, and he fell unnaturally silent. It took the rest of the boys a bit longer to wade through the unfamiliar language.

Daniel struggled to reconcile what he was seeing with what he had always believed. To him, Jerusalem was the center of the whole world. Surely, nothing could be grander! But his eyes were not deceiving him. The chief eunuch was not boasting, but merely stating a fact. Babylon was at least sixteen times the size of Jerusalem. And looking at the tower that dominated the skyline, not even Solomon's temple could compare in size and grandeur. It irked Daniel. Nothing should be more majestic than Jerusalem and the temple to Jehovah! But here, man had erected a monument to a false god that rivaled anything the Hebrews had ever done for their God. Daniel's irritation turned to shame.

He had to remind himself that no matter how grand the buildings and temples to the Chaldean gods were, they lacked the presence of the one, true God, Jehovah. Back in Jerusalem sat the ark of the LORD…unless Nebuchadnezzar had pillaged it. But Daniel hadn't seen the ark among the vessels taken from the temple. Many of the other vessels had been paraded before the boys—an effort, Daniel was sure, to prove Chaldean superiority and further discourage the Hebrew boys from thinking of escape—but not the ark. That gave him hope that the new king of Babylon had allowed the ark to stay in Jerusalem.

Daniel remembered suddenly the prophet Jeremiah talking about saving the ark. He'd nearly forgotten. A spark of hope blossomed in his heart. Perhaps the prophet had indeed saved the ark—somehow. He prayed it was so.

Regardless, if the ark remained yet in Jerusalem, then so did the presence of the LORD. It was why Daniel now prayed always toward Jerusalem.

"What now will become of us?" Daniel whispered to himself.

But the prince of the eunuchs heard and turned to the young prince, giving him a reproving look. Daniel had spoken Hebrew, yet he answered regardless, "Fear not, Belteshazzar, for thus it has been ordained that you might stand before the king of all the earth and serve him."

Daniel winced. Every time he heard his new name, he felt soiled, but he dared not complain. Not about that.

The chief eunuch continued, "Word has come that Nebuchadnezzar has been crowned king. He now stands as the vessel of the gods upon the throne of Babylon." He eyed Daniel and his friends as well as the other boys who had stopped when Babylon first came into view. His fat face, too big for his eyes, glistened with sweat. "You fear becoming eunuchs. I will not deceive you; it is not without pain, but the pain will pass, and then you may take your rightful place beside the king of all the earth. Harken, children of Israel. This is your only path forward. Because you are not of the Chaldean people, this is the only way you may stand before Nebuchadnezzar. It is better than the mines where death comes in short years."

Daniel's legs quivered. Since learning of their fate, there had been much talk about escaping among the four of them, but always the picture of Jokim's slit throat acted as an effective deterrent. No one could see a way out—except for taking one's own life. One lad, whom Daniel only knew in passing, had done just that, taking his own life by drowning himself in the Euphrates River, so great was his fear of becoming a eunuch. The body had been left to float down river, food for the carrion birds and other scavengers.

But ever since the covenant was made to the Babylonian gods, most of the captive boys from Jerusalem had surrendered to the Chaldeans' intentions to convert them to their way of life.

The prince of the eunuchs surged ahead suddenly toward a body of riders that had emerged from the city and were racing toward the captives. Daniel supposed it to be orders from the king as to the disposition of the returning army. Melzar, after a long, penetrating look at the four boys, hurried up to catch his master. Hananiah and Mishael joined Azariah up ahead, leaving Daniel momentarily alone as they completed the last leg of their journey to Babylon.

"He will not save you, Belteshazzar," a voice suddenly spoke in his ear.

Daniel jerked and spun around. "My name is Daniel," he growled out to the boy who had snuck up on him. "As yours is Ziph."

The taller boy shook his head. "No longer. My name is Naramsin, he who exalts Sin."

Daniel's eyes went flat. "And *do* you exalt the false god Sin?"

Ziph's smile would have looked at home on a jackal. "Perhaps, but I will exalt any who will exalt me. You had best remember that, *Belteshazzar*. I have been named captain of the Hebrew captives, and at my word you may live or die."

Daniel snorted. "You think too highly of yourself, *Ziph*. The prince of the eunuchs appointed you captain only because you were first to make the unholy vow to Marduk, but your power does not extend to me or to my friends. The God of our fathers will deliver us out of your hands."

Daniel's enemy quivered in rage. "You will bow before the gods of Chaldea, or you will die. I will not risk my head because of you. You saw with your own eyes what the Chaldeans do to those who disobey. So you will obey, *Belteshazzar,* or you will die. I will *not* die alongside you."

Azariah had finally spotted Ziph and strode toward them, his face as hard as granite and as sharp as a finely honed blade. Ziph noted the bigger lad and gave Daniel a crooked smile. "You will not always have your dog around to protect you. You will do as I command—as the Chaldeans command."

"I will obey my God, Ziph—no other."

"Then you will die."

Daniel nodded. "Then I will die."

Snarling, Ziph whipped around and darted away before Azariah could catch him. The large lad plowed up to Daniel, his eyes watching the retreating back of the son of Jucal. "What said he?"

"He spoke out of both sides of his mouth," Daniel said dismissively. "There was little truth in his words." But in fact, Daniel knew the lad's words carried a large measure of truth. If he became too problematic for the Babylonians, they would kill him. Of that he had no doubt.

"I like not that the chief eunuch appointed him captain over us," Azariah said emphatically.

Daniel nodded and began walking toward Hananiah and Mishael who waited up ahead. If he didn't get moving, the soldiers would encourage him to do so with spear and sword. "Beware of Naam also. I fear he would not hesitate to slay us in our sleep if he thought he could do so without recompense."

They joined the two sons of Elishama and moved toward the massive city awaiting them. Hananiah heard Daniel's last words and said, "We must walk a line. One step to either side and we may die. I like it not."

Mishael grinned mischievously, "What now, brother? I think you enjoy the danger much."

"Hold your tongue," his brother snapped. "I fear our fate. No matter the words of the chief eunuch, I fear becoming as he is."

DANIEL

Daniel heard the anguish in his friend's voice, but it was Azariah who surprised him by saying, "Aye, I would rather die."

The way he said those words caused Daniel to take note. An implacable resistance had sprung up in his friend's posture. One boy had already taken his life rather than be made a eunuch. No doubt others were considering a similar path, but Daniel had not thought that his friend would be among them. He had missed the signs, and seeing the determined set of Azariah's jaw, he knew his friend's life hung by a thread. He would take his own life if he must.

But Daniel felt sure this was not the path the LORD God of their fathers would have them take. He reached out and gripped Azariah's arms, forcing the much larger lad to look at him. "Say it not, my friend. Speak not of taking your own life."

"I will do as I must." The words were said with no angst, but with simple resolution.

"Nay!" The word whipped out of Daniel like a scourge, surprising all of them by its force. "You will not do this. Harken, Azariah, son of Michaiah, this is not the end of us, but the beginning. The LORD our God may allow this shame to come upon us, but for eunuchs who keep the LORD's sabbaths there are blessings upon his head. Is this not so, Hananiah?"

"You speak of the prophet Isaiah," the short lad said in a surprised tone. "I have copied his words under my father's eyes."

"What say those words," Daniel commanded, not taking his eyes off Azariah.

"Neither let the eunuch say, 'Behold, I am a dry tree.' For thus saith the LORD unto the eunuchs that keep My sabbaths, and choose the things that please Me, and take hold of My covenant, 'Even unto them will I give in mine house and within my walls a place and a name better than of sons and of daughters: I will give them an everlasting name that shall not be cut off.'"[1]

"Harken to the words of the prophet, Azariah. We must take hold of His covenant even as we are—as we will be—eunuchs. We

---

[1] Isaiah 56:3-5.

shall have a name better than that of sons and daughters, an everlasting name, that will not be cut off. Believe you those words?"

For a long moment, Azariah said nothing. Neither did he look at Daniel, but kept his eyes fixed on the approaching city of Babylon, the towering walls, the moat that ran around the city, and the towering ziggurat that rose from the earth like a blot upon the land. It was a dark land, an evil city that they would soon call home. All of them knew it. All of them feared it. But as Daniel had said, this was not the end.

When Azariah spoke, he surprised Daniel. "I am *not* a dry tree."

Daniel thought on those words, turning them over in his mind. "This is true. Of a surety, we are *not* dry trees. This is our crucible. It will change us forever." He paused, thinking of the prophet Jeremiah's words. "He is the potter and we the clay. Though marred, He may remake us into a vessel of honor."

"A name better than sons and daughters?" Mishael asked.

"Aye, vessels of honor."

Azariah finally looked at Daniel and bowed his head. "I will endure, Daniel, son of Elnathan, at your word and the word of our God. I will endure this crucible and be His crucible."

"We all shall," Daniel whispered, coming to terms with the dual meaning of the word crucible. With acceptance came determination as they walked into the shadow cast by Babylon. "As we four shall be."

26

Jeremiah couldn't stop the muscles in his cheek from twitching nervously. So, he paced. The movement helped him focus on something other than his dread. Baruch had been gone a long time, much too long in Jeremiah's estimation.

Only Nehushta and a maid currently remained with him in Elnathan's house, where for the last three months or so, Jeremiah had recited the words of the LORD to Baruch who had faithfully written them down upon a scroll.[1] The fast day appointed by Seraiah the high priest had finally come and Jerusalem was filled with people from throughout the land of Judah, all come to fast and pray for deliverance from Babylon.

How King Jehoiakim justified this fact to the Chaldean delegation left behind by Nebuchadnezzar, Jeremiah didn't know and didn't care. Knowing the king, he had found some way to deceive the Chaldeans.

---

[1] Jeremiah 36:17-18.

Nehushta broke the silence as she came into the outer chamber of the house. "There has been no word yet, my lord?"

Jeremiah looked at her askance. He didn't understand the woman. That she was intelligent and cunning was beyond dispute, but until recently, she had been willing to serve other gods if it pleased her husband the king. Since being put away for the abominations done in her flesh by the Chaldeans, she had leapt at the chance to aid Jeremiah and her father. Her insight and advice had been invaluable, but the prophet couldn't help but feel that the former queen had vengeance in her heart. He kept finding himself wondering if she was with child. Reports made mention that two others of the former wives of King Jehoiakim were now with child. The fate of those children would not be pleasant. Jehoiakim had already sacrificed one young son to the arms of Molech not two years past, and these children would remind him only of the shame done to him.

Jeremiah started, realizing he had not yet answered her question. "Baruch has yet to return, my lady."

She snorted softly, almost wryly. "Lady no longer, my lord, but I am most grateful for the comfort."

Jeremiah hadn't meant to comfort her. He cleared his throat. "Is there some service I may render you, my lady?"

"Nay, it is *I* who wish to serve."

Her olive skin glowed in the firelight from the hearth meant to ward off the winter chill, and her slightly slanted eyes narrowed as she regarded him. Jeremiah grew uncomfortable and unconsciously looked around for the maid. Naturally, the girl had made herself scarce, leaving him alone with the former queen. It was unseemly.

"Forgive me," Jeremiah said, "but what service may you render?" His words had bite to them, and he saw Nehushta flinch ever so slightly.

"Perhaps little, my lord, but what I have, I offer. My shame has covered me and will remain until the day I die, yet I have great love for my land, and I offer what knowledge I possess of the king."

JEREMIAH

She had already done that. Jeremiah opened his mouth to respond when the door burst open and Baruch slid inside, slamming it shut behind him. A cold swirl of air accompanied him, fighting momentarily against the fire trying to keep the house warm. The scribe was breathing hard, his flat face, protruding brows, and boney cheekbones dripped with sweat—or precipitation. Dark clouds had been threatening rain all day.

The scribe caught sight of Jeremiah and gasped, slumping down against the door. "My lord prophet, they take the scroll to the king!"

Jeremiah forgot all about Nehushta and rushed over to his friend and helped him back to his feet. "Come, sit and tell me what you know."

The prophet helped the scribe to the low table and then sat near, waiting impatiently for his friend to speak, pushing a cup of wine toward him. The scribe gulped it down and wiped his mouth, still struggling to control his breathing. At length, he said, "I did as you bade me, my lord. I read the roll in the ears of all the people in the new gate of the higher court of the LORD's house.[2] You had the right of it. The fast has drawn much of the people in Judah to Jerusalem to seek deliverance from the Chaldeans."

"Were you accosted?"

"Nay, it was as Elnathan said. After I finished reading your words, Michaiah, the son of Gemariah went to the king's house and to the chamber of the scribes where awaited Elnathan and the other princes of the land. There he declared all the words which I had spoken while I remained safe in the house of the LORD."[3]

"Did the king hear of this?" Nehushta interrupted.

Baruch yelped in surprise, his eyes growing as large as wine jugs, and he shrunk back against the pillows. "My lady! You affrighted me!"

"Forgive me, scribe." She bowed to him.

---

[2] Jeremiah 36:10.
[3] Jeremiah 36:11-13.

Baruch licked his lips and turned his eyes to Jeremiah, who nodded. "Nay, my lady," the scribe said, regaining his composure somewhat. "But he will soon, for they show the roll to the king even now."

"How know you this?" Jeremiah demanded.

"After the princes heard the words, they sent Jehudi the son of Nethaniah to me to bring me and the roll before the princes of Judah.[4] So I took the roll in hand and went down to the king's house." Baruch's eyes widened even more, and he swallowed hard. "I freely admit that I greatly feared the king would discover my purpose."

"So you read the roll in the ears of the princes?" Jeremiah prompted.

"Aye. I sat down among them and read it in their ears."[5]

"And?"

"They were afraid, my lord." Baruch shivered. "The words fell hard upon their ears. They questioned me most stringently as to how I came to write the words. I told them that you spoke, and I wrote your words with ink. They were greatly concerned, my lord, and together they decided to bring the roll to the king and read it in his ears."[6]

Jeremiah sighed in satisfaction. "It is as we hoped. Let us pray that the king will heed the words and return with all his heart to the LORD God of Israel. Perchance we may yet avert the coming wrath."

Nehushta, who had risen from the table, looked down upon the two men, her expression unreadable. "He will heed the words," she promised. "I know my husband, and the words written in the roll are of the LORD. He will heed them."

"We can but pray," Jeremiah said.

"I must retire, my lords. I thank you for not sending me away." She called for her maid who appeared on the instant from wherever

---

[4] Jeremiah 36:14.
[5] Jeremiah 36:15.
[6] Jeremiah 36:16-18

the girl had hidden herself. The pair of women left then, retiring into one of the inner chambers, with Nehushta whispering fervently to her maid.

Jeremiah dismissed the women from his mind and leaned closer to Baruch. "Tell me, did all the princes heed the words?"

Baruch sighed. "Nay, my lord, some were most displeased, but the words of Elnathan, Delaiah, and Gemariah prevailed upon them, and they held their peace. But I fear Jerahmeel the son of Hammelech and Shelemiah the son of Abdeel, among others, will seek to turn the king's ear from the words of the scroll."

Jeremiah knew of them. Their voices in opposition would not be alone. He drummed his fingers on the tabletop, trying to think of his next move. Finally, he asked, "Have you anything to eat?"

"Nay. It is a fast day, and I would fast and pray this day as do others."

"That is well," Jeremiah approved. "The LORD favor you and hear your prayers."

At that moment, Nehushta's maid, a slip of a girl of fourteen summers, darted past the two men and out the front door, likely on some errand for her mistress. Jeremiah waited until the door closed before asking his next question. "You heard the words of Nehushta. Do you truly think the king will heed the words on the roll?"

"I know not," Baruch admitted. "Because his youngest son was taken captive—though why the Chaldeans refused to take Jeconiah and Mattaniah is beyond my ken—it may be that he will heed your words because of his love for his son."

Jeremiah rubbed his face, feeling his gritty beard. He had not washed appropriately in the last few days due to his haste in finishing the roll so that it might be read on this fast day. "I fear that the youngest son of the king is not in favor. Nehushta's son, Jeconiah, is in much favor, and he remains in Jerusalem."

"But why take the younger son and not the older?"

"I know not of a surety. I suspect much, howbeit." Jeremiah glanced around to make sure Nehushta was not near enough to overhear and lowered his voice. "Jeconiah and Mattaniah lack what the Chaldeans sought. Perhaps they lacked the wit or the cunning. Mayhap, they were not deemed fit to stand before the king of Babylon."

Baruch nodded. "And now Nebuchadnezzar is king."

Word had reached them a month back that Nabopolassar had died and that Nebuchadnezzar had been crowned king of Babylon. They now knew why the Chaldean prince had left so quickly and why he had gone north instead of south. "Aye, and his son is a cruel man. I fear what he might do unto Jerusalem if King Jehoiakim rebels against him."

"But king Jehoiakim has made overtures to Pharaoh of Egypt!"

This was, of course, an open secret, hidden perhaps only to the small delegation of Chaldean administrators left behind by Nebuchadnezzar. No response yet had been received from the king of Egypt, but one was expected any day. It was a measure of the king's desperation that he was willing to sacrifice those seventy sons, including his own, in order to pull himself out from under the yoke of the king of Babylon. That the princes of Judah would allow him to risk their sons was troubling beyond Jeremiah's comprehension.

The prophet rubbed his sore eyes. Sleep had been a luxury that had escaped him often of late. "I fear this to be an ill sign. Only submission to the king of Babylon will avert the coming wrath."

The scribe heaved another sigh. "We can but pray."

"We can," the prophet agreed.

The door opened again, and the maid returned, bearing a bundle of cloth in her arms. Her eyes, somewhat hidden behind her veil, flickered to the two men sitting around the table. She buried her face in the linen and silk and hurried away to find her mistress. Put away and shamed Nehushta might be, yet she still loved her finery and would not do without it.

The girl had left the door open and cold air seeped in, like a fox finding a bird's nest. Jeremiah went over and closed it absently, returning to his seat without saying anything further.

JEREMIAH

The conversation died then as each of the two men became lost in their own thoughts and worries. Jeremiah knew that the future of Jerusalem and her people rested upon a knife's edge. He had done all that the LORD had bidden him to do—to the point where he had never taken a wife or begat any children. This had been a command of the LORD when Jeremiah had yet been a young man.[7] The words had been hard to hear, and they had been words he had added to the roll Baruch had written. In those words, the LORD had promised such misery and woe—grievous deaths from sword and famine. Indeed, the LORD had sworn to take His peace away from the people of Israel, even His lovingkindness and mercies.[8]

But even after those words, the LORD had spoken more words, but this time they were words of restoration and redemption. Hope had laced those words, but not for this generation. They were given for a generation to come. One phrase alone, stuck out to Jeremiah and had been seared into his memory so vividly that he could never forget them: "'Therefore, behold, the days come,' says the LORD, 'that it shall no more be said, "The LORD lives that brought up the children of Israel out of the land of Egypt," but, "The LORD lives that brought up the children of Israel from the land of the north and from all the lands whither He had driven them." And I will bring them again into their land that I gave unto their fathers.'"[9]

Perhaps young Daniel would live to see that day, but Jeremiah already knew he would not. And there would be no seed of his to see that day either. His obedience not to have a family of his own weighed heavily upon his shoulders. On days like this, it weighed even heavier.

Jeremiah had no idea how long he and Baruch sat there in silence, but his recollections were shattered when the door burst open and Elnathan stumbled in. With his turban askew and nearly

---

[7] Jeremiah 16:2.
[8] Jeremiah 16:3-13.
[9] Jeremiah 16:14-15.

falling off his head and his coat open from running, he staggard toward the back of the room, shouting, "Betrayal!"

The prophet and scribe found themselves on their feet in an instant, Jeremiah not even remembering moving. "What has happened?" he shouted at Elnathan.

The prince of Judah spun around, his face a mask of rage. "Flee! You must flee!"

Jeremiah's heart nearly stopped, and he clutched at the front of his tunic as his friend's panic transferred to him.

"My daughter has betrayed you and sent word where you may be found. Even now, men come for you!"[10]

Almost Jeremiah darted from the house, but he had to know. "What of the roll? Did the king hear the word of the LORD?"

Elnathan gripped the tabletop with knuckles turned white. "Nay. He cut it with a penknife and burned the rest in the fire after only a few leaves were read.[11] I could not prevail upon him to save the roll.[12] You must flee. He comes for you." He glanced at Baruch. "He comes for both of you."

The fugitives exchanged only a single glance and then ran out the door.

---

[10] Jeremiah 36:26.
[11] Jeremiah 36:22-23.
[12] Jeremiah 36:25.

27

"Where should we go?" Baruch whispered, the sound carrying too loudly for Jeremiah's liking. Darkness of a winter night surrounded the pair as they made their way quickly into the heart of Jerusalem. Baruch's house would no longer be safe and neither was Elnathan's. Jeremiah had no house in the city. His home was in Anathoth, a small town about an hour walk north of Jerusalem. If he could get there...

"Jeremiah?"

The prophet shook himself and looked around. "Hold your tongue," he hissed back at his frightened scribe. "Give me leave to think."

"No time," Baruch hissed back, his eyes nearly rolling in fear. "They have reached Elnathan's house!"

Jeremiah looked back. Torches lit up the prince of Judah's house and men milled around the building like a kicked anthill. The fugitives had only just escaped the house before soldiers led by Jerahmeel surrounded it. Somehow, the king had discovered their whereabouts. But how? Elnathan had mentioned his daughter, but she had never left the house.

"The maid," the prophet muttered, remembering the girl leaving and returning. "She used the maid to send word to the king."

Baruch jerked, blinking. "It matters not! We must flee!"

Pulling the scribe after him, Jeremiah fled down the dark street, pulling the hood of his cloak carefully over his head. It would not do to be recognized even in the dark. Winter had come, and unseasonably cold weather had settled around the city. Rain came and went, and the stone streets were slick with it. Dark clouds hid the moon and stars, and only light from the houses gave the pair any light by which to see.

They moved quickly down the western hill of the city toward the Pool of Siloam. With the recent rains, the king had ordered the flow of water from the Gihon spring to be reduced since the reservoir was being filled now with water running down the central valley, and the spring was not needed. The tunnels of Hezekiah might be their only chance of escape. No one would think of looking for them there. And there was a house in the City of David that he could hide in until he could figure out a way to escape Jerusalem altogether.

"Come," he whispered, "we must move quickly."

Baruch saved his breath for running. Their sandals slapped against the wet stone, echoing loudly to the prophet's ears, but they kept moving, ever downward, toward the central valley and the pool. Twice, they slipped on the slick stones, but Jeremiah ignored the pain in his knee and kept on going, running to the frantic beat of his heart. All the while, he prayed that the LORD would hide them.

Suddenly, shouts filled the streets behind the fugitives. Jeremiah pressed his friend up against a wall, stopping their flight. "Be still. I must listen." Over their pounding hearts, Jeremiah listened, trying to gage if pursuit followed on their heels or if Jerahmeel had quit the chase and returned to his master.

The shouts grew closer.

Biting back a fear-induced oath, he pulled Baruch along. "Come!"

They hurried along the narrow streets, turning ever eastward and south toward the pool. Finally, Baruch seemed to realize where they were going. "My lord, there is no place wherein we may hide there!"

"There be," Jeremiah said tersely. "Have faith!"

Now, if only Jeremiah could dredge up some of that needed faith for himself. He bitterly regretted speaking up in the name of the LORD. It had truly brought him nothing but trouble and pain. And now he was running for his life. It was not justice. Not at all. The street ended at the top of a broad stone staircase that descended into a valley.

A few drops of rain struck the prophet in the face. He scowled. Not only did he have to flee for his life, but it was also raining. And cold. But perhaps the foul weather would impede their pursuers. Perhaps.

They scrambled down the steps to a sharply cut channel at the bottom of the valley. Water, perhaps calf deep, ran through it. They splashed across—the freezing water sending stabs of shock up his legs—and turned to follow the opposite bank, heading almost due south now toward the pool.

They reached it presently. Above them and to the east rose the old wall of the City of David atop a steep ridge. The only way into that part of the city was through the Valley Gate to the north. Jehoiakim would most certainly have that route guarded. It was the only way into the City of David—under normal conditions. With the rain, the water from the spring didn't need to be diverted to the Pool of Siloam. If the king followed a prior pattern, he should have ordered the spring to release its water into the Kidron Valley instead of diverting it to the pool through the tunnels Hezekiah had built over a hundred years ago. Of course, that all depended on if the rain had been enough to warrant such an action. But if the king had given the order, then the tunnels beneath the City of David should be clear and navigable.

There were a lot of ifs and shoulds in that.

A stone walkway had been built all around the pool, giving easy access to the women who came to fill their pitchers with water. Part of the pool had been separated for ritual bathing, but Jeremiah had no interest in either. He went immediately to the base of the steep slope beneath the City of David, looking for the tunnel entrance. He found it quickly. It was secured by an iron grate across the opening. Only a small trickle of water flowed out of the tunnel.

Jeremiah heaved a sigh of relief and pointed. "There is our escape."

Baruch balked. "Beneath the city!" He sounded frantic.

"It is the only way, my friend." He pointed back along their path of retreat. Torches, lighting the way for patrols, dotted the city as they flickered in and out of view, moving ever in their direction. They had time, but not a lot. "We are being herded."

"But how may we see?"

That was a problem.

Rain began to fall harder, and faintly, they could hear soldiers of the king calling one to another. "We must persevere," Jeremiah said to his friend. "The LORD has provided. He will hide us."

The scribe eyed the dark opening as one might a sepulcher with his name chiseled in the stone above the entrance. Baruch shuddered. "I will follow."

"Good man." Jeremiah slapped him on the back, trying to force a bit of courage in the man's spine. Hopefully, it would bolster his own flagging courage. "Let us go."

They found the grate heavily rusted. With little effort, they pried it away from the opening and squeezed into the dark interior. They replaced the iron grate as best they could and then turned to follow the tunnel. It would eventually be obvious to someone looking that the grate had been removed, but if God favored them, perhaps that would not happen for days.

JEREMIAH

Within moments, they were in utter blackness. Fortunately, the tunnel was narrow, and they could feel their way along the slippery incline with both hands on the stone to either side. The water was cold. The stone slick. The darkness absolute. Baruch began praying aloud, his voice echoing in the narrow tunnel. Jeremiah didn't prevent him. The sound, other than the flow of water, was all he had to cling to for his sanity's sake.

Afterward, Jeremiah couldn't rightly recall how long they were in the tunnel. It seemed to stretch on forever. At times, they had to crawl up sharp inclines—two or three times after they slipped back down. Not being able to see, Jeremiah still knew his knees, hands, and elbows were scraped bloody. Once, Jeremiah, who led, smacked his head on a low hanging ceiling. That had hurt. But they made steady progress.

After what seemed to be an eternity, they emerged into a large cave over which a building had been erected. It was lit by torches around the top, reached by a winding, stone staircase. The light was blinding, and it took several moments to adjust. They'd come to the Gihon spring at last.

Baruch, despite his dark tones, looked so pale that his skin had turned nearly white. And he shook like a leaf in a storm. Jeremiah didn't feel much better. Carefully, they went up the stone steps and exited through an arched building that lay close to the outer wall. They'd emerged onto the eastern slope of the City of David.[1]

The city lay asleep. King Jehoiakim's search had not made it this far east. Doubtlessly, since the Valley Gate was guarded, the king wouldn't think of looking for him here—assuming the king believed Nehushta. But why would he not? The woman clearly wanted to regain her husband's favor. What better way than to turn over to him his most hated enemy? Jeremiah should have never trusted the woman, but her beguiling words had lured him into incaution. He wondered if she had intended such from the very first when Elnathan had offered his home as a sanctuary to Jeremiah.

---

[1] The winding tunnel is 582 yards in length or about one-third of a mile.

Shaking his head, the prophet, climbed into the city, shivering in the damp night air. He needed a place to dry out and clean up. There was a house near. The owners had died when Nebuchadnezzar had come through the city. They had resisted, and the Chaldean king had ordered their slaughter as an example. No one went near the house now. And as cold and rainy as it was, he could light a fire within, and no one would take note—not at least until the morning.

Right now, he was ready to risk it all for a little warmth.

They found the house near the temple wall not far from Baruch's house just as Jeremiah had suspected—abandoned. They entered after a careful watch up and down the street. The furniture inside had been smashed and everything valuable taken. But with a little work and an oil lamp left hanging from a rafter, the two cold servants of the LORD were able to get a fire going.

It felt good beyond belief. The two huddled near the blaze, desperate to soak up as much warmth as they could.

With chattering teeth, Baruch asked, "Now what, my lord? Are we safe?"

"For the moment," the prophet replied, rubbing his chapped and bleeding hands. "We will stay for a time, but I think it might be best if we leave the city and go elsewhere."

The scribe's head bobbed. "That is well spoken. The king's wrath will not be so easily assuaged."

"Aye." Except Jeremiah didn't know how to get out of the city. By morning, word would have reached all the gates leading out of the city to be on the watch for Jeremiah and Baruch. And he didn't know how long until the king's attention turned elsewhere. His pride had been cut to the quick when so many of the princes had joined with Jeremiah. Some, including Elnathan, might not be safe, especially once the king ferreted out how long Jeremiah had stayed hidden in his house. But whatever the king did, he had to be wary around the Chaldean delegation watching over him. Perhaps that

JEREMIAH

would afford the princes of Judah some measure of protection. Perhaps.

Then a warmth filled the prophet from his toes to the top of his head that had nothing whatsoever to do with the fire. And he heard the LORD's voice. His body stiffened as he listened and despite the overwhelming power of the visitation, dread still filled him at the words. If King Jehoiakim disliked him now, he would be filled with an unholy wrath after he heard what the LORD had just said to him.

"We cannot yet leave the city, Baruch."

"What is this?"

"We cannot yet leave. The word of the LORD has come to me yet again." Jeremiah took a deep breath. "We are commanded to take yet another roll and write all the former words upon it that King Jehoiakim burned with fire."[2]

Baruch was silent for a long moment. Just when Jeremiah determined he would not speak, he said, "That is not all that the LORD has commanded you. I see it in your eyes."

"You are perceptive, my friend. In His name, He has commanded me to say to Jehoiakim, king of Judah, 'He shall have none to sit upon the throne of David, and his dead body shall be cast out in the day to the heat and in the night to the frost. And I will punish him and his seed and his servants for their iniquity. I will bring upon them, and upon the inhabitants of Jerusalem, and upon the men of Judah all the evil that I have pronounced against them.'"[3]

The scribe stared at Jeremiah as if he had turned mad. The prophet hardly blamed him one whit. He offered the stunned man a feeble smile and said, "I doubt me that he will harken to these words any better than the first."

His mouth hanging open in astonishment, Baruch nodded weakly. "We will be surely slain for this." His voice cracked, and he swallowed hard.

---

[2] Jeremiah 36:28.
[3] Jeremiah 36:29-31.

Jeremiah reached out and put a comforting hand on his scribe's arm. "Fear not, my friend, we are in God's hand. He has hidden us, and He will succor us as long as we abide in His will."

"And what of Urijah, the prophet slain by King Jehoiakim? Was he not in the LORD's will when he was slain?"

Jeremiah's mind flashed back to that day, months ago, when the prophet of the LORD had been callously slain by the king of Judah. The LORD had permitted it. He had no good answer, so he said in all honesty, "I know not. But live or die, we are called to be the LORD's vessels. We are in His hands, and He will mold us to the shape and use of His choice. We can but yield or not yield."

Jeremiah watched a transformation take place in the scribe's posture. He sat straighter and his shoulders no longer slumped. "Crucibles of God," the scribe said softly. "We are tried in His crucibles to become His vessels."

"Is there anything better?"

"Nay. For this, I will die gladly."

Jeremiah found a grin spreading across his face. "Then we must find you new instruments of writing and a new roll. For we have much to write as we did afore, though the LORD has bid me to write many more such words."[4]

Baruch flexed the fingers of his writing hand, his eyes staring at them. "Mayhap that I know where we can find what is needed."

"Then we will do so in the morning. Perchance God will see us alive until the work is done."

"Until the work is done," Baruch echoed, his voice sounding more at peace than ever.

Jeremiah also basked in the peace that had descended upon him. No, he reveled in it, for he knew that soon, trouble and pain would once again become part of his life. But in this moment, he gave thanks to his God for His wonderful mercies.

---

[4] Jeremiah 36:32. This is very likely the book of Jeremiah we have today.

EPILOGUE

69 YEARS LATER

Nitocris, queen of Babylon, wished her husband, Nabonidus, would return to the city. His absence, though necessary in his eyes, had only promoted their son's excesses. And with her husband gone, Belshazzar, their unimaginative son, ruled in Babylon, and there wasn't a thing Nitocris could do to stem his seemingly obliviousness to the realities around him. If her husband was only home—no, she couldn't think like that. Her father, Nebuchadnezzar, had taught her better. A queen did not give in to despair.

A queen ruled.

Nitocris sat in an ornate chair, gilded in flowers—a gift from her husband from his plunder taken during his campaign against Tayma—and tapped her long, painted nails on the beautiful armrest. Several waterfalls fell over open windows on their way down to ground level. Birds and other animals—imported from as far away as India and Ethiopia—created a cacophony of subtle and soothing noise meant to put one at ease.

It wasn't working.

"Mother," Ennigadi-Nanna said in her soft, musical voice, "What weighs upon your mind?"

Nitocris looked over at her daughter and suppressed a sigh at the vacant look displayed on the woman's face. None of her children possessed the cunning and intelligence of Nitocris' father—or of herself. She wished it otherwise, and often wondered if the gods had cursed her. Not that her only son Belshazzar wasn't cunning. He had, after all, orchestrated the assassination of King Labashi-Marduk and managed to install his father upon the throne of Babylon, making Nitocris queen. But Belshazzar, like his sisters, lacked…insight and prudence. Her son's aptitude for rule was mitigated by the fact that her husband yet lived. For some reason, Belshazzar simply thought his father could fix whatever mess he created. It was absurd.

Nitocris lifted a hand toward Ennigadi-Nanna. "You need not worry, daughter. I was only thinking of your father and how I wished for his return."

Ennigadi-Nanna's face screwed up in obvious confusion. "Is not Father putting down the rebel Ugbaru?"

"He is," Nitocris agreed.

Ennigadi-Nanna sat back on a bed of cushions as if the matter was now settled and snagged a cluster of grapes to plop into her plump mouth. The girl ate too much. With the overconfidence born to the ignorant, she said, "Then all is well."

But it wasn't. Ugbaru, angry at the religious reforms her husband was trying to impose upon Babylon and upon the many provinces overseen in the kingdom, had rebelled and turned to the Persians under King Cyrus. Nitocris knew something of the Persian king. He was resolute and determined. In fact, he reminded her of her late father, Nebuchadnezzar. Cyrus had granted Ugbaru a military command, and even now the rebel was leading a massive force of Persians and Medes toward Babylon. With them came some upstart Mede who called himself King Darius. But all word about the conflict had stopped coming days ago, and Nitocris knew that for an ill sign.

Unfortunately, her son, instead of readying the defenses of the city, had decided to throw a massive feast for a thousand of his lords.[1] Much like his sister, he too had been dismissive of the

---

[1] Daniel 5:1.

EPILOGUE

rebellion and of the Persians. After all, as everyone did know, Babylon was the greatest city in all the world, defended by a double wall of sixty-five cubits high and half as thick. A moat surrounded the entire city outside the walls. It was a wonder of the world, and no army had even come close to breaching the walls. It was inconceivable that any army ever would.

Nitocris hadn't been invited to the feast—not that she would have gone anyway—but apparently, it was unseemly to revel in a drunken feast when one's mother was in attendance. Belshazzar's wives had been commanded to attend, but not a single word to his mother, Nitocris. She had been hearing music from the feast for some time, loud and raucous—though it had stopped of a sudden about half an hour ago. Well, the musicians surely needed a break.

The queen brushed some of her graying hair aside and prayed to Sin that her son would put away his childishness and attend to the realm as a proper king should. In her experience, the gods were fickle, so she didn't expect much to come of it.

A eunuch burst into the room, his eyes wild and fear clearly etched into every line of his face. "My queen! You must come!" He fell to his knees and then to his face, his body quivering.

Nitocris rose to her feet, feeling the aches in her joints. Age had caught up to her at last, though many would still call her beautiful. "What ails, you?" she demanded. She cast a quick look at her daughter, but the girl only stared wide-eyed at the eunuch, a grape frozen halfway to her mouth and juice running down her chin to stain her robe.

"The gods have delivered a message to the king!"

"My husband or my son?" she snapped, unsure where this was going.

"Your son, O queen! The hand of a giant did appear to your son while he feasted and wrote upon the plaster with a finger of gold!"[2]

---

[2] Daniel 5:5.

A spike of fear slithered up the queen's spine. "You have seen this handwriting? The hand?"

"I have, my queen! As have all who were at the feast. The king, your son, has called all the astrologers, soothsayers, and wisemen of Babylon to attend him and interpret the writing on the wall."[3]

"Interpret? What says this writing?"

"None do know. It is in a tongue none do understand."

Nitocris adjusted her robes. "Well? What say the wisemen?"

"They know not!"[4] the eunuch wailed. "We are forsaken and cursed!"

"Hold your tongue or I will have it removed," the queen snapped in irritation.

No one could read the script? None in all Babylon? Such a thing would spell disaster and could easily mark her son for death in the eyes of the inhabitants of the city. If no one could read it…inspiration lit her eyes. No, there was yet one in Babylon who could read it, one in whom the wisdom of the gods resided.

"Take me to my son," she ordered, sweeping by the eunuch and her still reclining daughter. "Make haste!"

The eunuch leaped to his feet and ran out ahead of the queen, snapping orders in a tremulous voice. Nitocris did not truly need an escort and she didn't wait. She knew where to find her son. She set off with the determination she'd inherited from her father, Nebuchadnezzar.

The walk to the lower throne room was a misty, humid one. The hanging gardens built by Nebuchadnezzar for her mother, Amytis of Media, was beautiful, but perhaps impractical. She had to take a winding course to reach the feasting hall. The massive double doors were open, so she strode in unimpeded—and unannounced.

No one was looking at her. They were all staring in slack-jawed silence at the precise handwriting engraved in the wall over against

---

[3] Daniel 5:7.
[4] Daniel 5:8.

EPILOGUE

the candlesticks.[5] The words seemed to glow to Nitocris' eyes. She couldn't imagine the hand that could write such words. Elegant and done with such perfection that all the craftsmen in Babylon could not match, the writing fairly blazed upon the wall. But, much like everyone else, they were unintelligible markings to her eyes.

"Mother! Do you see?"

The voice that struck at her quaked and cracked. She tore her eyes from the wall and found her son. Belshazzar stood before the writing, one hand holding tightly to a table. His knees were knocking together so that she could hear it. His robe was stained with more than wine, and a stink emanated from him.[6]

"None do know what the words say! None can read it! What evil has befallen me, Mother! I must know!"

With narrowed eyes, Nitocris realized that her son's sanity hung by a narrow cord. Never a brave man, this had so unnerved him that he was nearly undone. She needed to put a backbone in him. Taking a deep breath, she chose her words carefully. "O king, live forever, and let not your thoughts trouble you, nor let your countenance be changed. There is a man in your kingdom, in whom is the spirit of the holy gods."

It was working. Belshazzar's eyes left the writing and focused on her. Now, she needed to remind him of the strength of the blood he came from.

"In the days of your father, light and understanding and wisdom—like the wisdom of the gods—was found in this man, whom king Nebuchadnezzar, your father, the king, I say, *your* father, made master of the magicians, astrologers, Chaldeans, and soothsayers. Forasmuch as an excellent spirit, and knowledge, and understanding, interpreting of dreams, and showing of hard sentences, and dissolving of doubts, were found in the same Daniel, whom the king named Belteshazzar."

---

[5] Daniel 5:5.
[6] Daniel 5:6.

This Belteshazzar had better not make a fool of me, she thought, still eying her son, *or I will have him flayed.* In truth, she hadn't seen Belteshazzar—Daniel—in years. Ever since her father had died, the Jewish prophet had lived in obscurity, possessing an untouchable quality that had kept the hands of each succeeding king off him. But now, like as before, the man was needed.

She finished, "Now let Daniel be called, and he will show the interpretation."[7]

Belshazzar regained some measure of his composure. He nodded. "Find him. Bring him here!"

Guards darted from the room, and then there commenced the longest wait of Nitocris' life. She had no idea where this Daniel now lived, but surely someone in the city would know. She was certain he was still alive, for surely his death would have caused no small stir among the Babylonians who regarded him as near a god in human flesh as any man among the priests.

Finally, an old man was escorted into the banquet house. Above eighty years of age, the man was still not bowed down with the years resting upon his shoulders. He walked lightly for such an old man, his shoulders straight, his brown eyes undimmed. Nitocris remembered him with dark hair, but that had long since fallen to gray. A reddish birthmark shown against his olive skin at the nape of his neck. His face, hairless was now lined and seemed to hold the hardness of granite, and whatever fears he once carried, they had long since been purged with age and experience. He walked like a king should—like Nitocris wished her son would walk.

King Belshazzar nearly stumbled toward the old man. "Are you that Daniel, which are of the children of the captivity of Judah, whom the king, my father, brought out of Jewry?"[8]

Daniel's eyes flickered around the room, resting only momentarily on the writing upon the wall. They lingered longer on the gold vessels that lay strewn about the house. Only then did

---

[7] Daniel 5:10-12.
[8] Daniel 5:13.

EPILOGUE

Nitocris realize that these were the same gold vessels plundered from the temple in Jerusalem by her father.[9] She wondered if she'd made a mistake to call Daniel here.

The old man bowed before the king. When he straightened, he spoke in a surprisingly powerful voice for one so old, "I am, O king, *that* Daniel."

Belshazzar's eyes widened in sudden hope. "I have even heard of you, that the spirit of the gods is in you and that light and understanding and excellent wisdom is found in you."

Nitocris winced. Her son lacked imagination, repeating her words right back at Daniel.

"And now," her son continued, "the wise men and the astrologers have been brought in before me that they should read this writing!" He flung a shaking finger toward the wall. "And make known unto me the interpretation thereof, but they could not! But I have heard that you can make interpretations and dissolve doubts. Now, if you can read the writing and make known to me the interpretation thereof, you will be clothed with scarlet, and have a chain of gold about your neck, and will be the third ruler in the kingdom."[10]

Nitocris' eyes bulged. What was her son thinking? Third put this Daniel right after her husband and son! He couldn't do such a thing—shouldn't do such a thing. Her hands tightened on her robes, but she held her peace. After Daniel had read and interpreted the writing and her son had time to calm down would be the right moment to guide him away from such madness.

Daniel glanced briefly again at the wall and then bowed once more. When he straightened, Nitocris could see the younger man she'd once known. "Let your gifts be to yourself and give your rewards to another. Yet I will read the writing unto the king and make known to him the interpretation. O king, the most high God gave Nebuchadnezzar your father a kingdom, and majesty, and glory,

---

[9] Daniel 5:2-3.
[10] Daniel 5:14-16.

and honor. And for the majesty that He gave him, all people, nations, and languages trembled and feared before him. Whom he would, he slew, and whom he would, he kept alive, and whom he would, he set up, and whom he would, he put down."

Daniel's eyes seemed to bore into the king who stepped back from the intensity of them. Indeed, everyone suddenly moved back, leaving Daniel in a space by himself. The reminder of Nebuchadnezzar's power and might had struck a chord among the nobility in the room.

The old man continued as if nothing had happened, "But when his heart was lifted up and his mind hardened in pride, he was deposed from his kingly throne, and they took his glory from him. He was driven from the sons of men, and his heart was made like the beasts, and his dwelling was with the wild asses. They fed him with grass like oxen, and his body was wet with the dew of heaven until he knew that the most high God ruled in the kingdom of men and that He appoints over it whomsoever He will."[11]

Belshazzar looked confused. His eyes flickered to his mother and then back to the prophet. Everyone alive at the time remembered what happened to Nebuchadnezzar, though no scribe or chronicler would dare put it in writing. It was still too much of a shame on a nation, those lost seven years. They all wanted it to die and be buried to history. Nitocris had become frantic during that time, and with the scheming of her older brother, the kingdom had nearly come to ruin. Only Daniel had somehow held the kingdom together long enough to allow sanity to return to Nebuchadnezzar. Without Daniel, things would have likely turned out much worse. But to bring up this shame now? It was dishonorable to even speak of it!

"I understand not," Belshazzar said, staring at the old prophet. "What mean you by these words? Does it have ought to do with the writing?"

---

[11] Daniel 5:18-21.

EPILOGUE

Daniel shook his head—sadly, Nitocris thought—and suddenly pointed an accusing finger at the king. "You, his son, O Belshazzar, have not humbled your heart, though you *knew* all this. In the stead, you have lifted up yourself against the LORD of heaven and they have brought the vessels of His house before you. Then you, and your lords, your wives, and your concubines, have drunk wine in them. You have praised the gods of silver, and gold, of brass, iron, wood, and stone, which see not, nor hear, nor know, but the God in whose hand your breath is, and whose are all your ways, have you not glorified!" Daniel's hand then shifted to the wall, again, with only a cursory look at the words written there. "Then was the part of the hand sent from Him, and this writing was written!"

No one moved, no one even remembered to breathe. Nitocris stood as if something had rooted her to the spot. An ill feeling had spread through her limbs. She wanted to rush forward and stop Daniel, to tear his tongue from his mouth—for she knew then that his next words would curse her son.

"MENE, MENE, TEKEL, UPHARSIN!" shouted Daniel, his voice ringing through the house like a trumpet call. "That is what is written. And this is the interpretation of the thing: MENE, God has numbered your kingdom and *finished* it. TEKEL, you are weighed in the balances, and are found *wanting*. PERES, your kingdom is *divided* and given to the Medes and Persians."[12]

The old prophet's arm dropped to his side, and he gloriously fell silent. But the damage had been done. Nitocris sought for words to try and undo what Daniel had done, but she could find nothing. The weight of his words settled upon everyone in the room with the conviction of truth so profound that none dared to contradict them.

Belshazzar was first to move. He swallowed and then stumbled back until he half sat on the table nearest him. Strangely, he no longer shook in fear. No, his mother realized, he had the look of a man who faced his own imminent death and knew he could not escape it. She saw resignation in him. Complete surrender.

---

[12] Daniel 5:24-26.

Before she could rush to him, he pointed at Daniel and commanded, "Clothe him in scarlet, and let it be known throughout the kingdom that Belteshazzar, also known as Daniel, is now the third ruler of all. Only my word and my father's word will be greater."

Daniel didn't say anything further, but only folded his arms and stood resolutely. Nitocris finally found strength in her legs, and she rushed to Daniel, clutching his arm. As if her movement had been a signal, people silently slipped away, disappearing into the early evening, the festivities forgotten as they sought to get far away from those words written upon the wall. Even King Belshazzar left, tears streaming down into his braided beard.

But Nitocris had to know. In a voice only he could hear, she asked, "O Daniel, is there not mercy to be found that may avert the disaster you speak of? You speak of the end of my son and of my husband!"

Daniel did not try to pull away, but he stood there resolutely, gazing up at the words that had been emblazoned on the wall. "Long ago, O queen, your father decreed that if any people speak amiss of the God in whom I serve, then they shall be cut in pieces and their houses shall be made a dunghill.[13] Perhaps you remember my friends, Shadrach, Meshach, and Abednego, whom I knew as Hananiah, Mishael, and Azariah?"

Nitocris did remember them. They were powerful rulers under her father, all dead now, having passed on peacefully years ago. She vaguely remembered that decree as well. It had come after her father had returned from Dura and the dedication of his golden image.[14]

"I remember." Her whisper forced the aged prophet to cock his head to hear her better.

"That decree," Daniel said softly, "has returned upon the head of your son. Behold the violation of the LORD's vessels."

---

[13] Daniel 3:29.
[14] Daniel 3.

EPILOGUE

All strength left her then, and if she hadn't been clutching the old man's arm, she would've collapsed to the glazed tiles of the floor. The golden vessels taken from the house of the Hebrew God seemed to mock her. But somewhere inside her, she found a measure of anger to demand, "Who are you to so prophesy?"

Daniel's head tilted the other way as if listening, and then she heard it too. A chorus of triumphant trumpets. Persian trumpets. Her heart nearly stopped.

"Who am I?" Daniel whispered back. "I am the crucible of my God." He fixed her with a look of iron. "I am your crucible."

THE END

In the next book, Children of the Captivity, *the story of Daniel, Jeremiah, and Nebuchadnezzar continues where chapter 27 left off. Daniel and his young friends must come to grips with being eunuchs in Babylon, and Jeremiah is still hiding from King Jehoiakim who seeks his death. Each will seek to navigate their changing world where friends and enemies sometimes become interchangeable.*

ADDITIONAL BIBLICAL AND HISTORICAL EXPLANATIONS

Facts, Truth, and Interpretation

Stating a fact and interpreting the fact are not the same. By themselves, facts don't represent truth; they are merely facts. Truth is a fact that has purpose and meaning—often what is called a philosophy—that gives the fact a means to interact with your life and become relevant to you and thus meaningful. This then becomes a truth for you.

Jesus said that He is truth. This means that when we see life through His eyes, we find purpose and meaning in the Christian life and in Scripture. Jesus is indeed truth, my truth, and I trust your truth as well. But even among Christian circles, perspectives vary enough that our "truths" are often not quite aligned with someone else's. Welcome to individual soul-liberty.

Though I try to incorporate all the facts that the Bible speaks of in these stories, I am still going to interpret what those facts mean for the characters and events described. Not everyone will agree with my conclusions.

However, when you interpret a fact, your "truth" of the event shifts. Your understanding of it changes. And how you relate to the fact and how it becomes meaningful to you also changes. This

EXPLANATIONS

becomes your truth and understanding of the stories mentioned in the Bible. Preachers do this all the time with their interpretations of Scripture as they embellish a biblical story during a sermon.

These novels represent my interpretation of the facts into a cohesive and, hopefully, noncontradictory story that will entertain but also spark your fascination for the Bible, the characters, God's interaction with men, and ultimately your own relationship with Him.

I do not expect everyone to agree. But I do hope these novels will inspire you to delve into God's Word in a much more personal way and see that the characters in the Bible had real lives and that it is in those lives and stories that God wanted you to see Him.

Dialogue, Diction, and Word Choice

I thought long and hard on how I wanted to present this story. Much like the Davidic Chronicles that I wrote, I wanted an air of ancient ambience to pervade over the entire story. The men and women lived and died thousands of years ago. I didn't want them to sound like your neighbor or a hillbilly from Tennessee.

They thought differently, loved differently, hated differently, and worshiped differently than we do today. I wanted to reflect the morals of the time and not impose modern day morality on the story. To accomplish these goals, I used the King James Bible as my basis for dialogue and diction of the story. I didn't follow it exactly, but the pacing and air of ancient tone, in my opinion, is best portrayed using the King James Bible. Frankly, it even *sounds* godly, and I find comfort in that.

Regardless, the end result is that, without a doubt, I failed.

Keep in mind that I wrote this using Elizabethan English, for the most part, because I wrote for an English audience. Ancient Hebrew and Aramaic pacing, diction, and tone were certainly very different, and there was no way, in English, to capture it.

This was the best I could do and keep the story much like a modern novel that most people have become used to.

The Ark of the Covenant

Let me be clear: *I have no idea what really happened to the ark of the covenant.* In this story, Jeremiah hides it in a cave beneath Mt. Nebo. I choose to run with this theory for two reasons. First, it references the oldest historical source I could find as to what happened to the ark, mentioned in the apocryphal book of 2 Maccabees. Second, it fit well with the story of the characters presented in this novel.

There are many theories as to what happened to the ark. Some believe it was taken to heaven by God. Others think it was captured and ultimately destroyed by the Chaldeans. Another theory states it went down to Ethiopia. I have even heard that Israel has the ark today and is only waiting for the right time to reveal it. Several people have told me the ark is buried beneath Calvary, and when Jesus was crucified, His blood seeped down through a crack and dripped upon the mercy seat of the ark. Of course, according to Spielberg, it is now buried deep in the US National Archives in Washington, DC.

Whatever the truth is, I don't know it.

Fact and Fiction

Where the Bible clearly states what happened, I do my best not to change it but keep it exactly as written. I also try to stay as historically accurate as possible to what happened. I do, however, elaborate on the story *between* the facts. For example, we are told nothing of Daniel's life while in Jerusalem. We don't even know his lineage. So, using what historical information I could find, I created a background story and relationships that would not contradict the biblical or historical facts but would ultimately lead to the facts we do know of Daniel's life. That is the essence, in my mind, of biblical fiction.

For Daniel in particular, I hint at an unusual wisdom and intelligence granted to him by God. A fourteen-year-old boy back then is not comparable to a fourteen-year-old boy in our modern world. Back then, at fourteen, most boys were long doing a man's

EXPLANATIONS

work. The whole concept of a teenager didn't exist. They had to grow up faster, mature faster, understand life faster, and were exposed to harsh realities much faster than modern boys in first-world countries of today. So yes, Daniel sounds like a much older and wiser man than any boy of equal age today. Likely, he was.

Where I could, I used people mentioned in the Bible or, failing that, people mentioned in other historical records. A few times I invented a character to fulfill a specific role, but generally speaking, I tried to keep the story within the framework that was already given both biblically and historically.

It is true that I also tried to incorporate some of the more well-known historical elements in the story that didn't necessarily need to be included. An example of this is Jeremiah's escape through Hezekiah's tunnel. Obviously, I have no idea if such a thing ever happened, but the tunnel was available and referencing it will help the reader mentally picture ancient Jerusalem better.

Character personalities were based, as much as possible, on what Scripture and history tell us. Where there is no information, I invented their personalities. My goal was for the reader to become immersed in the ancient story, to learn something, to find intrigue in the Bible, to be entertained, but mostly to see God in the story.

Timelines

If there is any area where I take the most liberty, it is likely with the biblical and historical timelines. There is much contradiction as to when things happened and in what order. An example is when Nebuchadnezzar learns of his father's death. In my research, some scholars claim he learned of it before ever coming to Jerusalem and others after and when he was nearly to Egypt in his conflict with Necho II. For this example, I chose a middle ground that worked best with the story.

Regardless, there are times when the timelines and sequence of events are compressed for the novel's sake, but generally, they are as true as I could make them based on the biblical and historical records.

Standing in the Gap

The prophet Ezekiel is told by God in Ezekiel 22:30 that He had sought for a man to stand in the gap between Him and the land that He might not destroy it, yet He found none. This is an interesting statement considering that Daniel, Jeremiah, and Ezekiel were all alive during that time. If any could stand in the gap and make up the hedge, surely these three would have qualified.

Interestingly, though, God said that even if Noah, Daniel, and Job were in the land, He still would not spare it (Ezekiel 14:14-20). I don't know if this is the same Daniel of the book of Daniel, but the other two were certainly righteous men who should have qualified to stand in the gap if they lived in Daniel's day.

Why then could no one fill the gap and intercede between the land and an angry God?

The answer, I believe, is in the fact that there are four groups of people mentioned in Scripture and in this novel and, that of those groups, there was no one who had the ear of the people whom God could use to stand in the gap. Jeremiah wasn't listened to. Daniel and Ezekiel went into captivity, Daniel being too young to have earned the ear of the people anyway. Both Job and Noah are examples of individuals who were abandoned and ignored by friend and neighbor. None of the righteous men mentioned had the ear of the people. There was no one of influence that people would listen to who could come forward to stand in the gap, so God judged the people.

The four groups are mentioned in Ezekiel 22:24-31.

1. The people
2. The priests
3. The prophets
4. The princes

EXPLANATIONS

There was no one in the above groups who had the right influence to turn Judah back to God. This is why no one could stand in the gap and why God judged Judah and allowed them to go into the Babylonian captivity.

Judean Kings During the Time of Daniel

Following is a list of kings that ruled Judah during Daniel's lifetime.

s. = Son | m. = Married to

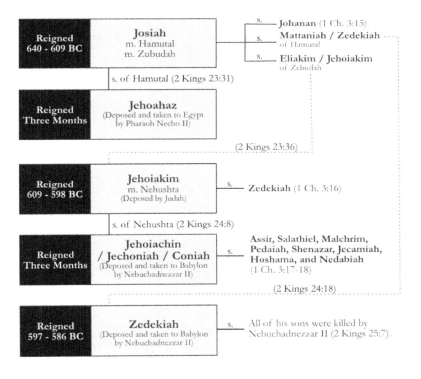

Babylonian Kings During the Time of Daniel

Following is a list of kings that ruled Babylon during Daniel's lifetime. In his life, he witnessed both the rise and fall of what scholars refer to as the neo-Babylonian era.

s. = Son | d. = Daughter | m. = Married to

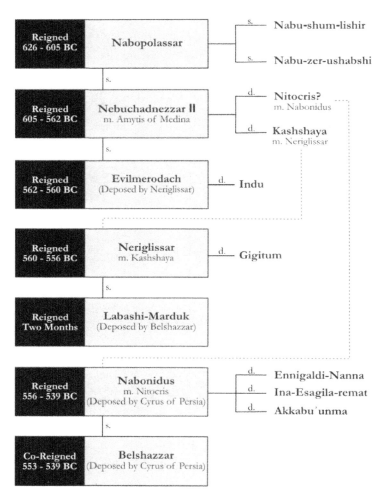

Of the kings listed, only Nebuchadnezzar, Evilmerodach, and Belshazzar are mentioned in the Bible.

BLOOPERS AND OUTTAKES

That Never Happened

Nebuchadnezzar glanced at an attendant standing nearby. "Fetch Ashpenaz." After the man ran off, Nebuchadnezzar turned to his captain. "I would have the chief eunuch's counsel, for I have had a dream these last nights."

Nebuzaradan's eyes snapped to the prince's face, a tiny frown darkening the lines beneath his beard. "How many nights?"

"Since Hamath. The dream is always the same."

Both men knew that dreams contained visions of power and messages from the gods. They were not to be dismissed, and Nebuchadnezzar had no intention of doing so. They waited in companiable silence until Ashpenaz, huffing and wheezing like a herd of diseased swine, finally made it to the top of the hill.

After the eunuch had heaved himself upright, Nebuchadnezzar began. "Harken," he said to his two closest advisors, "for I have dreamed. I beheld men and women, strangely dressed, standing before a beardless man of some age, his hair gray. He stood upon a pulpit and wore a coat of blue. A scarf of red fell to his waist against his chest. Banners of red, white, and blue did flank him to either side, all bearing a square of white stars upon a field of blue. Sticks covered in moss thrust up from the pulpit toward his face. A closed gate in a wall did rise up behind him. And then he spoke these words, 'Mr. Gorbachev, Mr. Gorbachev! Tear down this wall!"

Nebuchadnezzar eyed his advisors, but they only looked back as if they'd heard such visions and dreams before and found them commonplace.

"Tell me what means this dream," he commanded.

Ashpenaz straightened. "O king, live forever, for I shall interpret the dream. The man in blue, O king, is you, and the banners of red, white, and blue are the strength of your might and power, blessed by the stars in heaven and covering the whole earth. The command is clear. We are to march to Jerusalem and tear down the walls of that rebellious city!"

Nebuchadnezzar stared at his chief eunuch. *Tear down the walls of Jerusalem?* He could do that. Simple enough. But something bothered him. "What then means these words: 'Mr. Gorbachev'?"

Ashpenaz shrugged. "It is a spiced dish from India, my prince. Of fish and sheep…and…and goat." He licked his fat lips in anticipation, his eyes bright. "Definitely goat."

The Chaldean prince blinked. Truly, his chief eunuch was a great fool.

* * *

Shaking his head, he drew his sword and pointed it at the cowering priest's face. "Herald, say thus: open the doors and go in or I will slay you here and now to appease your God with your own cowardly blood that I may enter. Decide now."

Perhaps it was Nebuchadnezzar's calm voice, devoid of passion and completely lacking any compassion or care that convinced the sobbing priest to act. It was all the same to the Chaldean prince. With the cry of a man going to his death, the man pushed open the doors and fell inside, landing solidly on the floor of gold within. The man gasped sharply, clutched once at his chest, and then lay still.

Nebuchadnezzar looked beyond the man to see what would so frighten the priests. Two massive statues of cherubims, also sheathed in gold, stretched their wings from one side to the other of the square room. And between them sat the most beautiful ark Nebuchadnezzar had ever seen.

His breath caught as his heart beat faster. Entirely wrought in gold, the craftmanship rivaled anything the Chaldean prince had ever seen. But it was the rumors of what lay within that held his heart captive. He strode over to it and walked around it twice, looking at the ark from every angle. The top, the seat, was also a lid. It should come off with little effort.

Grinning like a fool, he gently lifted the gold seat off the ark and set it aside. Peering in, his grin slipped. Frowning now in confusion, he dipped his hand within and picked up a handful of white sand. *Sand?* He let the sand sift through his fingers, falling back within the ark.

All of this to protect sand?

The ridiculousness of it caused him to laugh, a full-throated belly laugh, the sound echoing off the cubed room of gold. *All of this for sand?*

And that's when the first beautiful ghost appeared before him.

* * *

The fat eunuch rubbed his hands together in pleasure, though Daniel could not tell if the man was relishing his answers or his coming death. "What sciences know you?"

Daniel took a deep breath. Now they were coming to the heart of the matter. He puffed out his chest. "I have advanced understanding of molecular biology and quantum mechanics, a branch of physics that deals with the behavior of matter on the scale of atoms or subatomic particles. Indeed, I am most interested in string theory as it relates to the unifying explanation of how all things consist. My research thesis as it relates to quantum gravity states—"

Ashpenaz held up a hand to stop Daniel. The eunuch looked bored. "If that is all you know, young Daniel, you are not fit to stand before the king of Babylon." He pointed off to one side. "Join your nephew and brother-in-law."

With his heart in his sandals, Daniel trudged over to join Jeconiah and Mattaniah.

* * *

The Elnathan spun around, his face a mask of rage. "Flee! You must flee!"

Jeremiah's heart nearly stopped, and he clutched at the front of his tunic as his friend's panic transferred to him.

"My daughter has betrayed you and sent word where you may be found. Even now, men come for you!"

Almost Jeremiah darted from the house, but he had to know. "What of the roll? Did the king hear the word of the LORD?"

Elnathan gripped the tabletop with knuckles turned white. "Nay. He cut it with a penknife and burned the rest in the fire after only a few leaves were read. I could not prevail upon him to save the roll. You must flee. He comes for you." He glanced at Baruch. "He comes for both of you."

The fugitives exchanged only a single glance and then ran out the door.

But once outside and no more than a score of cubits from the house, Baruch pulled up, spitting and sputtering, his choice of language colorful and bordering on blasphemous.

Concerned that the man might have swallowed something wrong, Jeremiah pounded the scribe on the back. "What ails you, my friend?"

Baruch pulled away, muttering half under his breath. "All that time. All that work. Gone! Arrggg!"

The ending scream jerked Jeremiah upright, and he glanced back the way they'd come, hoping the noise wouldn't bring down

BLOOPERS

King Jehoiakim's guards upon them. "Hold your tongue, man!" he hissed back. "What are you babbling on about?"

"He burned it! Burned it all!"

Jeremiah blinked. "The scroll?"

"Aye! All gone! Removed from under heaven!" The ugly scribe grabbed Jeremiah by the front of his tunic, his eyes boring into the prophet's stunned face with an intensity and anger he'd never before seen on the man. "Do you not see? Have you no understanding? Arrggg! I have fallen prey to the bane of every scribe! I forgot to save my work!"

SOURCES AND REFERENCES

Much research goes into a novel like this. I wanted to stay true to the biblical account but also stay true to the era and times. This meant understanding both the customs and political environment of Daniel's world. The sources below represent the majority of the information about customs, manners, and geography that I incorporated into this novel. Those not mentioned only corroborated what I found in the sources below.

Disclaimer: Undoubtedly, I missed or didn't learn aspects about ancient life that should have been incorporated, and so the astute reader may discover historical and geographical errors. Feel free to write me about them—as long as you corroborate them with sources—and I will attempt to incorporate them into future editions of the novel.

Websites

- owlcation.com/humanities/The-Mechanics-of-Scripture
- padfield.com/2008/carchemish.html
- en.wikipedia.org/wiki/Urartu
- bible.ucg.org/bible-commentary/Jeremiah/Defeat-of-Necho's-army-at-Carchemish-and-further-retreat/
- arsbellica.it/pagine/battaglie_in_sintesi/Carchemish_eng.html

SOURCES

- padfield.com/2008/carchemish.html
- livius.org/sources/content/mesopotamian-chronicles-content/abc-5-jerusalem-chronicle/
- historymuseum.ca/cmc/exhibitions/civil/egypt/egcrga3e.html
- historyten.com/mesopotamia/babylonian-deities/
- en.wikipedia.org/wiki/Marduk
- talesoftimesforgotten.com/2020/04/23/were-the-ancient-egyptians-black/
- christianstudylibrary.org/article/veil-tabernacle
- aleteia.org/2018/07/23/watch-king-solomons-temple-rebuilt-in-3d
- en.wikipedia.org/wiki/Nebuchadnezzar_II
- theologyattheedge.co.uk/tears-in-god-s-wineskin/30-tigw-part-2-eunuchs-eunuchs-in-the-ancient-near-east
- en.wikipedia.org/wiki/Jewish_views_on_astrology
- myjewishlearning.com/article/jewish-astrology/
- en.wikipedia.org/wiki/Nabopolassar
- amazingbibletimeline.com/blog/babylonian-king-nabopolasser/
- britannica.com/biography/Nebuchadnezzar-II
- britannica.com/topic/Aramaic-language
- dainspires.wordpress.com/tag/shach/
- livescience.com/28701-ancient-babylon-center-of-mesopotamian-civilization.html
- en.wikipedia.org/wiki/Etemenanki
- en.wikipedia.org/wiki/Amel-Marduk
- worldhistory.org/article/221/the-mesopotamian-pantheon/
- britannica.com/place/Babylon-ancient-city-Mesopotamia-Asia
- kadingirra.com/palaces.html

- bibleq.net/answer/1904/
- en.wikipedia.org/wiki/Neriglissar
- en.wikipedia.org/wiki/Labashi-Marduk
- en.wikipedia.org/wiki/Nabonidus
- en.wikipedia.org/wiki/Nitocris_of_Babylon
- en.wikipedia.org/wiki/Belshazzar
- wikitogo.org/en/Ina-Esagila-remat-8828088006

Books, Articles, and Research Papers

- The King James Bible.
- jbqnew.jewishbible.org/assets/Uploads/352/352_Ark.pdf
- Beaulieu, Paul-Alain, *A History of Babylon 2200 BC – AD 75,* (John Wiley & Sons Ltd, Hoboken, NJ, 2018).
- Kriwaczek, Paul, *Babylon, Mesopotamia and the Birth of Civilization* (Thomas Dune Books, New York).
- Seevers, Boyd, *Warfare in the Old Testament* Grand Rapids, MI: Kregel Publications, 2013).
- Herzog, Chaim and Gichon, Mordechai, *Battles of the Bible – A Military History of Ancient Israel* (Barnes and Noble Publishing, 2006).
- Wight, Fred H., *Manners and Customs of Bible Lands* (Moody Bible Institute of Chicago, 1953).
- Deursen, A. Van, *Illustrated Dictionary of Bible Manners and Customs* (Grand Rapids, MI: Zonderzan, 1958).
- Hourly History, *Babylon – A History from Beginning to End* (2018).
- *Archeology and History of Eighth-Century Judah,* Edited by Zev I. Farber and Jacob L. Wright (SBL Press, Atlanta, 2018).
- **Adele Hazel Esme Asher, *Judah and Her Neighbors in the Seventh Century BCE* (1996, a thesis).**
- Adamo, Nasrat and Al-Ansari, Nadhir, *Babylon in a New Era: The Chaldean and Achaemenid Empires (330-612 BC)* (Journal

of Earth Sciences and Geotechnical Engineering, Vol.10, No.3, 2020, Scientific Press International Limited).

Commentaries and Dictionaries:

- James Orr, M.A., D.D., General Editor, *International Standard Bible Encyclopedia*.
- John McClintock and James Strong, *Cyclopedia of Biblical, Theological and Ecclesiastical Literature* (1895).
- Canne, Browne, Blayney, Scott, and others, with introduction by R. A. Torrey, *Treasury of Scriptural Knowledge* (1834; public domain).
- *John Gill's Exposition of the Bible* (1746-1766, 1816; public domain).
- *Jamieson, Fausset and Brown Commentary - A Commentary, Critical and Explanatory, on the Old and New Testaments* (1871; public domain).
- *Adam Clarke's Commentary on the Bible* (1810-1826; public domain).
- *Joseph Benson's Commentary on the Old and New Testaments* (1857; public domain).
- *Albert Barnes' Notes on the Bible* (1847-85; public domain).
- *Matthew Henry's Commentary on the Whole Bible* (1708-1714; public domain).
- *John Wesley's Notes on the Bible* (1755-1766; public domain).
- F. B. Meyer, *Through the Bible Day by Day – A Devotional Commentary* (1914; public domain).
- *Dr. Kretzmann's Popular Comentary* (1921-1924; public domain).
- Mclaren, Alexander, *Expositions of the Holy Scriptures* (1904-1910; public domain).
- *Expositor's Bible Commentary* (1887-1896; public domain).

- *Keil and Delitzsch Commentary on the Old and New Testaments* (1866-1891; public domain).
- Hawker, Robert, *Poor Man's Commentary* (1917; public domain).
- *Sermon Bible Commentary* (1888-1893; public domain).
- *The Cambridge Bible for Schools and Colleges* (1882-1921; public domain).
- Bullinger, E.W., *The Companion Bible* (1909-1922; public domain).
- *The Preachers Complete Homiletical Commentary* (1892; public domain).

ABOUT THE AUTHOR

Greg S. Baker has been writing novels for over twenty years. His books are widely read and enjoyed. His primary focus has been on his popular biblical fiction novels and his engaging young adult adventure novels. He has written a number of other helpful books for the Christian life. He has a passion for expanding the Kingdom of God within the kingdom of men.

He lives in the southwest with his wife, Liberty, and their boys. Much of his writing has been for them, desiring to provide entertaining stories that teach and inspire biblical truths.

He attended Bible college in the late 1990s, pastored a Baptist church in Colorado for thirteen years, and now works as a writer, a freelance Christian editor, and a programmer from his house. He remains active in his church, serving God in a variety of capacities, but focusing mainly on teenagers and young single adults.

He loves being a husband, dad, and Christian, playing chess and sports, hiking, and, of course, writing.

You can connect with Greg through his website GregSBaker.com. He loves hearing from people and engaging with them as an active part of the writing process for his future books. If you love reading, then stop on by.

GregSBaker.com

Printed in Great Britain
by Amazon